America Victorious

Part A

The Dunkirk Option

By Kim Kerr

2020

Chapter One: August 1942

The English countryside appeared peaceful. A robin flitted through the branches of a nearby ash, while in the distance Sergeant Chuck Randel could see the road leading to the small town of Calver. The country around him rolled away in waves. Fields cut by stone fences sat just beyond the forest in which his tank was parked. A road, the A625according to his map, ran down along the edge of the Grindleford valley. Somewhere to his left the picturesque Derwent River flowed under stone bridges, running south until it reached the River Trent some twenty miles away.

Of course that was in German-occupied England. The high-water mark of Rommel's advance had almost washed up against the Mersey in the east and Lincoln in the west. In the end Liverpool didn't fall, with the panzers running out of steam at Wrexham and Stoke-on-Trent. The northern coast of Wales was still in allied hands as the 23rd Panzer Division reached the Peak District. The Canadians held Sheffield while American divisions dug in around the

Lincoln Wold. English divisions were still reforming but would soon be ready to reinforce the allied lines.

The four tanks of his platoon were camouflaged under nets within the forest. German planes weren't as numerous as they had been in July but the Allies didn't have air superiority. US Kittyhawks were as likely to be seen as Fw 190s. Three days earlier, four of the stubby German fighter planes had attacked his platoon of tanks. Luckily the aircraft weren't carrying bombs, so despite the noise assaulting his eardrums as bullets drummed against the armour, the M3s were undamaged.

Private Olaf Magnusson sat reading a copy of *Stars and Stripes*.

"London can't hold," he muttered to himself.

"What's that?" asked Private Freddy Spencer.

The big loader looked up. "I said London can't hold. East Anglia is gone and the Germans are moving into Kent. The capital is surrounded and even though the paper is full of stories of the heroic defence, the writing is on the wall."

"They've got no supplies," said Troy Ohlsen, the driver of the M3.

"The moment Rommel cut the country in two they were goners," said Spencer.

"Doesn't change our job. Churchill says the British will keep fighting and we are here to help them. The Krauts threw their lot in with the Japs so we have to beat them," said Randel. "If London falls, well it doesn't change anything."

"I'm not saying it does Sarge, I feel for the people who live there is all. The poor civis who are hidin' in their cellars and sneaking out to find food and water must be doin' it tough," said Magnusson.

"Yeah, thank God it's not happening at home," said Spencer.

Ohlsen cocked his head and everyone stopped talking. "I can hear a plane," said the driver.

Randel looked through the tree branches and saw a strange aircraft flying in circles over the valley. The twin-engine machine appeared fragile with a long thin frame and a centre cockpit area of glass panels. The Fw 189 continued circling above them and Randel hoped the camouflage over his tanks would fool the enemy reconnaissance machine. He knew the Germans were only a mile and a half away at Calver.

"Everyone get in the tank," he ordered.

The plane circled closer as Randel clambered into the commander's hatch on the top of the tank. The whistle of shells didn't surprise him and he quickly dropped inside the turret, closing the hatch. Explosions rocked the M3 and shrapnel pattered against the armour like hail. Outside, trees were torn apart by 105mm shells while the campfire disappeared, swept away by the barrage. Randel guessed it was probably the smoke from the cooking fires which had given away their position. The barrage rolled away over the forest and a few minutes later returned to the position of his platoon. The heavy shells landed within feet of the M3, making the tank shudder.

Inside, the crew were quiet as each man tried to control his fear. Only a direct hit threatened them but even then it might only disable the tank. Randel knew all of this, however sweat trickled down his back. The barrage built in intensity and then stopped. Lieutenant Myers ordered all of the crews to stay put for a few more minutes in case the Germans began firing again. On this occasion the enemy didn't renew the barrage and Randel was able to open the hatch. He peered out onto a burning forest. Trees lay on their side and the underbrush smouldered. The trunks of large oaks were scarred by shrapnel and craters pockmarked the forest floor.

The sight saddened Randel and he wondered how long it would take for this patch of woodland to recover.

"We are moving, Sarge," said Magnusson from inside the tank.

Randel glanced around for the pots and kettles his men had been using, and only managed to find the coffee pot. It lay in two pieces, neatly cut in half by a flying shard of metal.

"Alright. Start her up Ohlsen," he said.

V

The Pacific Ocean glimmered in the late afternoon sun. Ahead, the carrier grew in size as Commander James 'Pug' Southerland guided his Grumman F4F Wildcat toward the USS Enterprise. He could see the Australian carrier HMAS Tasman nearby. These were the only two allied flat tops in the area and constituted a major portion of the navy's striking power in the Pacific. The deck became larger as he lowered the Wildcat's undercarriage. Southerland glanced at his instruments before looking back to the carrier. The Landing Signal Officer (LSO) stood with his paddles raised slightly above his shoulders, indicating that Southerland's approach was a little high.

He eased the throttle and felt the plane drop. The LSO extended his arms out to his side showing that Southerland was safe to land. The arrester hook was down and the deck continued to grow. He always appreciated it when the landing area no longer reminded him of a postage stamp. The LSO signalled for him to cut power even further and the Wildcat dropped down onto the deck. The arrestor hook caught one of the cables and jerked his stubby little fighter to a stop. Deck crew ran out from various positions as Southerland opened his canopy and breathed in the humid air of the tropics. He guided his plane carefully over to the refuelling point. Southland would have time for a coffee and a toilet break before returning to the sky.

Overhead, the Australian Sea Brumby fighters flew combat air patrol (CAP). The pilots of those aircraft were veterans, having fought at both Midway and the battle of the Timor Sea. He supposed he was also an experienced fighter pilot now. He'd shot down a Japanese Val dive bomber during the battle. Whilst flying from the Enterprise. The ship had still been hit twice but the damage to the flight deck had mainly been superficial and the carrier was repaired in six weeks. He remembered the HMAS Tasman taking three hits to its flight deck with only one of the bombs actually penetrating the armour. Again, damage was compartmentalised and the carrier fixed quickly.

Three of Japan's heavy carriers lay at the bottom of the ocean, as did two of their smaller flat tops. Another carrier being repaired was the Kaga. That left two heavy carriers out there somewhere as well as the Hosho, a training vessel that was now moving aircraft between Tokyo and Rabaul. Losses for the US navy and the Commonwealth were worse. The Hornet, Saratoga, Lexington, and Yorktown had all been sunk at various battles or at Pearl Harbour. Two were destroyed at Midway as well as the Commonwealth carrier, the Ark Royal. The latter was hit by three torpedoes and sunk very quickly, taking at least two thirds of her crew down with her. Midway cost both sides dearly, with four of the five Japanese carriers also being sunk. The New Zealand carrier Eagle was also gone, and the HMAS Melbourne was in California being repaired.

At the moment the Allies were trying to hold the line at Vanuatu and Northern Australia. New Guinea had fallen and enemy bombers were raiding Cairns and Townsville. At least the Australians had managed to bring back three of its most experienced divisions from the Middle East, as well as many of its best pilots. No one knew what the Japanese planned to do and Southland hoped the USA would strike the next blow. He was sick of his country reacting to the enemy.

"No action today?" asked Lieutenant Stanley W. Vejtasa.

"No, Swede. I know that the Japs are in range. I mean we are what, halfway between Fiji and Port Vila?"

"Something like that," answered Vejtasa

"So a Zero might reach us here from Guadalcanal, and their twin-engine birds definitely could."

"True enough."

"But there's no sight of them."

"So what are we doing here?" asked Swede.

"I flew south on an anti-sub patrol yesterday. There are more of our ships out that way. I saw destroyers and light cruisers as well as troop transports."

"So you think we are covering reinforcements to where?"

"Espiritu Santo, or maybe New Caledonia, I don't know. The admiral dropped me off his Christmas card list."

Swede snorted. "I thought with your lofty rank he'd be checking in with you regularly."

"Well, I'm still a grade above you."

"Don't I know it, even though I have more kills."

"Yes, but I'm better looking and can read," said Southerland. The other pilot laughed, but the sound of his voice was drowned out by the noise of sirens. Both of the pilots looked into the bright sky. Swede shielded his eyes and pointed to the north.

"There they are, two float planes," he said.

Southerland could see them now. Black puffs appeared near the two as the heavier anti- aircraft weapons tried to bring the machines down. The Aichi E13A, or 'Jake' to the Allies, was a reconnaissance aircraft flown by the Japanese Navy. This pair were operating out of San Cristobal and were at the full extent of their range.

The two aircraft started to lose altitude and moved closer together.

"The Jake has a rear gunner," said Swede.

From somewhere the big pilot had grabbed a set of navy binoculars and was watching the two aircraft.

"Here come the Aussies," said Southerland.

Three of the Sea Brumbies were turning to maneuver behind the float planes, the fourth plane turned sharply and approached the Jakes from a beam position.

"Smart, whoever is in that fighter will be clear of the Jap gunners," said Swede.

"Yeah, but he will have to take a deflection shot," said Southerland.

The art of firing in front of an enemy aircraft, and it flying through a fighter's burst of fire was something few pilots managed. If you started shooting too soon then the bullets and cannon shells passed in front of the enemy machine and it could change direction, if you waited too long then the burst would pass behind the target. The pilot of the Brumby was Lieutenant George 'Screwball' Beurling. He was actually a Canadian, not an Australian. This wasn't unusual as the Commonwealth navy often was forced to mix personnel from different countries in order to crew the ships which fled England in 1940.

Beurling only fired a single one second burst. It shattered the engine of one of the Jakes and the Japanese aircraft fell away in flames while the Brumby flew in a tight loop over the remaining float plane.

"That was some fine shooting," said Swede.

Beurling had already participated in the Battle of the Timor Sea and the Battle of Midway. He'd missed most of the Carrier's time in the Red Sea when aircraft from the Tasman attacked targets in Italian

East Africa, only managing to shoot down a single Fiat G 50 before the ship was sailed back to Australia. The sea plane was his tenth victim.

"He's coming at the last one head on," said Southerland.

It was over quickly. The Jake didn't have a forward firing gun and tried to turn away. Beurling anticipated this and fired at the maneuvering aircraft. This time the four point five inch calibre machine guns ripped off a float and caused the right wing to catch fire. The Jake went into a flat spin and crashed into the ocean with a large splash.

"Whoever he was, that pilot can certainly fly," said Swede.

"Yeah, but he left his flight. Obviously, he's not big on teamwork. If he tries that stunt against a bunch of Zeros it will be a different story," said Southerland.

"You could be right. More importantly, the Japs have found us. We could be in trouble."

"It's late in the day. As soon as it's dark we'll change direction and perhaps we will be lucky."

They were. Vice Admiral Jack Fletcher ordered the fleet on to a new course the following day. The carriers turned back to Suva in Fiji, while the more southerly troop convoy continued onward, protected by P 38s based at Port Vila. The US navy wasn't ready to risk its remaining carrier in another battle with the Japanese just yet.

V

Construction of the Detlev-Rohwedder-Haus had started when Reichsmarschall Goering was still alive and the huge structure housed the Ministry of Aviation. Reichsmarschall Kesselring thought it was one of the ugliest buildings he'd ever seen, yet it was where he spent most of his time. Albert Kesselring wondered on how far he'd come. The head of the Luftwaffe was a long way from being the son of a school master. Still, here he was, trying to run an air force and win a war.

Glancing at his clock on the wall, he sighed. General Wagner was due to meet him in a few minutes and the man was annoyingly punctual. The meeting was supposed to be about the development of new transport aircraft. Wagner was acting more in an advisory role, as his command had been stripped back to rail transportation. Kesselring knew this decision was connected to politics more than any failure on the part of the general. Really, the man was a supply genius and his work in the east allowed the panzers to keep moving, when they otherwise would have been stranded for lack of fuel. Wagner was also involved in the carriage of oil back to the Reich from the fields at Krasnodar and Grozny.

Other topics would come up. Wagner's reputation as a pessimist preceded him. The General's attitude to the problems Germany faced stood in stark contrast to Kesselring's own opinions. That didn't mean he wouldn't listen to the man. Wagner and the so called 'Gang of Four' had been correct when they'd pushed the Reich into preparing for a long war back in the autumn of 1941. Kesselring found himself swept up in the rationalising of Luftwaffe production and the increased emphasis on pilot and air crew training.

There was a knock at the door and his adjutant introduced General Wagner. The sharp-faced man reminded Kesselring of a bird of prey. He shook the man's hand and gestured to a chair. Coffee and cake was ordered.

"My dear General. You have heard of the Heer's success in the advance on Stalingrad?" said Kesselring.

"The advance was going well, until a few days ago. Yes, I've heard many optimistic projections," said Wagner.

"The 13th Panzer Division and SS Wiking have reached the Volga! The Sixth Army has captured Kalach and crossed the Don. We are in sight of victory."

"I'm struggling to supply the panzer armies with the fuel they need. Trains are being taken away and used for," the man hesitated, "other tasks."

Kesselring knew of the Final Solution, but tried to ignore the reality of what was happening to the Jews.

"The 4th Panzer Army is guarding the northern flank and has stopped its advance. Won't that take some pressure off the supply situation?" asked Kesselring.

"Some, though the 1st Panzer Army is stuck. The trains have taken the fuel as far as Morozovsk, but two lines are not enough for two armies. These tracks have to supply the 6th Army as well. As for Wiking and the 13th, if it weren't for the air transport units they wouldn't have reached the Volga at all. Now they are almost out of fuel and under heavy attack."

"They'll hold and we will take Stalingrad," said Kesselring.

"You know our northern flank is held by our allies?"

"Backed by the 4th Panzer Army."

"Which is down to one panzer and two motorized divisions."

"As well as nine infantry divisions. I keep up to date, General. We also have two corps reforming in the east. True, they are still at fifty percent of their strength but that situation is improving. In England we are about to take London."

"But Churchill fights on and Rommel's thrust north has run out of steam. He didn't reach Liverpool, and now the Americans and Canadians are arriving in increasing numbers."

"General, General, the situation isn't as dire as you think. Compare the circumstances to the last war. Our armies are on the Volga!"

"In the last war the Russians surrendered, and we still lost."

"That won't happen again. The Führer has guided our country to a level of military success beyond anything it has ever experienced."

Wagner frowned and thought for a moment. "Do you still agree it will be a longer war than many first thought?" he asked.

Kesselring may have been an optimist but he was also an intelligent man. "Yes. The Americans will fight for quite some time. The Japanese advance seems to have reached its high-water mark, though there is a chance they will invade Australia. We haven't taken Moscow and any advance to Saratov seems unlikely. The Volga is as far as we will go this year. Then our armies need to hold against any counter strike."

"There are some in the High Command who speak as though the Soviets are finished."

"Not me. I fought in Russia in the last war. Stalin won't surrender and the Communists will keep fighting until their country is destroyed."

"Isn't that part of the problem? Our goal is to wipe Russia from the map. I wouldn't surrender if I were them either. The choice is to fight until the country is destroyed or surrender and watch the country be shattered."

"The Slav and Jews will finish us, if we don't do it to them first."

Wagner snorted, then fell silent.

"Well, you are here to talk with me about your recommendations for new transport aircraft. The British planes are wearing out and we need new designs," said Kesselring.

"You have to go with the Ju 252. I know there is an argument we should build the new transport planes out of wood and use other engines. Maybe there's some truth to this notion, but don't let it stop you building the 252 now. It's almost ready. Any redesign will put back the project by at least a year."

"What about the Ju 290?"

"That's another good plane but from what I've seen and heard, you should use that as a long range reconnaissance machine or a heavy bomber."

"Germany doesn't have the fuel to run a fleet of heavy bombers."

"They are needed to hit the Russian tank factories in the Urals; however, this isn't my area of expertise. Perhaps if you had a hundred of them? Maybe one day they will be able to reach America?"

"We have a Messerschmitt bomber for that. The prototype has just flown but it has a few problems. The wing loading is too high. There are other designs but they are on the drawing board and we need something sooner rather than later."

"I hope it works out. Creating a large surface area for the wings doesn't sound too difficult, however I don't know the first thing about building a plane."

"Your advice will be considered. If you can send me something in writing it would be extremely helpful. I'm currently looking at other designs as well and some have been abandoned altogether."

"I heard whispers about the Me 210 and 410," said Wagner.

"Both are off the table. What a waste of resources! At least I can use the engines on the new Fw 190C high altitude fighter. We will soon stop production of the Bf 110, as well as the Do 217. I'm trying to rationalize wherever I can. All efforts will go into making more Ju 88s."

"What about the jets, if you don't mind me asking?"

"I'm going to take a slow and careful approach with them. They will receive more resources but I want them thoroughly tested before bringing them into action. They won't be ready before the spring of 1945."

"So what will come in before then?" asked Wagner.

"There are a few exciting machines waiting in the wings. The Fw 190 C is a very promising high altitude interceptor if we can solve the problems of the engine overheating. The Do 335 is a project I've fast tracked and hope to have ready by the summer of 1944. The Fw 190 C should be in limited production by the end of the year and two other variants of the same fighter are due by the winter of 1943/44, along with another high altitude type by the start of 1945. We are putting a lot of effort into working out the bugs in the engines, particularly the overheating."

Wagner nodded and stood up to leave. “I wish you and the Luftwaffe luck. I’ll have my recommendations on the transport aircraft to you by the end of the week.”

Kesselring thought the General’s sudden ending of the conversation abrupt, but Wagner was known for his strange mannerisms.

“I look forward to it,” he answered.

V

The ground shimmered with heat. There were few trees and only the occasional balkas (shallow gully) cut through the area, providing little cover for Private Roza Shanina and her platoon. The young woman had to pinch herself. She wanted to avenge the death of her brother and fight for Russia, but given her age of eighteen, believed that wouldn’t be allowed. However, the situation was desperate for the Soviet army and with only six month’s training Roza had been sent to the front. With only a short period of time at sniper school, her company commander handed her one of the few Mosin–Nagant rifles with a 3.5 PU scope and told her to start killing Germans. He didn't even allocate her a spotter.

There had been little time to establish the positions of the 87th Rifle Division. Since Roza had arrived, the German 14th Panzer Division had crashed through the Russian positions splitting the Soviet formation in two, with two regiments being forced north and one south. The Nazis had now reached the Volga in two places, though Roza didn't know about the success of the Wiking Division further south. The Germans were attacking Stalingrad from the southeast, the east and even trying to push along the bank of the Volga River from the southwest.

She could hear tank tracks grinding and saw T-34s appear from the north, stirring up clouds of dust. Men clustered like flies on the backs of the armoured vehicles as the counterattack swept into the German corridor. Soon the order came for Roza's company to advance and they moved forward to the Borodkin Collective Farm. The railway line was only a few kilometres to the west and there was a shallow river to the south. Roza could see for kilometres in all directions and wished for more cover. The concrete buildings and sheds of the farm provided some protection, but her platoon was ordered to dig in near a shallow creek bed which ran along the edge of one of the fields. Here, a few dry bushes and small trees allowed the company commander to build a camouflaged position for his headquarters.

Roza thought the choice was foolish. The patch of brush was obvious. It's the first place the enemy would target. She crept away along the creek bed to the south with an old sergeant and three other men. They dug into the walls of the balkas and spread out a dirty tarpaulin. The sergeant placed this over his DP-27 light machine gun before glancing at her.

"Make sure you don't give us away girl," the older man said.

"I won't," Roza replied.

"The Captain will be along soon. He may move us, or maybe he won't. We have overlapping fields of fire with the other two guns, not that he'd notice," said the sergeant.

"He is new?"

The sergeant laughed. "Most of the division is. This is the third time we've been reformed. First time was after the frontier battles, then they rolled the airborne boys in with us after the losses they took around Kiev. Now we are here. About one in ten are originals, like me."

"This is my first battle," Roza said.

"Yes, I'd noticed. Just stay close girl, and dig deep. You know how to use that gun?"

"I was trained for three months at the sniper school, then they said my training needed to finish."

"There's been a bit of that going on. Still, you've got more training than some we've been getting of late. You know we are the cork in the bottle here right?"

"What do you mean?"

"There's a panzer division and a motorized division to our east. They smashed through and reached the Volga. We just cut the corridor they made. What do you think will happen next?"

Roza thought for a second. "The Nazis will try and link up again. The men to the east are cut off."

"Yep, and we are goin' to be right in the middle of it." The old sergeant spat, then drank from a flask. He hesitated momentarily and handed it to Roza. She took a mouthful and almost choked as the raw vodka burned its way down her throat.

"Good stuff, eh! That will keep you alert."

The other men laughed and started digging into the embankment at the edge of the dry creek bed. Roza moved about twenty paces along the creek and dug her own fox hole. She did the best she could to camouflage her position, then walked back to the four men. They were sharing a cigarette and cooking potatoes in a pot of boiling water. She licked her lips as the smell of food reached her.

Pulling out a small piece of mouldy cheese and a broken slice of black bread, Roza broke off some and put it in her mouth.

"Have some of the water, girl. It'll taste of the potatoes and softens the bread," said a skinny private who carried an older PPD-40 but with the drum magazine. All of the men carried a revolver or a semi-automatic pistol. Roza decided if these veterans had side arms she better find one for herself. She chewed her bread and listened to the banter of the men.

One dark-eyed private kept sneaking looks at her. Roza knew that her blonde hair and trim figure attracted the attention of men. She discouraged this as she was here to fight and kill Nazis, not to form romantic attachments. Roza frowned at the dark-haired man, who couldn't have been more than a couple of years older than herself. The sergeant caught her look and glanced at the man.

"Yuri, go and get us some grenades, we are almost out," ordered the older man.

The soldier looked as though he was about to protest but the sergeant's face hardened and Yuri nodded, picked up his submachine gun, and trotted off down the creek bed.

"If any of the lads get out of line, make sure you slap them and if that doesn't work tell them Sergeant Potemkin will kick their arse, okay girl," said the older man.

"Thank you, Sergeant," said Roza. "He was only looking but I'm here to shoot Fascists. The Germans killed my brother near Leningrad."

Potemkin's face softened. "This war has taken so many of our people. I hope when it's all over the world remembers how Russia bled."

Yuri returned an hour later with a bag of grenades and a loaf of bread.

"This one has more flour in it than usual," he said smiling.

They sat and leaned against the wall of the creek, watching as the rest of the company finished digging in. Two 45mm guns were placed near a low building in the main compound of the collective farm, while other soldiers climbed to the roof of a small wheat silo. They had just reached the top when dark shapes appeared off to the west.

Roza shaded her eyes and peered at the approaching aircraft. “What are they?” she asked.

“Stukas. Nazi dive bombers, girl. You best jump in your hole and roll yourself into a ball. Keep your mouth open. It helps with the shock waves,” said Sergeant Potemkin.

The planes grew in size until they were directly above the farm. A few anti-aircraft guns fired at the aircraft from nearby but without any discernible effect. The Stukas rolled on their sides and dived toward the farm, firing machine guns as they came down. The howling sound from the sirens was deafening. It seemed as though the Nazi planes were screaming at her. Explosions followed, impossibly loud, trailed by more of the shrieking dive bombers. Roza tried to burrow into the bottom of her hole as shock waves rolled over the creek bed.

Somewhere she could hear screaming but this was washed away by more explosions. Over thirty Stukas from StG 77 hit the farm and surrounding trenches that afternoon. They destroyed most of the buildings and knocked out a 45mm gun and a nearby artillery unit. Four men from Roza's company were killed, with the same number being wounded. The company was just starting to move from their holes when the air filled with the sound of whistling shells. Corps level 17cm long range artillery was directed onto the farm by a circling Drache helicopter. Two batteries fired on target for five minutes before shifting to other targets. The sixty-three kilo shells tore huge craters out of the ground and buried men alive in their trenches. The heavy guns moved onto other targets, however divisional 105mm guns took over from the 17cm weapons smothering the area with shells for another twenty minutes. Roza thought she'd go mad. By the time it was over her head was ringing and dust covered every inch of her uniform.

She stuck her head out of the hole and stared along the creek bed. Large sections of the balka had collapsed. The buildings of the farm were nothing more than rubble, while two trucks burnt near the silo. The large wheat storage tanks had collapsed leaving giant white slabs of concrete lying on the ground like stranded whales. Roza tried to gather her thoughts but her mind was fuzzy, as though she had woken suddenly and didn't know where she was.

"Wake up girl. The Fascists are on the way," snapped Sergeant Potemkin. "Clean your rifle off. You'll need it soon."

Roza brushed the dirt from her rifle and opened the bolt. She quickly cleaned the barrel and greased the weapon before checking the scope.

"Here they come," yelled Yuri.

Advancing from the south, Panzer IIIs and IVs rattled over the flat ground, stopping occasionally to fire their main guns. Roza counted fourteen of them but there may have been more. German infantry jogged forward slowly, some of them huddling behind the armour. A couple of half-tracks also advanced, the machine guns on these vehicles shooting at the Russian trenches.

Oh my God, this is it, thought Roza. She slid under her tarpaulin and peered through her scope at the Fascists. A man came into focus running next to a Panzer III. He carried a rifle and wore glasses. She adjusted her aim and gently squeezed the trigger. The soldier fell, the bullet hitting him in the chest just below the heart. Roza realised she had just killed a man. Fighting down the urge to vomit, she tried to find another target. Tears filled her eyes and Roza stopped to wipe them.

"They killed your brother," she growled to herself.

She swung the sight sideways, wishing she had a spotter. Nearby, the light machine gun chattered and Sergeant Potemkin cursed. 75mm and lighter 50mm shells exploded along the edge of the creek. The air was filled with dirt and smoke, yet Roza's world narrowed to that little circle through which she viewed the world. Her breathing slowed and she counted deliberately under her breath. A Fascist carrying a pistol waved men forward. An officer. She slowly squeezed the trigger, but the man turned as she fired.

Her bullet caught the Hauptmann in the right shoulder, throwing him to the ground.

Time to move. Roza slid back into the creek and crawled to her second firing location. Around her everything was chaos. Men screamed and the air was thick. She struggled to draw breath and took a moment to take a mouthful of water from her canteen. The action steadied her and Roza eased herself into a second hole. She hadn't brought the tarp with her and decided to move back to her previous location after firing a few shots. A panzer stopped one hundred metres from her location and Roza saw the commander stick his head up in order to better direct his gunner.

"Just do that again, Nazi," she whispered.

The panzer commander popped up again and Roza was ready. Her shot hit him above the left eye and he slid back inside the Panzer III. She smiled fiercely and looked for another target. A roar further along the creek bed caused Roza to look away from her scope. Nazis were pouring over the lip of the waterway and a rolling melee had erupted. Men stabbed and slashed it each other while others fired pistols or submachine guns. Somewhere a grenade exploded, throwing three of her company to the ground. Roza turned and dropped to one knee. She fired methodically at any German she could see who wasn't grappling with a Russian soldier. Roza wasn't sure how many men she'd hit, but suddenly the enemy weren't in the trench. Bodies lay everywhere, some crawling away from the carnage, others moaning and pleading.

An officer walked around shooting the wounded Fascists while men removed injured Russian soldiers on stretchers. Roza didn't like watching the lieutenant doing his grizzly work. For some reason she felt as though the enemy should receive some help as well. This didn't fit with her hatred of the Nazis as the bodies of the enemy looked indistinguishable from those of her side. This was war and she would defend her country to the last drop of her blood, but her heart still went out to the dead.

"Clean your gun and count your bullets," said Sergeant Potemkin.

Roza jerked from her thoughts and stared at the older man. His eyes softened. “They’ll be back girl. This day’s far from done. Best see if you can find us some tea. We’ll make a brew. When the Fascists’ return we will at least have drunk something strong and be feeling a little better.”

Roza turned and looked at the pools of blood and the half dozen remaining bodies. She shook herself and nodded.

“I’ll find us a brew, Sergeant,” she answered and walked off determinedly down the battle-scarred creek bed.

Chapter Two: September 1942

The situation in Yugoslavia blew up so quickly it took everybody by surprise. Lang sat in the back of the Sd.Kfz. 251 half-track, looking at the map on his knees. The road to Belgrade lay in front of his command. Wide valleys through low mountain ranges dominated this area of the country, through which the Panzer Lehr Division was travelling. There was no doubt the unit wasn't ready for battle. It had just started pulling together the various parts which were needed for the new formation when the call came to move to Bulgaria. With the 10th Panzer Division a corps was formed and this attacked toward Belgrade from Sofia.

Further north the 233rd Reserve Motorised Division and the 155th Reserve Panzer Division were attacking out of Hungary from the north, toward the capital. Italian and Croatian divisions advanced down the main highway along the coast to Split. A Hungarian army with the 187th Reserve Infantry Division, the 188th Reserve Mountain Division and the newly formed 189th Reserve

Infantry Division attacked from the north. The Romanians also committed an army and made a substantial air force contribution. As the armed forces of Yugoslavia were at war with themselves, the High Command weren't expecting a lot of resistance. Lang had heard that before in Russia.

Yugoslavia was already a divided nation. After the defeat of England in 1940, two of the country's northern provinces had broken away. Both Croatia and Slovenia were now independent states with their own small air force and navy. Germany recognized these new countries and received a contribution from both nations to the war on the Eastern Front. Slovenia sent an infantry division which was in the line near Moscow, while the Croatians contributed with a motorized division and a squadron of Bf 109 E4 fighter planes. Slovenia's relationship with Germany was more problematic as the Führer expressed an interest in absorbing parts of the new nation into the Greater Reich. Slovenia's troops were therefore only sent to the quieter zones in Russia, and the country didn't receive any modern equipment from Germany.

To make matters worse, there were also problems brewing in Greece. Mussolini never accepted the friendly neutrality that Germany fostered with the Greek government. Now that relationship with Germany was coming apart, as food and oil shortages racked the southeastern European nation. Prime Minister Metaxas asked for supplies of both, and though they were promised none ever arrived. Metaxas was angry and now understood Hitler couldn't be trusted. So he turned to the Allies. By June of 1942, the Suez Canal had been cleared of Italian troops and in July the first Commonwealth ships returned to the Mediterranean. In August, two battleships and four cruisers sailed through the Canal to be based at Beirut. Cyprus was reinforced and the advance by Commonwealth forces to Cairo and the Nile Delta left the Suez waterway open for the Allies to use safely. Port Said was brought back to full capacity.

The USA reached out to Greece, offering modern military equipment, food, and fuel. Indeed, as a gesture of goodwill, fifty M3 tanks, eighty 105mm howitzers and twenty P-40 fighters were sent to Athens. As soon as this equipment arrived in August, the Greek government tightened its exchange rate with Germany. Then Metaxas restricted mineral exports and forbid any flights over Greek territory by the Luftwaffe. The Prime Minister later retracted some of these restrictions, but the damage was done. Hitler was furious and now worried about his southeastern flank. He was painfully aware that Romania, his main source of oil, was close to Greece. Germany also needed the small amount of rare minerals the country mined for heat resistant parts for jet engines (though at this stage Turkey was still exporting these minerals as well). For the moment Germany lacked the strength to invade both countries. The Führer could only take one of these countries at a time and this gave Greece time to prepare.

Metaxas was playing a dangerous game and he knew it, yet he wasn't prepared to let his people starve. He wished to placate Hitler by ceding a few islands as bases for the Kriegsmarine, while stalling for time. As the Allies built their strength in the Middle East, he anticipated one day they would be able to send troops to support his country if the need arose. He hoped that it wouldn't but one never knew.

Germany seemed to collect enemies like cow dung attracted flies, thought Lang. Now here he was leading the Panzeraufklärungs-Lehr-Abteilung, or reconnaissance battalion. The armoured cars for the unit came from various training schools, with Dutch M39s and Csaba armoured cars from Hungary. Eighty of these had been swapped for Italian Macchi 202 and a few, by circuitous routes, made their way into the German army. His unit even used old Panzer IIs and a single Panzer I. Virtually anything that could be taken by the new division was swept up in its move from Northern France to Bulgaria. Its sister division, the 10th Panzer, was only at eighty percent of its established strength but at least was equipped with German armoured cars and guns. Hell, his anti-tank guns were 47mm APX French guns with only twenty rounds each. He thought it was a crazy way to fight a war.

Ahead, older Do 17 twin-engine bombers from the Bulgarian air force attacked positions held by the Yugoslavian army. Leutnant

Scholler moved from where he'd been watching the countryside through his binoculars, and sat next to his commanding officer.

"Sir, those bombers have just plastered the village in front of us," said the junior officer.

"According to the map it's called Sinjac. A speck of nothing that just became swept up in the war," answered Lang.

"There's a hill and a gorge up ahead. The enemy are probably going to try and hold us here while they build a more substantial line near the bridge."

"We can't let that happen. See if you can whistle up some more air support. I want us to charge down the road, all guns blazing, and see if we can take the bridge on the bounce."

Lang knew the Yugoslavian Air Force had been caught on the ground on the first day of the war and largely destroyed. However, the air support for this campaign came from five different Axis countries and the Luftwaffe, like the army, had scraped together whatever it could find for this attack.

The aircraft, which appeared to attack the Yugoslavian positions in the hills, were Romanian IAR 80Bs with fifty kilo bombs, followed by twelve Stukas from the same air force. When Lang's command reached the village, only a couple of machine guns and a smattering of rifle fire greeted him. He sent two Stummel half-tracks forward to blast the enemy from their positions and then assaulted the ridgeline behind the village with infantry supported by mortars. The Yugoslavians ran or surrendered.

Two days later the reconnaissance battalion rested in the city of Nis. The 10th Panzer Division leapfrogged Lang's unit and made a dash for the capital. Everywhere the story was the same, with the Yugoslavian army as ready to turn on itself as to fight the invasion. Forces loyal to Prince Paul and the Regency fought against the coup leaders and the eighteen-year-old, King Peter. Serbian anger against the Tripartite Act bubbled to the surface as brother fought brother. Slogans such as, 'Better the grave than be a slave,' were painted on walls, and the weak government was only just clinging to power. As the Germans advanced, King Peter took power in Belgrade.

Pockets of ferocious resistance by units composed mainly of Serbs occurred in the north of the country, where fighting continued along the line of the Danube. Here, the Hungarians struggled to form bridgeheads across the river. It was only the intervention of the 155th Reserve Panzer Division that broke the stalemate, and the advance from the north resumed. The Italian Pistoia Motorised Division and the 2nd Cavalry Division moved almost unopposed, first Zenica and then Sarajevo were taken, while Mostar was seized by the Croatian army.

SS trucks and Kubelwagens pulled in across the town square ahead of Lang's half-track. He watched as the company formed up in front of an officer wearing a trench coat. The officer pointed at squads, then sent them toward various houses. Soon doors were being smashed open and civilians dragged out on to the street. Lang exchanged a look with Leutnant Scholler.

"Sir, General Rommel told us to keep a low profile," said the junior officer.

Lang frowned. "I know," he muttered.

Most of the people rounded up by the SS were men but a few women were also taken. A wife tried to hold onto the arm of her husband and was clubbed to the ground with a rifle butt. Then three men broke free and ran toward an alley. An SS Rottenführer raised his MP 34 and fired two quick bursts. People screamed and children cried out as the men jerked and fell. One almost made it to cover, then was hit in both legs. The officer in the trench coat drew out his pistol and shot the wounded man through the back of the head.

"Wherever we go Scholler, these dogs turn up," said Lang.

"I know, sir. Looks like they have one of their lists," said Scholler.

"Jews, anyone with leftist leanings, and intellectuals."

"Nearly all men at the moment though, sir."

"For the time being."

Shots rang out from an upper story window and two SS men fell. While everyone dived for cover, a few of the captives ran for safety. A grenade exploded near the Rottenführer and the man screamed. As he fell, a bearded man scooped up the fallen MP 34 and fired into the other SS men hiding at the rear of the truck. Lang saw some of his men reach for their weapons.

"Hold your fire, men," he ordered. Let the SS defend themselves, he thought. I'll say I was afraid to hit fellow Germans by accident if anyone asks.

The SS responded with indiscriminate small arms fire, killing the bearded man and other prisoners. An MG 42 started shooting at the window where the original shots originated, and soon squads of men were advancing down either side of the street. Lang could hear the distinctive sound of a Thompson submachine gun and the bark of rifles. He wondered where the Yugoslavians had found the American gun, as the SS and their assailants exchanged shots. Eventually there were multiple grenade explosions and the shooting stopped. Three dead men dressed in the uniform of the Yugoslavian army were dragged out on to the street, while the SS gathered more prisoners. The officer was yelling and pointing, as his command pulled women and children out on to the street as well.

He gestured and ten people, selected randomly, were taken to a wall at the edge of the square and executed.

"What's he doing?" growled Lang.

"He seems to be treating the incident as though it were a partisan attack," said Scholler.

"The dead enemy are clearly in uniform."

The SS officer shot a crying woman and an old man at random, then some of his men started firing into the crowd of prisoners with submachine guns, pistols, and rifles.

"He's lost control," said Scholler. The junior officer was pale and his eyes wide with shock.

Lang left cover and strode toward the SS men. "Cease fire," he yelled. Some of his men emerged from behind the parked half-tracks, while his headquarter's staff peered from the windows of a café where they had taken cover. He was forced to bellow at the top of his voice before the SS stopped shooting. As he approached the young SS officer, he could see the man was visibly shaking. He wiped at his small moustache and glared at Lang.

"What is the meaning of this Obersturmführer? Have you lost control?" shouted Lang.

"These people are hostages and will be executed due to an attack by bandits!"

"I'm your ranking officer and you will address me as sir! One, these people aren't hostages; two, your assailants clearly wear the uniform of the Yugoslavian army; and three, these operations are supposed to be carried out discreetly."

Only the last point made the SS officer hesitate. "This isn't an army matter, sir," he said.

"You've undertaken this operation without setting up the necessary security, putting my men and your own at risk. What unit are you from?"

"The 13th Regiment 7th SS Mountain Division Prince Eugen," the officer said. "We received orders to divert from the fighting in order to clear the rear areas of Jewish bandits and other undesirables."

"You were to execute them in the main square?"

The short man looked away. "No sir, we were to transport them to a holding area near Pirot."

"Have you been in action yet? I haven't heard of this division before."

"This is our first action, sir."

"So you failed to set up proper security measures and broke your orders, because, what, you are angry?"

"Sir, this area was supposed to have been cleared by the army."

"Don't you even dare to presume my boys haven't done their job. We've been leading the charge to the capital since the start of the invasion. My battalion was sent here to rest and resupply. We are back in the thick of it tomorrow. Where will your company be then? Fighting more bandits?" Lang gestured at the women and children. "I suggest you take only those who are on the list and leave. Stick to your orders."

Lang knew this would only save a few lives and the SS would return. Hopefully, the locals would have scattered by then and perhaps a few of the children might be saved.

"Yes sir," muttered the Obersturmführer.

"And your lack of control here today will be reported," said Lang. He understood that this would be a waste of time. Maybe if Rommel were here he'd make life uncomfortable for this swine, but Field Marshal Walther Model was in charge of this campaign and his corps was commanded by General Ernst Dehner, both committed Nazis.

The SS officer glared at him and gave his men new orders. His company gathered its wounded and dead, and scoured the town for those Yugoslavians who were on the list held by the Obersturmführer. In the end only fifteen were found, the others being dead or having escaped during the confusion of the fire fight. Eight women and four children had been killed, while others lay wounded on the ground. The SS soon withdrew, leaving Lang and his command in the square.

"Scholler, find the medics and treat the civilians. They can remove the dead for burial as they wish. Find someone who can explain this to them," ordered Lang.

"Gruber speaks English. That's our best chance, sir," said the junior officer.

Lang waved him away and walked back to his half-track. He hadn't exactly kept a low profile. If Rommel ever found out, he wouldn't be pleased.

V

The summer weather was fading, with the days becoming colder. Rain often swept down over the moors, drenching the green fields around Poundsgate. Maggie looked out from the barn over the wet cobbles and smiled. She liked it here. On sunny days she would walk down to the River Dart and fish with an old bamboo rod, spinning for brown trout or salmon. She'd even caught a couple of fish which pleased Aunt Mary no end. Uncle Peter sometimes came with her but he preferred to use a worm on a hook, and Maggie never saw him catch anything. She thought he liked to just sit and enjoy the peace of the river.

Today the pools near Spitwitch were the meeting place for the leadership of the local resistance group. Tod Greenwich and Samson Thistle were to meet her to discuss moving another Jewish family to safety. So far, four groups had been taken on a fishing boat to Ireland. A trawler leaving just after dark could reach halfway across the St. George Channel by dawn. Luftwaffe planes patrolled from Swansea but didn't reach the area until 10 a.m. and never approached the Irish coast. The danger to the fishermen and the

Jewish families were patrolling E-boats at night. A few of these fast-attack craft had radar but many of these vessels did not. Maggie believed the risk acceptable, and wanted to transport more Jewish groups to safety by using this method.

Watching German troop movements and protecting the small Jewish population of Devon was all her group had done so far. Maggie wished she could strike a substantial blow, but understood any attack upon enemy troops would precipitate retaliation from the local SS or the 207th Security Division. Notices were plastered on walls in Torquay and Exeter proclaiming any attacks on German units would lead to hostages being shot. Maggie didn't want to be responsible for the deaths of innocent English civilians.

She leaned back against the trunk of an ancient oak and listened. It wasn't long before Maggie heard the snap of a twig and the crunch of autumn leaves. Slowly she eased her pistol out of her coat and waited. Then she heard the dry, elastic tic sound made by a robin and smiled. Stepping around the corner, Maggie saw the bearded figure of Tod Greenwich. The middle aged man nodded at her and placed his fishing rod against a tree.

"Thought it a good idea to bring some gear, in case I bumped into a patrol," he said.

A few minutes later Samson Thistle arrived, stumbling along the path like a drunken deer.

Tod rolled his eyes and Maggie grinned.

"You have the bushcraft of someone from London," she said stepping into the open. "It's hard to believe you've lived here all your life."

The young red-headed man scratched at his square jaw. "Never been a hunter or a fisherman, just a farmer. Didn't see the need for sneakin' around, 'til now," he said.

Maggie shook her head and they all moved into a thicket of alder trees.

"The Freedmans are safe?" Maggie asked.

Samson nodded.

"And the Leibermans?" she turned to Tod.

"The youngest boy was a bit sick but he's better now. They're ready to move," the bearded man said.

"Alright, I'll guide them to the woods near Frenchbeer on the first night. That's about eight miles. The next day I'll take them to another forest on the northern side of the moors near Folly Gate. After that we have transport arranged which will move the two families to Chambercomb on the other side, on the northern coast of Devon," said Maggie.

"How are they to be shifted?" asked Sampson.

Maggie hesitated. "Best you don't know. We need to compartmentalise the different parts of the journey in case anyone is captured. The families don't know your names?"

"No Maggie. We did like you said," muttered Tod.

"Good. If they are taken, we don't want to make it easy for the Germans to find us. Moving them at night will mean the families won't have a clear idea of where they are."

"They're from Exeter and Exmouth, so that'll help," said Tod.

Maggie nodded.

It wasn't the first part of the journey that she was worried about. The hay cart to the coast was what concerned her. Moving people and mounds of straw seemed so obvious, yet the cart had a false bottom where people could lay flat. It wasn't comfortable but it worked, or had so far. As it was, Maggie was more concerned about the Germans shutting down the fishing boats. She was surprised they hadn't so far but thought it was probably an oversight. The 207th Security Division was occupying all of Devon, Cornwall, and Somerset. There were smaller Luftwaffe, Kriegsmarine, and SS units scattered around but there was no doubt the Germans were spread thin. The trawlers would soon either run out of fuel, or an enemy officer would finally realise it wasn't a good idea to allow the vessels to go to sea.

The Germans still inspected the boats when they left and returned, but it was easy enough to transfer people or goods to and from them in small boats at night, as long as the weather was fine. The area did lack hidden, or sheltered coves, so all of these operations were dependent on gentle winds and clear visibility. Bottom line though was this operation couldn't last. She needed to get as many Jews out this way before the Germans shut it down.

It was dark when Tod escorted the two families to the B3357 road at the edge of the moor. Two men and a female waited for her as well as six children, the oldest of which was a sixteen-year-old girl and the youngest a seven-year-old boy. Tod did some introductions and Maggie gave her name as Claire.

"Right, we are following the ridgeline all the way to the new reservoir at Fernworthy. There's thick forest around the new dam and we'll spread a tarp and sleep near the stone circle. The moors are open, but as we will be travelling at night that won't be an issue. We leave the road in a few hundred metres and then it's all walking tracks until we reach Folloy Gate. The last four miles of the journey are through farmland and you'll need to skirt the town of Okehampton, though I'm told there is plenty of woodlands near the castle and railway line. Anyway, you'll have a different guide for the last part of the trip."

"Miss Claire, do we have enough food? The children ate at the last farmhouse, but before that finding enough to eat has been a struggle," asked the woman called Hannah.

"I've brought bread, cheese, and cold chicken and some of my aunt's cake. Now, one final point. If I say drop, fall to the ground without hesitation. The Germans rarely patrol the moors but it's not unheard of. Do not rise until I give the all clear."

"We cannot eat the cheese," said the oldest male. "It isn't kosher."

"The children are hungry Jacob, they need food," said the younger male.

"It is forbidden by our laws, Isaac. We do not pick and choose when to obey them."

"I'll eat the cheese and you can have the chicken," said Maggie. "There are also some hard boiled eggs, which the children can eat as we walk."

"They may have unseen drops of blood in them," said Jacob.

"This lady is trying to help us," said the sixteen-year-old girl.

"Do not interrupt your elders, Rachel!" snapped Jacob.

"I think we can take the risk," said Hannah. "The children have a long walk in front of them."

The oldest man took some time to consider before giving a single sharp nod.

Maggie handed out the eggs passing one to the sixteen-year-old last. The girl stared at her.

"Are you carrying a gun?" asked Rachel.

"Yes, would you like to see?" said Maggie. She pulled out a Walther P38 and held it before the girl. Maggie was happy to have the pistol. Nigel said there was one at the weapons cache and she'd immediately swapped it for the lesser powered Muaser HSc she'd been given originally. Tod had her old pistol now.

"Can you show me how to use it?" Rachel asked.

"That is not appropriate," Isaac said sternly.

"Uncle, we are on the run from the Germans who are killing our people and you would stop me being able to defend myself?"

"It isn't your place to argue with me, or to learn how to use a weapon."

"This young woman fights," said Rachel pointing at Maggie.

"She isn't Jewish."

Maggie felt her hackles rise. "No, I'm just risking my life to save you. Your niece is right. The Germans are your enemy and mine, and everyone should be ready to fight them."

"This isn't your concern Claire, if that is your real name? I lead this family, or what's left of it," said Jacob.

Maggie frowned and tucked the pistol away. “We are leaving now. Make sure everyone keeps up,” she growled before walking to the front of the group.

They walked along worn tracks up a slight gradient to the top of a ridgeline. Somewhere to the west, the Walla Brook gurgled. Maggie led the group around the small farming community of Cator Court, before skirting the edge of Postbridge. The final stretch to the reserve of forest around the new dam took the group through open moor land and across the B3212. By this time, the children were starting to struggle and Maggie tried to think of a way to keep their minds off sore feet and drooping eyelids.

“Do you know the story of the Hair Hands of the Moors?” she said.

“No,” said Rachel.

“I’ve heard it,” said Isaac.

“Do you mind if I tell the children?” Maggie asked.

“No, it will certainly help keep them awake.”

“Well, it seems the stretch of road we just crossed is known for a number of strange vehicle accidents. The first incident happened in 1910 when a milk cart veered off the road into a ditch. The driver couldn’t explain it at the time, but said it looked as though the reins were jerked sideways and the horses spooked by something he couldn’t see. Other strange accidents occurred on the road with people mysteriously crashing their wagons or cars. Anyway, in 1921 an army captain reported that a pair of invisible hands took control of his motor bike, which caused him to veer off the road and into a hedge. Later, I think it was in 1924, a woman stated that she saw a pair of hairy hands trying to force open the door of her caravan. They disappeared when she made the sign of the cross,” said Maggie.

Jacob snorted. “The cross holds no power. Do not listen to this rubbish.”

“It’s just a story, uncle,” said Rachel.

"When we reach the stone circle in the forest we will be safe. The fairies will protect us," said Maggie, embellishing on the story she'd heard from Uncle Peter.

"Now you speak of fairies as well!" said Jacob.

"I'm trying to respect your beliefs. Many around here believe the stones contain power. Whoever put them there did so before the Romans arrived," said Maggie.

"Our people predate the Romans," said Jacob.

Maggie sighed. "I'm trying to keep the children going. It's a story, that's all."

"It's nonsense," said Jacob.

"Claire is trying to help, uncle and who is to say it's nonsense? The ways of God are mysterious," said Rachel.

"You know nothing of the Lord's ways, girl," snapped Jacob.

"Look, we all tired. Why don't we just concentrate on making it to the forest before dawn?" said Maggie.

The final stretch took the group over a mile of open moorland to the forest. The pine woodland here had been planted in the early 1930s, so most of the trees were only about three times the height of a tall man. It would provide Maggie with the cover she needed to hide the family for the day, then they could push on to the northern end of the moor. They would have to cross a brook, the River Taw, and the North Teign. This high up in the moors these crossings wouldn't be difficult, though she suspected that at least some of the group would get their feet wet. After sleeping for most of the day Maggie ate a little cheese and bread, and walked to the edge of the woodland. In the distance she could see a small group of roe deer grazing. The sun was low but it back lit the rocky tors and hills, creating a landscape of shadows and grassland.

"It's beautiful, in a stark kind of way," said Rachel.

Maggie hadn't heard the girl approach and started at her voice.

"I'm sorry, I didn't mean to intrude," said Rachel.

"No, I'm just angry I failed to hear your approach. I need to be more aware than that," said Maggie. "It's my job to keep us all safe."

Rachel shrugged. "There's no one out here," she said.

"I was taught to be careful at all times."

Rachel nodded and the two women fell into a comfortable silence for a while.

"Do you know why the Germans hate us?" asked Rachel suddenly.

"I've wondered that," said Maggie. She remembered Kurt briefly and his fear of his comrades finding out he was even part Jewish. "To start with they needed someone to blame for everything that went wrong in their country, the loss of the Great War, the collapse of the economy, the carving up of their country. The Jews are seen as a people who live apart. You are an easy target."

"It's more than that though, isn't it?" said Rachel. "Sometimes I think people just like to hate. It's as powerful as love."

Maggie turned and looked at the girl. She hadn't expected any thoughtful statements from the teenager. "You are correct. Then a sociopath rises to power, not a mad man, as some people say. Hitler is no raving lunatic. He is not the first of his type to rise to the top, nor will he be the last. Besides, his hatred watered fertile ground."

"It seems so unfair. My people don't want to take over the world. My Uncle talks of a homeland for our people but that's about it. I just want somewhere safe to live. Maybe America, or a country of our own, I don't know."

"We'll try and get you somewhere safe," said Maggie. She liked this girl and on the spur of the moment pulled out her pistol. "I want you to have this."

Rachel's eyes grew wide. "My uncle would never let me keep it."

"Then hide it. You need to be able to defend yourself. If the Germans find you and there is no hope of hiding your identity, then fight. First I'll show you how it works."

Maggie went through the safety features first and drilled them into the girl, then she talked about how to aim and the importance of taking cover.

"Get the first shot if you can. The Huns won't expect you to be carrying a weapon. Shoot the most important looking man first."

To begin with Rachel appeared frightened, then Maggie noticed a shift in the girl's expression. Her jawline firmed and her eyes narrowed in determination. Good, she's taking this seriously, Maggie thought.

"Don't ever use it unless there's no other choice," said Maggie.

Rachel nodded and then hugged Maggie tight. "Thank you," the girl said.

The following day they hiked the rest of the way across the moor, skirting Okehampton Castle and crossing through farmland to Folly Gate. Maggie stayed with the family at a barn near the Crossway Inn. She snuck away with Rachel in the middle of the night and quizzed her on the pistol. The girl answered most of the questions correctly. Maggie hoped she'd made the right decision. In the morning she said goodbye to the group and turned for home. So far Maggie hadn't seen a single German and her luck held until she reached Poundsgate three days later.

Rachel and her family travelled safely by cart to the coast and were transferred to a fishing trawler two days later. Poor weather held up the operation, with high winds preventing the rowing boat heading out to meet the larger vessel. Then the family clambered aboard and they all started sailing toward Ireland. Unfortunately, the Germans were experimenting with shore based radar in the area and noticed the unusual behaviour of the trawler. An E-boat patrolling out of Swansea was ordered to cut across the track of the fishing boat and question the crew.

Rachel thought she was safe. As she looked out over the sea and fought nausea, one of the young sailors approached her and handed her a dry cracker.

"It'll help. Also keep your eyes on the horizon," said the young man. Rachel saw the sailor had large brown eyes and long lashes. She thought he was very handsome. His eyes narrowed and she turned to look. In the distance a light lanced out into the darkness.

"Hells," he muttered. "You better get below."

Rachel moved away to a position behind the wheelhouse, while the young man went inside. A moment later he re-emerged with a Thomson submachine gun. She went inside and saw a rifle next to the captain, and another crew member instructing her father on how to use the .303 calibre weapon.

"It is similar to a gun I have used before," he said. "Burt why don't we just hide?" asked her Father."

“We aren’t set up with false hulls or hidden rooms. There is nowhere for you to hide,” snapped the captain over his shoulder. “If we don’t lose them, then they board us and we’ll all die, eventually.”

Rachel could see the tension in the broad shoulders of the captain. His bearded face was grim in the soft light of the cabin.

“Get the life preservers on the little one,” said the tall crew man who’d been instructing her father.

Rachel couldn’t believe this was happening. The light seemed to be getting closer. What the crew didn’t know was that land based radar was guiding the E-boat toward them. They were only fifteen miles from the coast and soon would be out of range of the German device.

“Skipper, maybe we should give up, if they spot us,” said the skinny crew member.

"And end up in some Gestapo torture room, no thanks! We are running Jews, Bob. They'll want the rest of the network," growled the captain.

"But we don't know anything," said Bob.

"Do you think they'll believe you? Now grab some grenades and give one to Charlie. If we get close enough, one of those in their engine room might give us a chance. Rachel saw Bob go white. Her father's hands were shaking and a line of tears ran down her mother's face. She pulled the pistol from her pocket and cocked it.

"Where did you get that?" snapped Jacob.

"Claire gave it to me, so I could defend myself."

"Give it to me," yelled her uncle.

"No. I'm going to fight."

"Please hand the pistol over," said her father.

"I'm not going to stand by and let others shoot at me," said Rachel.

Calmness settled on her as she realised they might all die. The E-boat was less than a mile away and she felt sure it's light would settle on their vessel shortly.

"Let the girl fight," growled the captain. The bearded man stared fiercely at the girl.

"You know how to use that gun?"

"Yes, our guide showed me," she answered.

"Okay then, just don't start shooting until one of us does," he said.

The light swept over the trawler a moment later and a voice came at them from a megaphone ordering the captain to stop.

"Keep the guns hidden to the last second," said the bearded man.

"Then shoot anyone who looks important first," added Rachel.

The captain smiled. "Well said, lass," he muttered.

The captain put the trawler's nose into the wind to make the E-boat's approach more difficult. Rachel stayed hidden behind the wheelhouse with her family, while Charlie moved to the bow with a rope in his hand. The captain cut the engines and walked onto the deck. He'd left another gun hidden under a tarp and stashed a grenade in his pocket.

"What seems to be the problem?" he yelled up at the E-boat bridge.

The two boats came together at the bow with only the forward 20mm gun covering the trawler. Three crew members waited at the rail of the E-boat, the S-22 as the Germans called her. It was an older boat and only mounted the forward gun and a twin-mounted 20mm gun aft. An MG 42 was in position in the centre of the boat, fitted with a shield. The crew of twenty-four had seen action in the 1940 invasion but since then had little to do until the second attack on Britain. During this period they laid mines near Dover, but did nothing else.

Rachel thought the enemy vessel looked powerful and deadly. It was about a third longer than the trawler and seemed to bristle with weapons. As she watched, the captain pulled the grenade from his pocket and tossed it next to the forward 20mm gun. At the same time Charlie snatched up the Thomson and gunned down the three German sailors who were about to board. He then jumped across on to the enemy vessel. Bob fired a Sten gun blindly at the E-boat while her father stood holding the rifle, staring.

"Shoot dad, shoot," she yelled.

Rachel stepped around the wheelhouse, forgetting Maggie's warning about cover, and fired two rounds at a German who was cocking the heavy machine gun behind the bridge. The man yelped and grabbed at his ear, before dropping to the deck. She fired two more shots at the area before remembering to drop behind the wheelhouse.

Somewhere on the E-boat Charlie was firing his machine gun. There was another explosion and the young sailor fell into the water. At this point the two boats started to drift apart. The forward 20mm gun had been knocked out by the first grenade and the E-boat crew caught off guard. Now Rachel could hear yelling in German, then the sleek vessel turned slightly. She fired her pistol at the bridge until the firing pin clicked on an empty chamber. Her father worked the bolt on the rifle, firing steadily.

The noise of the aft 20mm cannon was deafening. Rachel could see flashes of fire from the muzzle, then saw pieces of timber fly from the deck as shells tore up the area at the bow of the trawler. Bob dropped his gun and ran inside the wheelhouse. The engine roared and the trawler lurched toward the E-boat. As the distance between the two vessels was only fifty metres, the fishing boat didn't gain a lot of momentum before it struck. The blow was only glancing and the E-boat pulled away easily.

Bob swung the trawler around and the captain fired his weapon. Rachel picked up the Sten and pulled the trigger. She was surprised how the weapon shook in her hands. Now the Germans gathered their wits and turned the E-boat side on to the fishing trawler. Both 20mm cannons and the machine gun ripped the boat apart. Shells punched through the wheelhouse killing Bob and sending flying glass in all directions. Rachel stood transfixed as a stream of projectiles tore up the railing and hull. She pulled the trigger again, emptying the magazine of the weapon. A powerful blow hit her in the middle of the chest and she slumped against the shattered wheelhouse. Her father reached for her, but he fell with a grunt across her legs. She placed her hand on his head and watched as her mother and two little brothers jumped into the sea. The other children were still inside the cabin of the boat. Rachel didn't feel any pain, only a type of wonder. I think you'd be proud of me Claire, she thought, then she died.

Everyone on board was dead and the trawler was sinking by the bow, its thin hull riddled with cannon holes. The E-boat's powerful light swept the water and a surprised crew pulled the two children and a badly wounded woman from the water. The sailors didn't find any other survivors. The Germans suffered four dead and three wounded, one of the crew having lost most of his ear due to an accurate pistol shot. A very annoyed Kapitanleutnant turned his vessel around and headed for base.

When the E-boat made it to shore, the German navy sent the wounded woman to hospital and alerted the Gestapo. The children were sent to a local orphanage as the navy personnel weren't sure what to do with them. This snap decision saved the children's lives. Hannah died of her wounds before the German security services could interview her. By the time anyone thought of the children, the Catholic nuns had moved them to Wales. All of the documentation said the children had gone to Swindon but when SS enquires were made they were redirected to another parish at Oxford. The two children were never found by the Germans and after the war were reunited with other relatives in Northern Ireland.

Maggie didn't hear about what had happened for over a month. An E-boat had returned to port carrying children. Some of the crew were wounded and the ship itself a little battered from the grenade explosions and pock marked with bullet holes. The children were whisked away but there was no sign of Rachel. Everyone else involved in the encounter was presumed dead. On hearing the news, Maggie cried for days. In many ways the news of Rachel's disappearance struck her harder than Kurt's death. The girl was so full of life and promise and now she was gone. Maggie hoped she had used the pistol. Uncle Peter tried to console her but she felt a deep depression settle on her. In the end her Aunt Mary pulled her aside.

"The Jewish girl is but one casualty in this war. You need to put it behind you and find a way of helping it motivate you."

"What can I do, Aunty? The Germans hold half the country and nobody seems to know how to beat them," Maggie said.

"We don't give in, even if they take all of England. How can any of us look in the mirror if we let this Hitler and his cronies run Europe? They are filled with hate. We must stop them."

Maggie sighed. "You are right. It's just she reminded me of myself. I really liked her."

"Make them pay. Find a way."

"I will Aunty, I will."

V

Reichsmarschell Kesselring looked at the reports from the Russian Front, as his Mercedes drove toward the airfield. It looked as though the XXIV Panzer Corps had bounced Stalingrad taking the northern half of the city while the rest of the 6th Army, reinforced by the 1st Panzer Division from Army Group Centre, helped hold a corridor open to the city. The 4th Panzer Army attacked from south of Stalingrad while the III Panzer Corps made up of the 13th Panzer and Wiking Divisions were stranded on the Volga at Zubovka and Chyorny Yar, one hundred and twenty kilometres further southeast. The long northern flank was guarded by a Romanian army but held mostly by the 1st Panzer Army, with units such as the 22nd Infantry Division pulled from reserve to help.

The Romanians were now in possession of ninety Marder IIs, courtesy of General Wagner. This had been one of his last acts as head of supply in Russia before the Führer transferred him to the reserve army in Germany. Kesselring's information led him to believe these tank destroyers had been scattered among the four divisions of the Romanian army, along with twenty-five converted T-34s. This had been done on Wagner's orders and infuriated German generals in Army Group Centre. Before being sent west, Wagner had argued that the anti-tank capacity of Germany's allies was woeful and something needed to be done to strengthen them.

The last time he'd seen the man, Kesselring thought he was having a breakdown. Wagner had complained about the flow of reinforcements east going to the wrong front, how the transportation system he'd built was now falling apart, and the loss of rolling stock to the SS for the Jewish solution. Kesselring didn't want to know about the last issue. The Führer's plans in this area were none of his business. He was a military leader, not a political one. All he wanted to know was that more planes were being built and more air crew being trained.

Around Krasnaya, in the high peaks of the Caucasus Mountains, the Italian Alpine Corps had broken through the Russian lines and reached Alder on the coast of the Black Sea. From here the two mobile divisions allocated to the Georgia area attempted to break out along the coast road to reach the rebel-held town of Poti. They only made it to the town of Sokhumi, until dwindling supplies and stiffening Russian resistance forced them to halt. Neither the German or Romanian mountain units managed to force a path over the high peaks further east into Georgia or Azerbaijan.

There had been border clashes between Soviet forces and the Turks, leading toward some hope that Turkey would enter the war as an ally of Germany. Fw 190s had fought Russian La-5 fighters, and artillery exchanges occurred around Batumi on the coast. The reports in front of Kesselring suggested the Americans were trying to calm the situation and the initial aggression was dissipating.

Yugoslavia was now occupied by the Axis powers. The campaign had been a whirlwind of lightning advances, marred by the bombing of Belgrade. Kesselring didn't regret the decision to bomb the capital as he was sure it had helped speed the decision of the rebels to flee to the interior of the country. Now it looked as though the Führer would order the invasion of Greece. All the divisions used to attack Yugoslavia had moved south to be joined by three partially rebuilt SS panzer divisions. Kesselring wished the attack weren't necessary, as he'd had to scrape together Luftwaffe units to support the army. He'd pulled the Kampfgeschwader (KG) 53 from northern Russia, Sturzkampfgeschwader (St) 5's 1st Gruppe from Leningrad, and all of Jagdgeschwader (JG) 1 from Germany, to support the coming attack. The Bulgarians had promised all of their air force to support the attack and the Italians also were sending three bomber wings and four fighter wings. The problem was that the Bulgarians only had thirty Br 109 E fighters and a similar number of Stuka dive bombers. They had recently purchased twenty Caproni Ca.309 light bombers from Italy but by the standards of 1942 these aircraft were already obsolete. The Regia

Aeronautica aircraft and pilots were better than they were at the start of the war, but that wasn't saying much.

Now the Greeks were receiving US Fighters, bombers, artillery, and tanks, Kesselring agreed that Germany had to move quickly before the new equipment was integrated into the Greek armed forces. Kesselring thought Prime Minister Metaxas was a fool for making deals with the Americans. What he didn't know was the number of deals Hitler had made with the Greek leader and broken. The country was on the verge of starvation, industry was collapsing as Germany didn't keep its promise to deliver oil, and Italy was still pushing for territorial concessions from Greece. The USA had managed to fill a Greek freighter with grain and sent two small tankers to Athens. This was now possible as the Suez Canal was open and being used by the Allies.

The Italian position in Africa appeared to be in real difficulty. The Commonwealth, under an Australian, General Heathcote Hammer, was performing exceedingly well. With scarce resources, the Commonwealth forces had taken Cairo and advanced across the

Nile Delta to Rasheed. Only the main branch of the Nile and a distance of forty kilometres separated the Australian 2nd Armoured Division with its Sentinel tanks from Alexandria. The Italians were now virtually cut off from their colonies in the Horn of Africa, with only a tenuous overland route remaining open. The Führer was looking at ways to support Mussolini but there was no spare capacity.

The Italian navy failed to stop the Americans delivering food and fuel to Greece. The difficulty was that the goods were transported in Greek registered ships, and the leadership of that country had made it clear any attempt to prevent the grain or fuel arriving would be met with aggression. This led to a clash between two Greek Greyhound class destroyers and three Italian Turbine class destroyers. Both sides lost a vessel in the exchange before eight newly purchased American B-25 Mitchell bombers attempted to attack the retreating Italian ships. All of the bombs missed.

It was a mess, but Kesselring could understand the Führer's anxiety at leaving Greece unoccupied. His reason for the coming attack was similar to that used to invade England. He could see these neutral countries being used by the Americans as a base from which to bomb important German resources. In the case of Greece, Kesselring could see the possibility of US Flying Fortresses attacking the oilfields in Romania. In England, the airfields in East Anglia were the main concern. From there, US heavy bombers could reach Germany.

Unlike England though, whose armed forces were weaker in 1942 compared to 1940, the Greek Army was stronger. It had originally purchased anti-tank guns from the Hungarians, then was forced to manufacture its own equipment, much of it copied from Czech examples. Its air force, until recently, struggled to purchase modern machines; the best being thirty Bloch MB 51 fighters from France. The Yugoslavian home-produced Rogozarski IK-3 fighter proved to be the equivalent of the British Hurricane. It was completely out classed by the Bf 109 and Fw 190 but now these were being replaced by the recently delivered American P-40 Kittyhawks.

In England Luftflotte 3 had lost all of JG 27 to supporting the Italians in Egypt. These eighty fighters supported the sixty Ju 88s of KG 77. Both these units had been recently built up to strength and were supposed to go to Russia. Now they were in Africa. The figures in front of him showed that the Luftwaffe, as of a week ago, had four thousand five hundred serviceable combat aircraft. This was a powerful force, but it was scattered across Europe and North Africa. He needed the Greek campaign to end swiftly so the aircraft could be moved to other locations. Germany had been stripped bare of planes, with only part of JG 53 and two Nachtjagdgeschwaders remaining to protect the country, while other bomber units trained and formed near the capital. At least he'd be able to send over a hundred He 111s to the east soon. He hoped they would bomb Baku and the oilfields still held by the Russians, though he understood they might be needed to hit rail links to Stalingrad.

Kesselring wasn't worried about the Allies intervention in Greece. He believed his air units would soon be released to other fronts, though some would need to stay to defend the Aegean Sea.

The Commonwealth was also stretched thin, with the Japanese threatening Australia. US forces were building up in the Middle East, but recent intelligence reports suggested that only their 3rd Infantry Division was there in full strength, while part of the 9th Infantry Division was supposed to be gathering at Jerusalem. Most of the American strength seemed to be gravitating toward the Pacific or England. Both the 1st and 2nd Armoured Divisions were somewhere around Liverpool, and at least two other infantry divisions had been encountered in Britain. This could be added to three Canadian divisions and six English divisions north of the rough line from the Wash to Chester. Rommel was holding this line with six German divisions and three from the Italian 8th Army. Sitting in reserve were the 23rd, 24th and 25th Panzer Divisions (the 27th Panzer was rolled into the 25th), while the 7th Panzer was withdrawn to France after handing over much of its equipment to the other units. Three divisions kept London under siege while slowly grinding into the city. A paratrooper division also assisted in this process.

Kesselring was confident the capital would fall soon. Unfortunately, that didn't mean England would surrender.

His other concern was that the Luftwaffe didn't control the skies over the front in England anymore. Any air operation north of the line from Bristol to Norwich could expect to meet enemy aircraft. P-38s, P40s, Canadian Spitfire Mark Vs, and Hurricanes contested Luftwaffe control. Kesselring was now worried that Northern Germany was in range of the American B-17s. At the moment though the US Army Air Force was more interested in supporting their ground forces or dropping supplies to the beleaguered defenders of London.

Finally his car arrived at the airfield at Rechlin, one hundred kilometres northwest of Berlin. He could have flown there, but had used the hour in the Mercedes as an excuse to read through the operational reports for the various fronts. The drive had also given him time to think. He was no more convinced than ever that the Luftwaffe needed more effective fighters, especially high altitude ones, as soon as possible. The jets were promising, in fact exciting, but he couldn't see them really being ready, with acceptable engine life until 1945. Speaking of which, the engine life of the Fw 190 C was still far from being optimal. At least it lasted longer than the Jumo 004 which powered the Me 262. Those power plants only lasted ten hours. The latest report said the engine life of the new Fw 190 was ninety hours. This wasn't good enough. The latest news was the engineers were suggesting that the Luftwaffe give up working on the unit, and move to developing the Jumo 213. Kesselring wasn't prepared to do that. With the scrapping of the Do 217 and the Me 410, there were plenty of the new engines available. Kurt Tank, head of the project, was certain he could make the troublesome engine work.

He exited the car and met all the usual officials. Kesselring asked the standard technical questions before finding himself alone with the designer, Kurt Tank. Nearby, an Fw 190 C with its four blade propeller and strange air scoop, sat parked on the runway. He turned to the man, noting the high forehead and receding hairline.

"Will it work?" he asked Tank.

"Yes, in time. There are still problems with the engine but we are making definite progress. Yesterday, the plane made seven hundred kilometres per hour at seven thousand metres altitude. The engine itself is extremely promising."

"I've heard the Jumo 213 could be a better option." Said Kesselring.

"It's nowhere near as ready and it's a bomber engine," said Tank.

"I'm going to continue developing it as well, and I want you to see how it would fit into a similar airframe."

"I thought you might say that, and the first prototype will be ready to fly in October. I'm calling that machine the Fw 190D"

Kesselring was surprised yet pleased. "Good, we need a couple of options. The Fw 190 C could be a high altitude interceptor, while the D model might prove to be a multi-role model. Kurt, I want these aircraft ready by mid to late next year. The Americans are coming and we need to maintain the technological edge. The Jet could be rushed, and maybe I'd have them online by autumn of 1944, but they wouldn't be properly tested. Mark my words, they are still the way of the future, but we need something in the interim. Your Fw Ta 152 is still being considered and there is even thoughts of a twin-engine machine. The P231 from Dornier looks very promising, but the devil will be in the detail. It always is."

"So you still think the war might last some time?"

"I have since I was visited by certain people in late 1941. I don't think you know General Wagner?"

"I've heard of him. He was sticking his nose in a while back, telling the engineers what they needed to do in order to make a good transport aircraft."

"Well, I hope they listened to him, though I think that issue has been resolved. No, the man may be an absolute pessimist but for a period of time he and some powerful friends managed to convince me to prepare for a long fight. Now I'm glad they did."

“You fear the Americans?”

“I’d be stupid not to,” said Kesselring.

Chapter Three: October 1942

A rain squall drenched the flight deck of the Enterprise. Commander James 'Pug' Southerland was sitting inside the cockpit of his Wildcat Grumman F4F-4, waiting for the all clear to take off. He was the first of his flight to take to the air today. The sun had just touched the horizon and he was to fly combat air patrol (CAP) above the fleet. The HMAS Tasman had also pulled into the wind and launched four Sea Brumbies. The rumour was that the Japanese were about to try and take Port Vila and maybe even Fiji. The Japanese had two heavy carriers and one lighter unit somewhere to the northwest. The Allies could only oppose them with two flat tops, and the Australian ship could only carry fifty-eight planes.

Southerland knew of the continuing raids on Luganville by the enemy. It was almost a six hundred mile flight one way by the Japanese, but the Zero managed the trip and escorted the bombers to targets around Espiritu Santo. This meant both sides could reinforce any naval battle with ground based air units. Southerland wasn't sure what the Japanese hoped to achieve by taking the island chain. He supposed it would make moving troops and materials to Australia harder, but otherwise he wasn't sure. This was the strategy of the Japanese High Command, but the enemy also wanted to engage the final remaining heavy carriers of the Allies and destroy them. Then they believed they could sweep as far as Fiji and Tonga. The aim was to create the greatest impediment to any US counter strike, and to hopefully force the Americans into a humiliating treaty.

Impractical schemes to attack the Panama Canal and the West Coast of the USA had been discussed and dismissed. Three huge submarines were being built and perhaps they could be used in the future to attack US soil, but for now it was not feasible to strike at targets so far from the Japanese island perimeter.

So far Southerland had destroyed four enemy aircraft. He was itching for more combat but was more concerned at the state of the war. Everywhere the Axis were on the march. Stalingrad had fallen, though the German advance in Russia seemed to have stalled sixty miles north of the city. However, it had made no progress at all in advancing east toward Astrakhan. London had surrendered a few days earlier to preserve its population and history. Now the Nazi flag flew above the Tower of London and the Houses of Parliament. The Allies needed a win. The rest of England was quiet and the only good news had come out of Egypt where Alexandria had just fallen. Even Greece looked as though it might fall under the heel of the Axis. The news throughout the ship was of the German attack across the border. It was too early to tell if Greece could hold out, or how much help could be sent their way.

Southerland took off and led his flight in a slow ascent to fifteen thousand feet. With a climb rate at between five hundred to one thousand feet a minute, it seemed to take an age to reach the required altitude. He still thought the earlier F4F-3 was a better aircraft than the F4. Sure, the extra guns and armour in the later model were nice, but they came at the expense of speed and rate of climb.

"Reaper One, we have a customer for you. Contact bearing three fifteen northwest, height fifteen thousand feet. Distance thirty-two miles," said a radar officer.

"Roger that, we are on our way," answered Southerland. He continued to climb to an equivalent height as the intruder, while leading only his wingman away from the fleet.

It didn't take long to find the enemy aircraft. The large Japanese float plane was flying west, following a destroyer which was scouting ahead of the US fleet, searching for submarines. It would soon spot the carriers, and then the enemy would be able to mount a strike on the Enterprise and the HMAS Tasman.

"She's an Emily, sir," said Ensign Lynman Fulton. The Kawanishi H8K was well protected with five 20mm cannons and plenty of lighter machine guns. They were a respected opponent.

"Reaper Two, come in from the north, I'll attack from the south. We'll try and split its fire. Aim for the cockpit area," ordered Southerland.

The two Wildcats split up and approached from different directions. At the same time, the Japanese float plane dived toward the ocean. He doesn't want us to get underneath him, thought Southerland. As he approached, the enemy aircraft tried to turn away from him. Southerland only managed to fire a short burst at the turning plane. Machine gun bullets peppered the fuselage just forward of the tail. He could see the tracers from enemy cannon shells racing toward his plane but managed to fly past the machine without being hit. Fulton came in from behind the big aircraft, taking fire from both the rear and dorsal turret. His six guns shot holes in the tail of the Emily and killed a gunner, but the Wildcat was also damaged.

"Flight leader, my engine temperature has gone through the roof. I have smoke in the cockpit," said Fulton.

"Can you make it back to the carrier?"

"The smoke is getting worse. Oh God, there's fire."

"Get out, Fulton," yelled Southerland.

He could hear screaming and saw the Wildcat below him streaming smoke and flames. Fulton was yelling and pleading. Southerland kept telling him to jump but something had gone wrong. Suddenly the fuel tank ruptured and the Wildcat exploded, ending his wingman's agony.

Fury washed over him and Southerland dived after the descending sea plane. He dropped in behind the shattered rear gunner's position and followed the Japanese aircraft through its twists and turns. From two hundred yards his six machine guns poured bullets into one wing and then the other. Eventually, the port engine of the Japanese machine caught fire, soon to be followed by an explosion in the inner starboard unit. Flames spread and the wing burnt through, causing the machine to crash into the sea in an explosion of spray.

He flew back to the Enterprise and finished his patrol in silence before landing. Southerland immediately realised something was up. He wasn't called for a briefing, just told to stay in his plane and wait for it to be refuelled. Southerland wanted time to think about what had happened to Fulton, to grieve for the man, but the Japanese fleet had been located and Admiral Fletcher wanted to beat the enemy carriers to the punch. In carrier warfare the first strike could be critical, so all efforts were being made to launch an attack as quickly as possible. Rather than attacking in two waves, every machine on both the Tasman and the Big E were being made ready.

A large enemy fleet was steaming south with carriers and battleships. A second group of cruisers and transport vessels followed about fifty miles further back. A flying fortress raid was going to be attempted on the enemy fleet, but it was switched to attacking enemy airfields on San Cristobal. This was an intelligent move as high flying bombers hadn't managed to hit anything of worth in attacks on fast moving ships so far in the war. The raids distracted Japanese ground based air power at a crucial stage of the Battle of the Torres Islands (often shortened to 'the Battle of Torres').

What Southerland didn't know was that a second strike was being formed on the airfields around Luganville. Here, Marine Air Group 23 (MAG 23) put together three squadrons of Wildcats and two of Douglas Dauntless dive bombers to attack the enemy ships. They would arrive thirty-five minutes before the naval squadrons and inflict little in the way of damage. However, two bombs hit the heavy Japanese cruiser Kumano. What the attack did was disrupt the Japanese defences and prevent two-thirds of the enemy strike force becoming airborne, before the US naval planes arrived over their fleet.

By the time the marine aircraft had arrived, the enemy had a good idea of where Fletcher's carriers were. At the very least, the missing Emily float plane gave an excellent indication of where to look. Thirty dive bombers and sixteen Zero fighters were already heading for the American fleet when the US and Australian planes started their attacks on the Japanese vessels. The Enterprise sent fifty-five aircraft and the Tasman forty more for the strike. These arrived over the enemy late in the morning. Commander James

Southerland led his flight toward the enemy, knowing that his job was to keep the Zeros away from the dive bombers and torpedo planes.

"Skipper, I can see the ships," said Ensign Peters. His new wingman had been transferred from another flight. Southerland was a little concerned that he'd never flown with the man, because teamwork was the essence of fighting Zeros.

"And at nine o'clock level I can see enemy fighters," he replied. "All right everyone, remember your training. Use the Weave to support your wingman. First attack will be head on."

The Japanese pilots were veterans and knew to avoid a head on confrontation with the Wildcats. The US planes hit harder and had more armour. Also, the Wildcats weren't the target for the enemy, the bombers were. Southerland's job was to protect the Avengers and Dauntless attack planes. This was difficult when the enemy fighters were faster and more maneuverable.

"Don't let them get past," he ordered.

The Zeros broke into two groups, forcing the American covering fighters to do the same. Southerland quickly found an enemy plane on his tail and yelled to his wingman.

"Turning toward you now," he called.

He maneuvered his Wildcat straight at his wingman as the Zero chased him. Cannon shells flew past his wing, a couple punching holes through the metal. He saw Peters coming straight at him and lifted the nose of his plane slightly. The Japanese pilot suddenly found himself flying straight at another Wildcat and panicked, pulling up. This exposed the belly of his plane to Ensign Peters. Six point five inch machine guns ripped into the lightly armoured fighter and it exploded in flames.

"Got him, Skipper," yelled Peters.

The two Wildcats turned above the enemy fleet and saw a pair of Zeros diving toward the dive bombers. Southerland understood this was the one area his plane might outperform the enemy fighter. He led Peters down after the Japanese machines, catching them a thousand meters from the Douglas Dauntless bombers. The two enemy pilots were intent on their prey and didn't see the Wildcats behind them. Southerland fired first, his bullets ripping into the wing of the Zero, causing the machine to crumple, and then explode. His attack warned the second machine which turned sharply to escape. Peters' attack missed the enemy fighter. His wingman tried to follow the Zero through his turn. Quickly the Zero turned inside Peters and fired two bursts that smashed the tail of the Wildcat and chewed holes in the wing.

Southerland hadn't abandoned Peters and had been trying to get behind the Japanese machine. Finally, at one hundred and fifty yards, he managed to fire a quick burst. Southerland was on target and the Zero's engine caught fire, with the enemy pilot quickly bailing out. Southerland had no time to wonder at the pilot's fate as other enemy machines swooped down toward the US attack planes.

The dive bombers were already entering their dives. Having rolled over they fell almost vertically toward the enemy carriers.

The air around them filled with anti-aircraft shells and two machines were hit. One flew straight into the sea and the other blew up. Many continued on toward their targets and Southerland witnessed at least one bomb explode on the Zuiho. He didn't know by this stage the Hiyo was burning and the Jun'yo was struggling to stay afloat after being struck by two torpedoes. The Japanese fleet had suffered a grievous blow. Not only were they to lose three carriers, but many experienced pilots died either in the air or on the burning ships themselves.

When Southerland arrived back over the combined US and Commonwealth fleet he could see smoke coming from the Tasman. The Australian carrier was hit five times by Japanese bombs. However, her three inch deck armour and heavy compliment of anti-aircraft guns saved her. The damage was heavy enough to force all of the remaining Australian aircraft to land on the Enterprise.

Everyone was in high spirits in the ready room, joking with each other and slapping backs. Even the Commonwealth pilots were buoyant despite the damage to their ship.

"Heard you made two kills," said Lieutenant Stanley W. Vejtasa.

"Yep, and you Swede?" asked Southerland.

"Just the one. They kept me back on CAP as you know. I got a Zero. That Canadian, Beurling, he shot down four of the Vals. Just flew through the fire of the dive bomber's rear gunners and shot them all down. There was flak exploding around him but he ignored it all. The Aussies call him 'Screwball'."

"Sounds like a good pilot," said Southerland.

"Yes and no. He's a bit of a lone wolf and went charging into those dive bombers alone. One of the Aussie pilots also said he is a cold fish. Beurling has actually told a few of the boys he loves the war."

"Live for the thrill, eh. It will get him killed eventually," said Southerland.

Swede nodded. "Yeah, well that's not our problem. As long as he shoots down heaps of Japs before he goes. I'm more concerned with finding out how big this victory was. If what I've heard is correct, we might be the only navy carrier still operating for either side in the Pacific!"

This wasn't quite true. The Japanese still had the Jun'yo, though this carrier only carried forty-eight aircraft. The enemy also had two carriers under repair but neither would be ready until February of 1943.

V

The rain had stopped and only wispy clouds now occasionally covered the sun. Sergeant Chuck Randel viewed the English countryside through his binoculars. Somewhere ahead of him the Italians had taken the high ground just north of Cawkwell. The enemy had thrown the Americans back ten miles and overrun at least one battalion of the 34th Infantry Division. Randel couldn't believe that the Italian 8th Army had defeated the US army. The Centauro 131st Armoured Division backed by the 2nd and 3rd Italian Infantry Divisions had launched a limited offensive into the Lincolnshire Wolds. A bombardment of US positions was followed by intensive air operations, where new Macchi C.205s and older 202s escorted Reggiane Re.2002 and Caproni Ca.314s as they attacked the Americans.

Taken by surprise and overwhelmed by the ferocity of the attack, the Americans retreated. They had been pushed all the way back from Horncastle, a distance of over ten miles. Further to the west the Germans were also launching a limited attack in order to seize Lincoln. The Axis were aiming to push the Allies all the way back to the Humber and outflank the Canadians and British further west. The 34th US Infantry Division had taken a battering, while closer to the coast the 1st US Infantry Division, The Big Red One, had been ordered to retreat to avoid being cut off.

What Randel didn't know was that the US Corps Commander, Major General Lloyd Fredendall, commander of the II Corps had panicked and ordered the withdrawal. The general's command bunker was sixty-five miles away back in York. Major General George S. Patton (who was soon to be promoted) had just taken command and ordered The Big Red One to turn around and attack. The 1st Armoured Division had been pulled out of reserve and sent to counter the Italian advance.

Sergeant Randal was with Combat Command B (CCB) as it moved to block the Italian armour. His platoon of four M3 Lee tanks was parked in a thin strip of forest next to the Caldwell Racetrack. To his southwest he could clearly see five hundred yards to the crest of the hill. From here though, the land dropped away into Cawkwell.

"See anything, Sarge?" asked Private Troy Ohlsen.

"No enemy units yet, but I can hear tracks. They're coming," said Randel.

The Italian tanks crept from behind a thick windbreak of trees and shrubs. The lead vehicles stopped, and a man climbed down and peered around through a pair of 6x30 binoculars. The Italians were veterans of Africa and Russia, with the infantry units having fought on the Eastern Front until early spring 1942. They'd then been withdrawn, reinforced, and reequipped before being sent to England a month ago. Paratrooper units, as well as other divisions, had also been attached to the Italian 8th Army.

"I don't know what the Italians are using," said Randel.

"Their tanks don't have a good reputation," said Private Freddy Spencer.

"Well, we might soon be putting that to the test. Lieutenant Gould has the rest of the company back in that patch of woods behind us and more of the command is near the large farm."

As he finished speaking the radio crackled to life.

"You see those tanks edging up to the Bluestone Road, Randel?" asked Captain Davidson.

Randel keyed his microphone and answered. “I can see them, Captain.”

“We are going to let them come a little further. As soon as we fire, then you join in.”

“Got it, sir,” he answered.

“I’ve other vehicles coming up the hill, Sarge,” said Corporal Freddy Spencer. The gunner was peering at the fields to the southeast through his sights. Randel looked through his binoculars and saw four squat shapes advancing along the Hornecastle Road straight toward him.

“Assault guns of some variety,” he said. He passed the information along to his captain who grunted.

“You hold them and we’ll deal with the tanks,” said Davidson.

“Skipper, I think the one at the back has a longer gun than the others,” said Spencer.

Four Semovente da 47/32 were moving slowly up the road, though the final vehicle had been reequipped with a Czech 47mm gun which had better armour penetration than the similar Italian weapons. Further to the northeast twenty Carro Armato M15/42s were advancing. Italian trucks moved along the road and even a few turretless T-34s (known as 'Cockroaches' to the Germans) were moving through the fields. These vehicles had been bought from the Germans and were used as troop carriers.

The noise of the first guns firing from the company caused Randel to jump.

"Fire when ready," he said.

The main 75mm gun boomed from its hull-mounted position. The 37mm gun fired next. Private Green often derided the smaller gun but he tried to hit the Italian vehicle.

"A hit," the red-headed man yelled. The small shell tore off the track, while the larger 75mm gun penetrated the Semovente's armour beneath the main gun. The armour piercing round (AP) smashed through the 30mm armour and caused the assault gun to catch fire. The rest of the platoon also fired, and another vehicle blew up as it was hit by three shells. The rest of the Italian Semoventes tried to back away while firing. Both were quickly hit though not before the last assault gun fired two rounds. One of which hit Lucky Lady, the second tank in Randel's platoon. At five hundred yards the shell penetrated 80mm of armour. The front of the hull on an M3 was only 51mm thick. The shell punched through near the old radio operator's position. It then bounced around inside the hull wounding the 75mm loader and gunner.

The M3s then started firing at the Italian infantry, truck, and Cockroaches. The sloped 60mm armour proved harder to penetrate with all of the 37mm rounds bouncing off the hulls. Even the larger 75mm shells had trouble punching holes through the turretless T-34s. Eventually, the two vehicles were knocked out but by this time the infantry they had been carrying had scattered. The Italian trucks retreated quickly.

Over to the east, near the forested Pewlade Hill, the rest of the Combat Command battled the 15th Armoured Battalion of the Centauro Division. Here, even though outnumbered, the M3s were winning. The thicker armour and heavier guns of the American tanks made life difficult for the crews of the Carro Armato M15/42s. The 47mm guns of the Italian vehicles could penetrate the Lee tanks, but they had to close to three hundred and fifty yards to do so.

Fourteen Reggiane Re.2002 dived out of the sun, dropping their five hundred and fifty pound bombs on the forest and farmhouse where most of the CCB were based. The fighter bombers then made a strafing run before retiring. The air attack disorganised the Americans, and Italian infantry and armour closed in on the US positions. Captain Davidson hadn't been idle. 105mm shells crashed down on the advancing enemy, driving them back toward the ridgeline and off the crest. The rest of CCB arrived with extra infantry and M3A1 half-tracks mounting M1897A5 75mm guns. These attacked with mortar support and soon US troops were on the edge of the high country looking down on the valley of the River Bain.

V

For a while it looked as though the invasion of Greece wouldn't occur. Prime Minster Metaxas had made a number of promises to do with the neutrality of his nation. He promised not to accept any more weapons from the Allies and to only take food deliveries; yet even as he was saying this, small amounts of American and Commonwealth supplies continued to arrive by air. This was only spare parts and small arms, but it was enough to infuriate the Führer. To the German leader this proved Metaxas couldn't be trusted, the hypocrisy of his position completely escaping Hitler. The risk of the Allies landing and making bases in the area, even if this was in the distant future, couldn't be tolerated.

Lang was near the end of the column riding in a half-track. The Sd.Kfz 250 was smaller than other varieties, but this one was especially fitted out with a powerful radio and other command apparatus. His reconnaissance battalion had been merged with a battery of StuG III assault guns, a battalion from the 901st Panzer Grenadier Regiment, a pioneer company, four attached Flakpanzer Is and a battery of towed 105mm guns. The Kampfgruppe was racing along the coast road toward Velika. Another stronger group was trying to force a passage over the pass near the Pineious River. Somewhere further inland the SS divisions were advancing, while the 155th Reserve Panzer Division waited at Kato Egani, after having forced a breach in the Aliakmon Line near Nea Efesos. Here the inexperienced unit had taken heavy casualties from artillery, as well as being attacked by Greek P 40 fighter bombers. The nearby hills were assaulted by the 233rd Reserve Motorised Division while the 7SS Mountain Division attacked the steeper country further west.

The Luftwaffe ruled the sky after eventually destroying the two hundred modern planes of the Greek Air Force. Now Stukas from St 5 were pounding any opposition the different panzer spearheads encountered. Since the early battles at the Metaxas line on the border, Lang hadn't seen an enemy plane. His thrust along the coast was an effort to try and outflank any Greek blocking forces in the mountains. So far the only opposition he'd faced was a few reserve units, mines, and destroyed roads and bridges. The coastal plain here was less than a kilometre wide, though ahead it broadened to over fourteen hundred metres.

Lang was aware that soon his Kampfgruppe would need to turn west and push over the hills to Agia. The country here was steep but it least it wasn't as rugged as the passes to the north. The Kampfgruppe was equipped with earth moving equipment and explosives to clear obstacles, and he hoped this wouldn't be needed. Hopefully his command wouldn't have to worry about any fighting until they reached the plains around Larissa.

He still couldn't believe that he was fighting along the same route that had taken Xerxes from Persia to Athens. Lang had stared at Mount Olympus in wonder with Leutnant Scholler.

"The home of the gods," he'd stated.

"Our leader would say we are the gods now," Scholler had answered.

The reason for the invasion actually made sense to Lang this time. The Greek Prime Minister couldn't be trusted, and Germany couldn't allow the Allies a chance to establish themselves on the European mainland. It was a similar reason put forward for the second invasion of England, but probably with a lot more justification. Lang wondered if Turkey would be next but knew that would be a difficult task. Germany would need to transport its army across the Sea of Marmara and even though that was possible, Turkey was a large country which had a border with the Allies. Such a move would open up a third, and probably ongoing battlefront. Once Greece was conquered, the troops used by Germany could go back into reserve or be moved to Russia or England.

The Greek 8th Infantry Division was a battered formation. It had fought in Thrace and been cut off by the German advance further west. Hastily evacuated from Thessalonica, it had lost much of its heavy equipment and was waiting for more artillery and vehicles. The division had managed to hold on to its new American anti-tank guns, though they were lacking ammunition.

Leading the German column was a light four-wheeled armoured car. The shell from the six pound gun hit the front tire, causing the vehicle to veer from the coastal road and crash into the sea. More rounds followed triggering the column to stop. Anti-tank shells hit the smaller group of German vehicles travelling along a road near the hills. Ahead, Greek troops started shooting at the German troops with American imported BAR automatic rifles and Commonwealth Bren guns.

Lang and Scholler jumped from their half-track and ran to the sheltering wall of a small hotel. Through the olive groves Lang could see muzzle flashes from the enemy anti-tank guns hidden on the slopes of a nearby spur of hills. He estimated the range to be a touch over four hundred metres, though the vehicles on the inland road would be less than one hundred metres from the guns. The Greek infantry seemed to be firing from small houses and taverns as well as from the thicker groves of trees.

"Get the StuGs onto attacking the anti-tank guns, and order the mortars and artillery to set up," he said to Scholler. The junior officer dashed back to the half-track to relay orders, while Lang continued to examine the lay of the land. He could see quite a bit of movement to the south and realised what was about to happen. Running back to the half-track he yelled for Scholler.

"Warn all units, the Greeks are about to attack," he screamed.

Scholler's head bobbed up from inside the half-track and nodded before ducking down once more.

The enemy had gathered in the woods to the west on the lower slopes of the hills, as well as in olive groves and patches of scrub. The Greek infantry had remained hidden when earlier scout cars had investigated the area. Now they were going to spring their trap. They emerged immediately after the firing of a red flare. One company came from the west and two from the south. The enemy jumped out of their fox holes and trenches and ran forward, firing all sorts of weapons. Greek EPK light machine guns, Sten guns,

French Lebel rifles, and even Thompson submachine guns were carried by the advancing enemy.

There was no subtlety to the attack, which amounted to a wild charge. Kubelwagens, half-tracks, and two light armoured cars were immediately overrun, with the German infantry finding itself in close quarter combat with the Greeks. Grenades exploded and there was a brief exchange of close range fire before the enemy swept onward. Though a German company was wiped out, it held the Greeks for a few precious minutes.

“The mortars are ready, sir,” said Scholler.

“Direct their fire on the southern attack and order those StuGs and Flak panzers forward,” said Lang. He gathered ten men and a machine gun, and ran with them to a nearby hotel. A soldat smashed the door in and Lang yelled for them to get onto the roof. The men stormed up the stairs and onto a flat area which overlooked the surrounding countryside. He pointed at running Greek soldiers and told the squad to open fire. The MG 42 ripped out short, sharp bursts and the other men fired their rifles. A non-commissioned officer (NCO) started to shoot with his MP 40. Lang peered over the edge at the advancing enemy and saw two positions where pockets of his troops held out. The Greeks attacked these men from all sides, while other groups continued forward.

Further to the south he spotted another enemy company moving forward, as well as a single M3 tank. A quick glance showed the enemy vehicle was battle damaged, but it still posed a threat. Lang ran quickly back down the stairs and returned to his half-track. He was clambering on board just as the enemy tank fired. One of the Flak panzers shot with its 20mm cannon but the shells bounced from the M3's armour. A single round from the Lee blew apart the small Flak panzer, while the smaller 37mm gun in the turret fired at the surrounding buildings.

"Where are those StuGs?" said Lang.

Scholler spoke into the radio briefly. "They're almost here, sir," he replied. A moment later the first assault gun drove up the road before stopping next to Lang's half-track. The commander stuck his head out and called for instructions.

"One hundred metres on the middle street running northsouth there's an M3 tank. It's main gun is powerful enough to knock you out," said Lang. The man pulled his head set back onto his ears and spoke briefly. Two more StuGs drove up behind the first vehicle before all of the assault guns drove off.

The M3 saw the StuGs and turned to face them. It fired with its 37mm gun first but that shell only bounced from the assault gun's armour, glancing off the metal above the driver's vision slit. The StuG fired next and at eighty metres it couldn't miss. The armour-piercing round smashed the M3's side gun mantle, killing the gunner of the 75mm cannon and wounding the driver. The Greek crew quickly bailed out as two more shells set the tank on fire. German mortar and artillery fire then swept over the advancing enemy troops, while the StuGs blasted them at short range. Greek casualties were very heavy and soon the attack fell apart and the enemy retreated, leaving many of their dead behind them. Lang later counted two hundred and fifty eight Greek bodies while fifty-two of his own men lost their lives. Reconnaissance units then located other units of the Greek 8th Infantry Division as they tried to form a defence line, and the Luftwaffe pounded the enemy from the air.

Later that day Lang turned his command inland and pushed his Kampfgruppe until it reached the inland town of Sotiritsa. He was almost through the hills and hoped the following day would take him and his men down onto the plains.

V

It was cold and wet. Junior Sergeant Roza Shanina watched, with her partner Anna Adamia. Both scanned the ruins of Kamyshinsky with binoculars and telescopic sight, looking for any sign of the Fascist. The ruins around her position were bleak, with most being not much higher than four to five metres. Over one hundred He 111 German medium bombers had hit the town a week ago and since then the area had been frequently pounded by artillery. The fish processing plant by the river was contested by what remained of her regiment and units of the German 60th Motorized Division. Both units were extremely worn down and consisted of exhausted veterans. Her division now had only two regiments, the 1379th had been broken up to provide reinforcements to the other two regiments. Even then, the 1382nd was down to six hundred and twenty effective soldiers. The only consolation was that their enemy wasn't much better. The German 92nd Motorized Infantry Regiment was also down to under seven hundred men.

"I've got movement," whispered Anna.

Her spotter gestured with her hands and soon Roza could see five men crawling from one piece of cover to the next. The Germans would have someone covering them, probably a machine-gun crew. She scanned the likely spots but couldn't see any glint of metal or other sign of movement. The Germans were getting better at this and she needed to be patient. She kept scanning and eventually gave up. The enemy's supporting units were too well hidden.

Roza settled her sights on the squad, and watched as they carefully scouted forward. The Germans were using every piece of cover they could find and she knew she'd only get one chance for a quick shot. Ahead of the patrol was a low wall. To pass it they'd either need to go over it or along it. In the middle of the structure was a small window. Roza placed her sights in the middle of the gap and waited. The first German crossed so quickly that she missed her chance. The second man tried to dive past the window, but she managed to pull the trigger. Her bullet hit the Nazi just above the knee on the side of his leg. He screamed and was dragged into cover as she worked the bolt.

Machine gun bullets chewed up the masonry around her. Roza heard the distinct tearing sound of an MG 42 as it fired, and only just managed to roll away from the stream of bullets. She crawled away from her position as mortar shells started to fall. Anna met her at a space between two destroyed buildings, and both retreated quickly to an area of tumbled concrete and twisted steel, between what would have been two of the processing buildings of the fish factory. Here they rolled under a thick steel girder and into a hollow in the concrete as the shells continued to fall.

"Did you kill him?" asked Anna.

"I think I hit the Nazi in the leg. He'll be going back to Germany, but his war mightn't be over," said Roza.

Her friend looked disappointed.

"Hey, there'll be more. I only had a chance to make a very quick shot. The Germans have become extremely cautious."

"I know."

Roza then heard Anna's stomach growl. They both smiled at the noise.

"Do you think there will be any food waiting for us when we get back?" asked Anna.

"Nadia said she'd make sure they kept something for us," answered Roza.

She hoped the attractive radio operator wouldn't get into trouble for hiding food for them, but then supposed that her powerful protector, Colonel Yekov would keep her safe. They crawled back through the ruins, moving slowly until they reached a line of blasted trees on the edge of a park. Here they called out the password before crossing over into their own lines.

After giving a report to the Captain they found Nadia Smenko outside the regimental headquarters. She smiled at her friends and gestured that they follow her into a reinforced dug out.

"I managed to bake some flour into a flat bread and found some lard, which I mixed with the dough," said the radio operator. She tucked her long dark hair into a cap and then turned holding a small white object in her hand. "And I boiled this for us to share."

Roza stare in wonder at the egg. It had been so long since she'd eaten anything her stomach clenched.

"An egg," groaned Anna.

"Yiri gave it to me," said Nadia, using the Christian name of the colonel.

Both of the sniper team looked away and their friend blushed.

"You don't have to eat it if you don't want to," she said.

Anna shook her head. "We don't judge *you* Nadia. The colonel is married and almost old enough to be your father."

The pretty radio operator shrugged. "He is a man with power and it's the way of the world."

Roza wondered at that. She believed if she wasn't such a good shot that some general might have insisted she warm his bed. Roza knew her blonde hair and attractive face caused men's heads to turn. She ignored their stares, and if any came too close, she went to Sergeant Potemkin and he would warn the offending men. He'd hint at how dangerous a misplaced grenade would be, or point out how in a fire fight bullets could hit a man from any direction. The offending soldiers quickly got the message.

The egg was delicious, and even though Roza only received a third of it she savoured it. The flat bread and lard almost filled her stomach, but after a short while she was hungry again. That seemed to be the situation these days. There was never enough food. The three women went searching for more food, first swinging past the unit's portable kitchen. Here they managed to scrounge a few potatoes but then Roza had another idea.

"There's a German tank, a Panzer III with a 75mm gun, anyway it was knocked out and didn't burn. It's near the high school," she said.

"Why hasn't it been investigated?" asked Nadia.

"Well, it's sort of in no man's land," Roza answered.

"Sort of! It's within fifty metres of the front line," said Anna. "There's no way we can reach it."

"That's where you are wrong. A building collapsed near the tank after the last bombardment."

"Then somebody has probably beaten us to it," said Anna.

"It's worth checking! The wall only fell a couple of days ago. Nobody might have thought of it yet."

"I think the idea is dangerous," said Anna.

"The Nazis often carry all sorts of goodies in their tanks. It's worth a look," said Roza.

The two women looked doubtful.

"Think of spicy German sausages and white bread."

Anna snorted. "Even the Germans don't get white bread."

"Well, what about a few cans of tomato soup? We know they often have that."

Nadia nodded. "I'm in."

Anna rolled her eyes but then nodded. "Alright, but let's grab some smoke grenades and Nadia, you'll need a gun."

"I've got my Reising."

"That US gun is piece of shit. It jams if you look at it. I'll get you a PPS-42. They're rough but it will keep working even if you drop it in the sand," said Anna.

The three women collected a bag of grenades and a new gun for Nadia, then slipped through the lines and into the jumble of broken down houses away from the river. They passed through the Russian picket line and into an area where only rats and the odd stray dog lived.

"We need to watch for German patrols," said Anna.

"And snipers," added Roza.

"I'm starting to think this isn't a good idea," whispered Nadia.

The three women found a tunnel of rubble between shattered houses and under slabs of concrete. Eventually they could see the Panzer III. The area appeared empty but Roza told her companions to wait.

"Let's just watch for a while," she said.

There was no movement around the tank but the view of the women was limited to a narrow gap between rubble and smashed buildings. Still, Roza knew patience was important and continued to wait. She scanned the area through her scope, looking for anything which she thought might be out of place.

"Can you hear that?" whispered Nadia.

A clanking sound, like someone banging metal on steel reached their ears. Then conversation drifted on the breeze.

"That's German. There are Nazis at the tank," said Anna in voice so quiet Roza had to strain to catch the sound.

"What do we do?" asked Nadia.

"Kill them," said Roza.

The radio operator went pale but Anna give a single small nod and pointed at a pile of rubble which lay on top of a wrecked ZIS-5 truck.

The three women crept forward, moving very slowly and carefully without making a sound. The wind was increasing, covering the slight noise their boots made and soon they were in a position where they could see the rear of the tank. Four men were working on the engine, while one watched. This soldier was smoking and carrying a Gewehr 41 semi-automatic rifle. All of the Germans wore black panzer crew uniforms and didn't pay great attention to their surroundings.

Anna placed her mouth against Roza's ear. "We can take them prisoner," she whispered.

Roza considered the idea. Five Germans would certainly be able to provide information on the enemy's disposition and strength. The problem would be getting them back through the lines. In the end she decided it was worth the risk. The panzer crew didn't seem to understand the danger they were in and she thought it should be possible to get the jump on them. She nodded at Anna and signalled the avenue of approach they should take with her hands.

It took another ten minutes to reach positions from which they could surprise the Germans. Anna stepped out first and called out for the Germans to drop their weapons. In her excitement she used Russian. The man with the gun raised it to his shoulder and Roza shot him in the chest. She then yelled "Hande hoch!" and the four surviving crew members slowly stood. Nadia appeared and trained her weapons on the enemy, while Anna moved to a spot where she could watch the surrounding area.

"Why here?" said Roza in broken German.

The oldest man gestured at the panzer and said something she didn't understand.

"Nadia, climb inside and see if you can find some food. After all, that's what we originally came for," said Roza. "Anyone else about Anna?"

"Not that I can see," her spotter answered.

"Alright, search the Nazis, but give me your gun first. I want to be able to fire a lot of bullets quickly if they get any ideas."

Anna carefully patted the men down, removing three Luger pistols and a single stick grenade. She also found some tobacco and some crackers wrapped in paper. The Germans didn't make any moves though a young blond soldier kept glancing at the man she'd shot.

"He's dead," she said.

The soldier sighed. "He was my friend," he said in passable Russian.

"You speak our language?" Roza asked.

"A little. I learned, university and picked up more when I was moved here."

Roza corrected the soldier's mistake and then wondered why she had bothered.

"We will take you back and you'll live. They will question you but if you cooperate then it should be okay," Roza said.

The man grimaced but didn't speak. She understood. In his position Roza wasn't sure what she would do. Giving the enemy information on her comrades was something she'd resist, but in the end, if it were a matter of life or death, then would she talk? It was impossible to know.

Nadia popped out of the tank grinning. "Canned meat, a jar of jam and two cans of tomato soup, at least that's what I think it is," said the radio operator.

"That makes all this risk worthwhile," said Anna.

"Alright, let's get out of here," said Roza. "Bind their hands."

"What with?" asked Anna.

Roza glanced into the engine of the tank. "Use some of the electrical wiring. If that doesn't work, use their shoelaces."

Anna tied the German soldiers' hands behind their backs, while Nadia watched the surrounding ruins. Roza kept the muzzle of the submachine gun pointed at the four Germans.

"We haven't heard good things about your treatment of prisoners," said the blond soldier.

Roza snorted. "That's good, coming from a Nazi."

"I'm not a Nazi," said the man.

Roza blinked a few times. She supposed it was possible that not all Germans were Fascists but it didn't really matter. "You're an invader. This is my country and you attacked it. Your people treat Russian prisoners worse than dogs."

"You were getting ready to attack us," said the German.

"Do you really believe that? Germany has attacked so many other countries and yet somehow they all asked for it, in one way or another."

The older German said something in a loud voice and the blond man fell silent. Anna strode forward and pushed the muzzle of one of the captured pistols against the older soldier's throat and then placed a finger against her lip, motioning for quiet.

The trip back with the four prisoners was slow but Roza and her friends were lucky. The 60th Motorized Division was preparing for an attack in a few days and positions were being consolidated. Soon patrols would go out to locate Russian strong points but that wouldn't happen until the following day. The attached panzer battalion from the 16th Panzer Division was also trying to gather its striking power, and that was why the crew of the Panzer III had been sent to see if their tank was repairable.

German strength in the area was centred on the motorized division and the 14th Panzer Division. A single infantry division and the 18th Motorized Division, with a battalion of panzers from the 16th Panzer Division, were also trying to push forward through the mud toward Saratov. The German supply lines ran back one hundred and twenty kilometres to the railhead at Stalingrad. The

German push north from the Don River bend had created a triangular shaped line running along the Volga River to the east and the Khopyor River to the west. German attempts to advance east from Voronezh had failed and renewed attacks along the length of the northern Don River bend had also stalled.

Roza tried to hand the four prisoners to her company commander but he ordered her to take them to the regimental headquarters.

"Maybe I should disappear for a bit," said Nadia. "I don't think the Colonel will like it when he hears I've been out in no man's land."

Roza arranged to meet the radio operator later when they could share the food they'd taken.

In the end the colonel wasn't at his bunker but two NKVD officers were. Roza saw the two men from the Soviet Secret Police and thought of trying to retreat with her prisoners but it was too late. A major with a scar on his cheek and a captain with a shaved head approach her and Anna.

"What have we here, comrade?" asked the major.

"I was on patrol with my spotter when we took these men prisoner. They were trying to fix a tank," said Roza.

The man ran his eyes over her, and Roza repressed the urge to shiver. He then turned to the Germans. Stepping forward he struck the oldest crew member across the face with the back of his hand.

"What is the strength of your unit?" he yelled at the man.

Roza was surprised at the sudden violence. "Sir, he doesn't speak Russian," she said.

The Major spun, his eyes blazing. "You have spoken to them?" he hissed.

"I had to give them instructions in order to get them back here, sir."

The man's shoulders relaxed just a little.

"The blond man sir, he speaks our language," Roza offered.

The captain drew his pistol and walked over to the prisoners before hauling the blond German away from his crew.

"Thank you, junior sergeant," said the major.

He stepped over to the man and punched him in the face. Roza saw blood fly from the impact and heard the man cry out. She wanted to stop the assault but the NKVD men scared her. These men were known as the agents of Stalin and held the power of life and death over the ordinary soldier. She must have taken a pace forward because Anna's hand gripped her shoulder. Her friend gave a tiny shake of the head and Roza froze.

"What is the strength of your unit?" the major asked.

The German soldier shook his head and this time the captain hit the man with the butt of his pistol, opening a shallow cut in the prisoner's cheek. The major asked again, and again the man failed to answer. To Roza this felt wrong. She fought the invaders of her country, killed them in battle and did what she could to drive them back. The beating of this man distressed her in ways she didn't understand.

"Grab one of the others," said the major after he'd tried beating the information from the German for five minutes. "You need to answer or I'll shoot your comrade," he said.

This is wrong, thought Roza. Shooting prisoners is what the Nazis do. The German was on his knees and there was blood in his hair. Roza saw the NKVD captain raise his pistol and point it at the oldest German. The dark-haired man said something to his comrades and then closed his eyes. The captain shot the German between the eyes.

"What did he say?" the major screamed the question in the young German's face.

"He told me not to answer," said the blond man through swollen lips.

“Maybe your next comrade won’t be as brave,” said the major. The captain turned to the next man and pointed the gun at his head.

“Major?” said Roza.

“Don’t interfere woman,” the man barked.

She didn’t like being dismissed as though she were a dog. Roza was a sniper with thirty-six kills and she deserved respect. She shook off Anna’s hand and stepped forward. Grabbing the stunned German she pulled him away. Roza wasn’t sure what she was doing, only having a vague idea of taking the man to the colonel.

“What are you doing?” screamed the NKVD major.

Anna trailed after her with wide eyes, constantly glancing back at the two officers. The explosion of the heavy mortar round took everybody by surprise. The Germans fired a short barrage of 120mm shells, which burst around the bunker and Roza only had a second to hurl the German inside before she and Anna dived in after him. Both the NKVD officers and the surviving prisoners were caught in the blast of the third shell. Mortar shells don't whistle so there was no warning. The barrage killed another two Russians before it stopped.

Anna and Roza crept from the bunker a few minutes later and found the NKVD officers lying mixed with the Germans. The major didn't have any legs and the captain was almost unrecognisable. The blond German staggered out and looked at his comrades. His face was pale and Roza saw tears in his eyes.

"We need to patch you up and find someone safe to hand you to," she said.

The German didn't speak and she felt a growing sense of sympathy for the man.

"Why did you come here? This is our country," she said.

"I'm a soldier. I did what I was told," he said.

Roza wondered how many more there were like this man. He wasn't a Nazi or a Fascist, just a human being who had been sent here by his leaders. She dug out the crackers in her pocket and a piece of moldy cheese.

“Keep these. I don’t know when you will find more food. She went to the bodies of the dead and found a crust of bread. She even found some RotFront chocolate on the major which she shared with Anna and the German.

“What’s your name?” she asked.

“Rudi Fischer, from Austria,” he said.

“So you aren’t even a German?” asked Anna.

“Hitler is from Austria,” said Roza to her friend.

“I’m sorry,” said Rudi suddenly.

“It’s a bit late for that,” muttered Anna.

“I didn’t know what we were doing. We were told that communism is a terrible thing,” he said.

“We are told the same thing about fascism,” said Roza. “My people won’t stop fighting until you are driven from our soil.”

Rudi just looked at her with his swollen jaw and split lip.

Roza sighed. "I'll find someone in authority who won't kill you," she said.

They handed Rudi over to a captain who was in charge of a field hospital. He was left with two other lightly wounded Germans to await treatment. Rudi helped look after wounded Russians for most of the day and then slipped away into the river that evening with the other two men. One was spotted and shot, but Rudi and his companion managed to drift with the current until they reached German lines. Both were so cold by the time they'd floated ten kilometres down river they could barely paddle to the bank. The two Germans were then sent to the rear for rest and debriefing, with Rudi receiving leave from his commanding officer. Later he was given a promotion and, in time, transferred to the Panzer Lehr Division. He never forgot the sniper who'd saved his life.

Chapter Four: November 1942

Field Marshal Wolfram von Richthofen was nobody's fool. Kesselring respected the man, and had called him back from the front to get his opinion on many different issues. He intended to keep him here for at least a week, allowing the Field Marshal to visit his family, as well as view some of the new aircraft prototypes the Luftwaffe was looking at adopting. Today they were on their way to inspect a new panzer. Kesselring wasn't sure why, but his advisors said it might be a perfect fit for the new Herman Goering Panzer Division the Luftwaffe was developing.

The two men drove to the test airfield north of Berlin. Kesselring enjoyed the time, being free with nobody to distract him as he rode along in the car. Richthofen sat next to him, silently leafing through some papers.

"The colder weather hasn't arrived in the east yet?" Kesselring asked.

"Not when I'd left. The mud was still shocking and nothing is moving. I wish that they'd left General Wagner in charge. Maybe he could have pulled another rabbit out of his hat," said Richthofen.

"The man is a pain. One of the biggest pessimists I've ever met."

"He managed to get us to those oilfields in Russia, and now the fuel is being pumped to the coast and brought back in trains. Hell, some of it's being used locally, now we have a couple of the refineries fixed."

"Then why is nothing moving? It's one of the questions I've been meaning to ask you," said Kesselring.

"Mud, terrible roads, poor railways, and not enough tracks. We can get stuff to Stalingrad but all the tracks from there are on the other side of the Volga, and that's Russian territory still. At the moment I can't fly anything in either. Besides, you've taken some of the transport planes."

"I moved them because the Führer wants to drop an airborne division on Crete. There are only Greek stragglers on the island but it will still be a major operation. Our leader also wants to be able to take Gibraltar."

"Really? Are the Spaniards going to help?"

"No, it will need to be another air attack. They will let us fly over their territory, that's all. The operation still may be cancelled."

"Well, I would have thought we have enough on our hands. Russia hasn't collapsed, and Britain fights on," said Richthofen.

"True, true, but Crete I believe is necessary, to stop the enemy having bases from where they could bomb the Romanian oilfields. I'm not so sure about Gibraltar."

"In Russia we could use those transport planes, and the helicopters would be really helpful."

"The Draches will fly some of the paratroopers to Crete."

"I understand, but the Luftwaffe is stretched thin. We can't supply the attack toward Saratov and the renewed attack in

Georgia has barely advanced. The drive from Voronezh due east has also only managed to move thirty kilometres. Winter is approaching in Russia and there will be a counterstrike," said Richthofen.

"We have a small reserve ready. I've spoken to the Führer and he knows of the dangers. Besides, the Russians are weaker. They can't access the oil in Azerbaijan as we have sunk most of their tankers on the Caspian Sea, and they are struggling to feed their people," said Kesselring.

"I think we will hold any Soviet offensive this time, but the point is that they still haven't surrendered. I'm sure the Russians are having to divert men and women into producing food and that must hit their ability to reinforce the Soviet Army. It will also have an impact on their production. However we are finding cans of food with American labels, and also fighting Russians who are flying P 40s or Airacobras. A pilot from JG 52 shot down a Liberator bomber three days ago. The USA is going to do its best to keep Stalin in the war."

“We will build a ring of steel. The Americans are fighting a war on two fronts as well. They don’t have the will to pay the blood cost it would take to beat us,” said Kesselring.

Later they reached the air base. Clear weather and a slight breeze greeted their arrival. The two men left their car and walked across to look at a strange aircraft and three panzers.

“Why are the tanks here?” asked Richthofen.

“The Skoda plant wants me to order some for the new Herman Goering Division. They think if I do, then they will be able to start making them and perhaps export them to other countries,” said Kesselring.

“And you don’t want to go all the way to Czech occupied territory to have a look?”

“I told Skoda if they wanted me to see this panzer, they had to bring it to me.”

“Well, it looks like they brought three. What’s the aircraft?”

"This is the Do 335, or it will be. It has projected speeds of around four hundred and twenty miles an hour. Later versions will be even faster if we can get the DB 603 engine working properly. We are using the engine in the new Fw 190C but it still has all sorts of overheating problems. Kurt Tank says he is getting on top of the issues, however time will tell."

"It looks strange, with an engine at each end."

"Placing the two engines in line with each other reduces drag. Dornier has experience with engines that push as well as pull, and it seems to work. The plane has been flown twice and there are few handling issues. Personally, I think the undercarriage needs strengthening, and with these engines the aircraft has only reached four hundred miles an hour. Still, it can carry one thousand kilos of bombs. I think, with the upgraded engines, it will be even faster."

"Well, let's have a look then," said Richthofen.

As the two men drove back to Berlin, Kesselring decided he was happy with the progress the Do 335 was making. He hoped it would be in service with the upgraded engines by the summer of 1944, or even earlier. The panzers were a different issue. Creating the Herman Goering Panzer Division had been his decision, brought about by Heinrich Himmler's bloody mindedness. When it was suggested that one of the new SS divisions be named after the founder of the Luftwaffe, the SS leader had prevaricated. In the end the Führer agreed that the German Air Force could create a single elite panzer unit to honour one of Hitler's earliest supporters.

Then the army became involved and blocked every attempt to supply the division with decent equipment. The Luftwaffe could supply the trucks, anti-aircraft guns, and even many of the half-tracks. Small arms were gathered from air force security groups, yet artillery and panzers remained a problem. The division was training with old Czech 38Ts and Panzer Is, but those two vehicles were useless on a modern battlefield. Kesselring decided he'd place an order for two hundred and fifty of the Skoda tanks. 100mm cannons were also going to be purchased from the firm, and now all he needed were mortars and anti-tank guns to fill out the division.

"When do you think those transport planes will be returning to the east?" asked Richthofen suddenly.

Kesselring smiled. "Sooner than you think," he answered

V

Three M3s smoldered on the road, while a fourth burned furiously in the middle of a field. Sergeant Chuck Randel scanned the woodlands carefully trying to find the German gun that had done all the damage. His captain and lieutenant were either dead or gravely wounded, and he was now in charge. Sweat dripped down his back. This was supposed to have been an easy advance by the company into an area recently evacuated by the Italians.

Instead, German infantry were fighting house to house in the little village of Donington on Bain, while the armour was held just north of the town by a single gun. His M3 was parked behind a patch of thick pine forest, while he scouted forward on foot with Private Olaf Magnusson. The big Dane had his trusty Thompson submachine gun and was furiously chewing a piece of gum.

"There's three spots the Kraut can be, down near this lake marked as Low Pond on my map, near this cottage, or in the patch of scrub to the west. My money is on the forest near the lakes," said Randel.

"Why Sarge?" asked Magnusson.

"There's cover behind it to fall back into, and it's closer to the village."

"Wouldn't the river block them?"

"River? The Bain at this point barely deserves the name creek. Nah, they're in those trees. Let's go back to the tank and I'll call in the air boys or see if the artillery can't work the woodland over. It's only a couple of hundred yards long and maybe twice that length."

They returned to the M3 and Randel radioed in. He explained the situation and asked for help. The officer on the other end of the line informed him that the air boys would take too long. Minutes later, two batteries of 105mm guns pounded the tree line.

Randel watched with his binoculars and despite the explosions, saw movement.

"It's a StuG and he's pulling back. Tell everybody to get moving," he yelled.

If he could reach the woods and skirt them to the western end, he might be able to find a firing position before the enemy assault gun could reposition itself. His platoon charged down the narrow road with Randel ordering his driver to crash through the hedge where the road turned a sharp left. His M3 had just travelled over a kilometre, most of it on road. Unfortunately for him, the enemy moved only six hundred metres. Most of that was across country with both vehicles moving at a similar speed. There was a slight rise between where the StuG stopped and where Randel halted his tank. This was where the extra height of the Lee didn't do the Americans any favours. The StuG could see the top half of his tank clearly.

The assault gun's first shot glanced off the turret, jamming the 37mm gun in place and making everyone in the M3 shout in surprise and pain, as the tank rang like a bell. Randel screamed for his driver to put the vehicle into reverse. The M3 backed away hurriedly, just missing Sergeant Tyloske's tank. The man had only just been promoted and this made Randel his superior in rank. The two vehicles pulled up next to each other and both commanders stopped and threw open their hatches.

"What the hell?" yelled Tyloske.

"That Kraut had the drop on us. Can you hold his attention?" said Randel.

"How?"

"Lob some high explosive (HE) his way. It will mask my tank's noise and keep his attention. I'm going to find his track through the forest and see if I can turn the tables."

Randel guided his tank quickly around the northern edge of the woodland until he found the position from which the StuG III had been firing from. He told his driver to stop, and jumped down on to the earth. There was a rough track between two small lakes.

He could see churned earth and broken branches, which clearly marked the German's path. Randel hoped the assault gun would be facing in the direction of his platoon and wouldn't see his M3. The German would need to turn his whole vehicle to fire at Randel which would give him a few seconds of valuable time to put a round into the StuG. With any luck the German commander would be inside his vehicle with the hatches closed. Randel could hear the shells exploding as the rest of his platoon lobbed rounds over the forest toward the enemy.

To the east the crackle of machine-gun fire could be heard. He couldn't see the fighting but would later learn that the Germans fought ferociously to hold St Andrew's church and the primary school. The northern half of the town had fallen, but a company from the 53rd German Infantry Division held the southern half.

All of the assault guns fighting in the area were from the 667th Battery. Leutnant Hugo Primozic was the commander of the vehicle that had ambushed the M3 company and had already destroyed three Canadian RAM tanks, Four British Valentines, and seven Crusader IIIs. He was a renowned German tank ace.

Randal clambered back into his tank and discovered that his crew had managed to unjam the turret so it would now be possible to use the 37mm gun once more. He guided the tank through the woodlands slowly, moving carefully to the southern edge of the forest. The StuG was clearly visible only three hundred yards away, across a field of cut hay. Randel didn't quite have the flanking shot he was after, but it was obvious that the Germans weren't yet aware of his presence. As he watched, a 75mm shell from his platoon dropped onto the ground in front of the StuG. It exploded in the yellowing fields, throwing up earth and steel.

"Right Spencer, now it's on you, and Green, try and hit the tracks," said Randel.

Both men grunted and a few seconds later both guns fired. The shells hit within a foot of each other on the front drive sprocket, blowing the track off the StuG and crippling the vehicle. The Germans jumped out of the assault gun and started to run for cover. Randel ordered Private Green to fire the top turret's machine gun at the fleeing crew but the recoil of the gun had rejammed the traversing mechanism.

"I don't want them getting away," yelled Randel. "Use the main gun. Fire HE."

The whole tank turned slightly and Private Olaf Magnusson rammed a high explosive shell into the breech. Unfortunately, these rounds had been designed for artillery pieces and were meant to explode when they hit the ground from a steep angle. Of course, when fired from a tank gun at a target that was only a few hundred yards away, the angle was very shallow. This problem had already been noted by American authorities and had been dealt with, however some of the older shells still found their way to American tanks.

This round hit the ground near the retreating StuG crew and then skipped off like a stone thrown in a pond. One hundred yards on, the shell hit an old oak tree in the middle of its trunk and detonated. The ancient giant was shattered by the explosion and pieces of timber flew in all directions. The Germans dropped to the ground momentarily, before jumping to their feet and running toward a drainage ditch flowed down toward the River Bain.

"Again," roared Randel.

The second shell skipped off the earth once and then again, before landing in a long dam down near the river. Randel saw the round throw up a fountain of water but it didn't explode.

"You have to be kidding," yelled Randel.

"Skipper, I can't see them anymore. We could chase them," said Corporal Spencer.

Randel thought about it for a second. He was tempted to go after the Germans. He knew that crew were experts at what they did. They would be given another StuG and then kill more of his comrades.

"No, we need to look around first. If I go charging into the open we could be hit by a hidden gun. We know there are more StuGs in the area," he said.

Randel cursed the fact the Germans had escaped, but later he and his crew celebrated. They were the first crew in the division to destroy five enemy-armoured vehicles. Better than that, they were still alive.

Later, the Germans fell back a few miles to the villages of Ranby and Goulceby. Randel and his unit were moved back into reserve where they received a welcome surprise. Sitting under the trees just north of the small village of Little London were ten new Sherman tanks. Randel looked at the vehicles and smiled. Later he'd discover the new tank had a number of fatal flaws, but at this moment he was a happy man.

V

The showers fell throughout the day. Maggie sat in the Tavistock Inn and stared out the windows. She could see the bare branches of the oak trees on the other side of the road. The fields were sodden, and the grey sky matched her mood. Sipping her beer, she tried not to think about Rachel and her family. The death of the young Jewish girl played on her mind, and Maggie couldn't shake the idea that her resistance network had in some way let the girl down.

What was she doing here? Her organisation managed to move fifteen Jews to safety and had reported on German movement in and around Devon. Truth was that the area was a backwater. Sometimes she would go to the other side of the moors and spy on the Luftwaffe base at Harrowbeer, but this was a small airstrip with only a single squadron of Bf 110s based there. All of the airfields were near Plymouth and another group, watched that area. The German base at Haldon wasn't in use with the main Luftwaffe presence being further east near Exeter. This was again someone else's area, which was just as well as it was over twenty miles away. When she'd first started operating in Devon, areas had overlapped and her little cell ranged far and wide. Now it was restricted to the area of Dartmoor and the country between Pondsgate and Torquay.

Samson Thistle poked his red head through the door of the inn, before shaking his umbrella. He nodded at Maggie, then made his way to the bar. After ordering a pint he came and sat next to her.

"Weather set to clear says my Da," he said.

"It's almost winter, the weather will get worse," Maggie replied.

"I know. Bad weather for flying, so strange that planes were about last night."

Maggie stopped, the glass halfway to her mouth, and looked around. Nobody was listening.

"Go on," she said.

"Commonwealth planes bombed Brest in France. One of their machines, a Martin Baltimore I think, didn't make it home. The plane came down near Holne so we didn't hear anything in the valley. The crew bailed out and drifted a long way on the south westerly. Two of them landed near the Spitchwich Manor grounds. The other two in the woods by the river.”

“My god, that’s only five hundred yards from here.”

“The wind was strong and the Aussies hit the ground hard. They bailed out high and blew a long way in the winds.”

“We have them?”

“Yes, but the Germans are looking for the crew. So far the patrols and door knocking have only gone as far as Newton Abbot and the few surrounding farms.”

“That’s only half a dozen cottages. It won’t take the Germans long to rule out that the crew didn’t land there.”

“With a lot of effort I managed to get them to St Peters at Buckland.”

“You had to get them across the river Webburn at night? You should have brought them to me, it would have been closer.”

“I thought of that, but decided it was best the crew didn’t know where our chief operative lived. The vicar over there doesn’t even know that there are four men staying in the caretaker’s cottage.”

“Fair enough. Alright, I need to think. Obviously, we need to move them, and quickly. The Germans however will be on the alert. We can probably get them on to Peter’s milk cart first thing in the morning and then move them to the Rugglestone Inn. Old Tom will hide them. He’s a supporter.”

“Maggie, I don’t know if we have that long. I can get them to Cator Court in my truck. We’d need to go now. You could walk them to the Warren House Inn. We have supporters there now.”

“As of how long ago?” asked Maggie.

“A couple of weeks. I didn’t tell you because you said to keep things on a need to know basis.”

“So we don’t know if they can be trusted?”

Sampson shrugged. “We have to take the chance at some point. David seemed like an upstanding man. That Inn has been in his family since it was rebuilt in 1845. He lost his son at Dover fighting the Nazis, so he has good reason to support us.”

Maggie sighed and nodded. “Let’s go then,” she said.

The drive to Buckland in the Moor was not straight forward, and as Sampson chose to take the northerly route it took a good twenty minutes. The trip was about four miles, but the roads were narrow and the weather foul. Then the distance back to the drop off point would be another five miles. This would put a big strain on Sampson’s remaining stock of fuel. The walk across the moors would be about as far as the drive, and that was what worried Maggie the most. Part of the trip was through pine woodland next to the Walla Brook, but the final stretch was across open country. In this weather and with one of the crew member’s legs broken, it would be tough going.

The four crew members were Australian. Two smaller men, not much taller than her, watched the door holding their revolvers.

A sandy-haired man with a face like a house brick sat by a bed. Propped up on some pillows was a man with black hair and eyes that were as green as new spring growth. She locked eyes with him and then hurriedly looked away.

"You don't find me at my best," he said. His accent had a slight drawl but not the gravelly sound of some Australians she'd met.

"This is Pilot Officer Peter Thompson; the two men at the door are Corporals Smith and McIntyre, with Flight Sergeant Bligh here by the bed," said Sampson.

Maggie nodded at the men and tried not to glance at the handsome pilot. "Can you move?" she asked him.

"I can hobble," said Peter Thompson.

"We'll carry Thomo if we need to," said Flight Sergeant Bligh.

"It may come to that. We'll need a stretcher. You can't stay here, as the Germans are looking for you. We have a safe place up on the moors where we can stay for a couple of days before we make more permanent arrangements," said Maggie.

The men hastily gathered their few possessions before Sampson gave them long farm coats. They all clambered into the rear of the truck and hid under a tarpaulin. Pilot Officer Peter Thompson sat in the front between Sampson and Maggie. She was aware of his close proximity but chided herself for feeling like a schoolgirl.

"The break is down near the ankle. I twisted it when I cut myself free of the chute," he said as he eased himself on to the seat.

"Where's your chute?" Maggie asked alarmed.

"Still in the tree."

"Oh great! When the Germans find it they'll rip the area apart looking for you. You should have told me," said Maggie looking at Sampson.

"He didn't know. I was found near the river, about a couple of hundred yards from where I landed. I told the old farmer who helped me," said Peter.

"There's nothin' we can do 'bout it now Maggie," said Sampson.

"No names! If the pilot officer is captured, the Germans could force him to tell them who helped him."

"Sorry," mumbled Sampson.

"I wouldn't talk," said Peter defensively.

"If the Huns torture you it would be difficult to stay silent. Or they might trick you, bug your cell, or place fake prisoners with you."

"They'd torture me?"

"Depends who got hold of you. The Gestapo would, the Luftwaffe, probably not. They'd use other methods," said Maggie.

The pilot officer went a little pale though Maggie wasn't sure if it was from the pain in his ankle or the thought of a German beating him to a pulp.

Sampson drove north, then west, recrossing the East Webburn River and passing by Shallowford farm. The truck splashed through the water, which was running a little higher than usual, before travelling the final mile to Cator Court. To Maggie the countryside was now as familiar as the back of her hand. The area held less than half a dozen houses and nobody was around. Sampson left the group next to a wind break at the edge of the moors. The double line of trees stretched off into the distance, giving the group cover from prying eyes.

She turned to look at the four men. "It's about a mile to the forest. Sorry about the weather but in some ways we are lucky. It will help keep people indoors, though Devon farmers are a hardy lot, so we can't count on that being the case. Then it is about a mile through the woods." She stopped speaking abruptly. It was best the

Australians didn't know of their destination, just in case the Germans found them.

Peter Thompson walked bravely, though Maggie could see the pain that moving caused him. He used a rough crutch to support himself but the ground was boggy and wet. She was wrapped in a rainproof coat and wore waterproof boots. The Australians were in their flying kit, which though warm, wasn't designed for hiking. After walking for a mile they reached the woods and Peter collapsed. His men ran to him and he waved them away. Maggie walked up and stared at the man as he hauled himself to his feet.

"I don't have time for heroics," she said. "It might be faster and easier to carry you."

"We don't have a stretcher."

"I brought a small axe from my friend's truck. We'll cut some branches and make a rough litter. In my pack are two blankets, a little food, and a knife. You can't walk out onto the moors unprepared," she said.

Maggie cut the two poles and Flight Sergeant Bligh helped her tie the blankets. Peter allowed himself to be carried by the four of them into the forest.

By now everyone was wet and cold. The rain eased to a misty drizzle but the wind carried a chill with it. Even Maggie was feeling the strain. The three crew members all took a position on the stretcher and Maggie insisted on taking a corner. After half a mile everyone was straining and muscles began to ache. Changing position allowed them to move through the rest of the forest, but when they reached the northern edge of the woods Maggie suggested they rest. Nobody objected.

Looking across the open ground she could just make out the tavern in the distance. The moors here were very exposed with the country dipping down to a boggy creek. If she followed the edge of the slope for seven hundred or so yards it would be possible to work around the swampy area, and there was a gully they could hide in. The rain picked up, obscuring the road and Warren House. Maggie decided to take advantage of the poor weather.

"Right, time to go. This squall hides us from the road. There probably won't be anyone driving around but you never know," she said.

The Australians groaned as they climbed to their feet and she walked over to Peter.

"Not far now," she said.

"Thank you, Maggie," he said. "Risking your life for us. If we do get caught, I won't talk."

Maggie blushed. She felt an almost welcome heat flush through her cheeks.

"We all fight the Germans in our own way," she said.

"My boys don't have to live with the fear of being discovered every day. Sure, when we are flying we are in danger, but back at base there's nothing to worry about."

Maggie shrugged. "You get used to it."

Peter stared at her and then his body shook.

"Are you feeling alright?" she asked.

"You said no heroics, didn't you, well I think I might have caught a chill," he said.

Maggie felt a spike of anxiety. If Peter became sick, it would be difficult to move him from the inn to a safe house further north. She swallowed her concerns.

"You've done the right thing telling me. I didn't mention where we were going but the Warren House Inn has a story about its fire. It's said that it hasn't gone out since it was first built in 1792. When the inn burnt down in 1845 and they rebuilt it, the owner carried the embers across the road from the old site. My point is you'll soon be warm."

"Don't have stories like that where I'm from. The Aboriginals do, but I haven't really spoken to them much," said Peter. He coughed loudly.

"We need to get you to the inn," said Maggie. She turned to the rest of the crew. "Alright, we're moving."

They picked up the four corners of the makeshift stretcher and walked out of the forest into the wind and driving rain. The area before them was covered in low grasses with small outcrops of rock. The rain pelted down, running from Maggie's face, and finding its way into her boots. She looked at the rest of the crew and saw the strain on their faces. They weren't as well dressed for the weather as she was, though the coats provided by Sampson helped.

After struggling across the slope they reached a gully which marked the halfway point. The creek at the bottom was usually a boggy patch which dried up completely in summer. Today, the water ran knee deep. Everyone was soaked and the icy torrent running into their boots didn't help. They climbed out of the depression panting and cursing until the group reached a walking track.

"Not far now," said Maggie.

Around them the wind picked up, making coats flap, and chilling them all further. Peter coughed and shook in the stretcher, while Maggie felt blisters forming where she held the wood.

"We need a rest," said Flight Sergeant Bligh.

"The inn is less than half a mile from here. Just hold on a little longer," urged Maggie.

Somehow the group struggled on, eventually reaching the main road. There was a slight smell of wood smoke and Maggie turned them toward a whitewashed building that was now visible through the gloom. The inn appeared in front of them and Maggie felt a wave of relief. They entered a small cloak room that stuck out of the two storey building, and the warmth and comfort that came from being out of the wind was glorious. Lifting Peter from the stretcher, they stumbled into the main room.

"By God, you lot are dripping all over my floor," growled a large, bearded man from behind the bar.

"You must be Desmond," Maggie said. "I've been told a lot about you."

"And who are you lass, to muddy up my floorboards?" asked Desmond.

Maggie glanced around and saw that the only other person in the room was a middle-aged woman who was tending the fire. She stepped over to Flight Sergeant Bligh and eased his coat open, showing the Commonwealth flight uniform. Desmond's eyebrows shot up.

"You were told to expect us?" said Maggie.

"No, I was informed I might have to help the odd traveller but I didn't realise it would be so soon."

"Well, here we are. Our trip across the moors was tough, and one of my companions has a broken ankle and is sick."

"Come over to the fire. Best get you out of your wet clothes. Ruby here knows what I do." Desmond turned to the woman. "Luv, can you bring in my old clothes and maybe bring some of your clothes for the young woman."

"I'd do introductions, but its best you don't know. Call me Claire," said Maggie.

"Alright then. We can get you dry and then I'll get some rabbit pie. You must be hungry."

"The pilot is ill. Do you have any soup?" asked Maggie.

"We are an isolated inn lass, not a restaurant."

Maggie's face tightened and she stared at the man. His small blue eyes slid away from her.

"I'll see what I can find," he mumbled.

Desmond disappeared and she turned to the crew. "He's a grumpy old man, or so I've been told. His heart's in the right place. The reputation of Warren House depends on whether you obey his rules or not. We broke the first one with our wet boots and coats. He also has some strange rules regarding dogs and children, but they obviously won't affect us," she said.

"Are we safe here?" asked Flight Sergeant Bligh.

"We are in occupied territory, so no. However, the Huns only use this road occasionally. The main route is further south on the A38. It's the road between Plymouth and Exeter. Sometimes the enemy comes up here to train but that's only happened once. Even then, that was in the northern part of the moors."

"I suppose safety is relative here," said Peter before coughing.

Soon Ruby arrived with a pile of clothing and the men went into the next room to change. Maggie found some dry items that fitted her while Ruby took out the wet items.

"I'll dry these in the kitchen lass," said the thin lady. "Put a little more wood or peat on if you're cold."

The men walked back in wearing a variety of ill-fitting clothing and smelling slightly of mothballs. Ruby came in carrying a small container of camphor.

"The young gentleman should rub this on his chest, not too much mind. It will help with his cough," said Ruby.

The smell of rabbit pie wafted into the room as Desmond returned carrying four plates. The scent reminded Maggie of how hungry she was. The crust of the pie was perfect, and soon she was taking large bites of the steamy meat and enjoying the sensation as it almost burnt her mouth. The men were all similarly engaged.

"There's soup on but it won't be ready for a bit," said the bearded man. Maggie nodded.

"That's fine," she said through a mouthful of food.

"Ruby is making up some rooms. We have no guests at the moment. No one's walking the moors and there's little traffic. No fuel for sightseeing these days."

"We have some funds and I'll see some come your way Desmond. It's important you stay open," said Maggie.

"That'll be appreciated, lass."

Maggie slept well that night, though in the morning she was disappointed to hear that Peter was worse.

"He'll need to stay here," said Desmond.

Outside, the weather was grey with a misty drizzle keeping visibility to a few hundred paces.

"I should move the rest of the crew to the safe houses further north, but I need them to help carry the stretcher," she said.

"I have enough food to keep you all going and young Peter should be alright in a couple of days."

"The longer we stay, the greater the risk."

"Do we have a choice, lass?"

Maggie sighed and went to see Peter.

The pilot lay shivering in his bed. He gave her a sad smile as she entered.

"I'm sorry for all the bother," he said.

"It can't be helped. You came down in terrible weather and none of you had a chance to dry out properly until we arrived here. Desmond thinks we should be safe but he did mention that German dispatch riders often stop at the Warren for a pint on their way to Plymouth. They occasionally take the moors road just so they can drink here."

"So we should set a watch?"

"We wouldn't see them until they were on us in this weather," said Maggie.

"Then we keep a low profile?"

"Yes, and don't talk to anyone unless you can help it. If you have to, try and sound English, not Australian."

"I can do a BBC accent," said Peter in an upper class accent.

Maggie smiled. "That will pass. We could say you're part of the local gentry."

Peter coughed and then wiped his mouth. "My men won't be able to pull it off."

They spent the following two days waiting for Peter to recover. The crew chopped wood, though most of the fuel for the fire was peat. Maggie helped cook and clean, and gradually the pilot's condition improved. During that time everyone enjoyed the view south across the moors as the weather cleared. The crew watched for any traffic but the only vehicles that passed were trucks delivering food and a few of the locals driving to Plymouth. No Germans were seen.

Peter often spent time with Maggie downstairs before napping. His strength improved and the swelling around his ankle receded, leaving an angry purple bruise. He still couldn't put any weight on the limb, but he managed to hobble around nimbly on a crutch that Desmond made in his small workshop. Sometimes he'd read to his men from a collection of Sherlock Homes novels he found in one of the bedrooms. The group would speculate on the plot, and try and solve the crime from the available clues. Late in the day Maggie decided they would try and push across the moors to the next safe house.

The motorbike arrived just before dark. It had a sidecar and carried two Germans from the 207th Security Division. The wind was blowing from the south so they didn't hear the machine until it was at the inn. Outside, a bright moon was climbing into the sky and Maggie saw the silhouettes of the two Germans clearly as they walked to the door chatting. Two of the crew managed to make it upstairs but Flight Sergeant Bligh and Peter were caught in the bar.

One of the Germans, a big man with extremely short hair, carried an MP 40 submachine gun on his back, while his bespectacled companion wore a holster carrying an unknown pistol on his hip.

The smaller man smiled at everyone and nodded. Then he turned to Desmond.

“One of your famous ales for me please, innkeeper,” he asked in English. “My friend wants to try your Scrumpy.”

Without a word Desmond turned and started to pour. No one spoke for a moment.

“Usually the bar is empty when we drive through,” said the Gefreiter.

“You speak good English, old boy,” said Peter in what Maggie thought was a passable English accent. She also noted he didn’t answer the German’s implied question.

"Oh ja, I learned it at university. You have injured yourself?" said the German pointing at the crutch.

"A little tumble walking across the moors. Soon be right," said Peter.

The bespectacled man nodded, but the big German squinted and stared at something before turning away. Both men sipped their drinks and spoke very quietly in German.

Maggie glanced in the direction of the big German's earlier gaze and noticed the boots both Peter and the Flight Sergeant were wearing. She felt for the Walther pistol in her pocket, touching the cool metal, and her grip tightened around the handle. The bespectacled German then turned and stared at the boots. Maggie caught him saying something in German and she definitely heard the word Luftwaffe. The man was reaching casually for his pistol and his large companion was slowly swinging the MP 40 off his back.

Swiftly, the Walther was in her hand. She shot the big German through the throat and he fell clutching at the wound. The Gefreiter scrambled for his side arm but Maggie fired again. The bullet went through the right lenses of his glasses before exiting the back of his head. She took a step forward and shot the big man again in the head.

There was silence for a moment before Peter yelled. "What the hell Maggie?"

"They picked your boots as air force. My guess is they'd been told to keep a look out for the crew of a downed bomber. I saw them staring at your boots, then the big one said something about air force. But they were too casual with their guns."

"Oh my God, oh my God, there are dead people in my inn," yelled Desmond.

"We will hide the bodies and the bike. I want to grab the papers they were carrying as well," said Maggie.

"You shot them in the head," said Desmond.

"They're not the first Huns I've killed. They never seem to give me a lot of choice. I think we can sink them in the Fernworthy Reservoir. We'll need to ride the motor bike up one of the trails. If somebody puts the bodies in the side car, then maybe the driver can take Peter up into the woods."

"Smithy knows how to ride a motor bike," said Peter.

Maggie glanced at him and noted that he seemed to have taken the death of the two Germans in his stride.

"Right, let's get moving," said Maggie.

Later she drew a map for Corporal Smith while the other crew members tied the two dead Germans into the side car. Handing Peter the MP 40, she raised an eyebrow.

"I know how to use it," he said, giving her a smile.

Maggie liked it when he smiled at her. She shook her head. It was important to keep her mind on the task at hand. She'd only recently shot two men and now she was having lustful thoughts about the handsome man. What was wrong with her? Was killing becoming that easy?

Walking back into the inn she found Desmond cleaning his floor.

"There is no reason for anyone to ever know what happened here," she said.

"I'll know," muttered Desmond. "Ruby will know."

"Won't it just add to the collection of local ghosts?"

"You can't make light of this, lass. I didn't sign up for killin' people."

"You joined us to fight the Nazis and on this occasion it led to death. This is war, Desmond."

"I don't want to see you again; you're not welcome here."

Maggie rolled her eyes. She didn't have time for this. Going back outside she saw everyone was ready to move. The motorcycle started up and the corporal eased it up the track. Maggie looked around and saw that the moors were empty. She marvelled at the stark beauty, then thought about what she needed to do. They still had to hide the dead Germans and get clear of the area.

The walk to the reservoir was familiar to Maggie, and she tried hard not to think about the last occasion she'd been here with Rachel and her family. This time she moved quickly. With the help of the three mobile crew members they sunk the motorcycle and the Germans in deep a water. Dropping the machine and the bodies from the wall of the dam ensured they wouldn't be found if the water level decreased. Maggie wasn't to know the two Germans had actually told their commanding officer they would be taking the A385 to Plymouth. Instead, they'd taken the route through the moors especially to stop and drink at the inn, and because the big man thought the B3212 was actually a little faster.

Maggie handed the crew over to her contact at Sticklepath on the northern side of the moors. She had mixed feelings about saying goodbye to Peter. On one hand it was a relief to send him on the next part of his journey, but there was a part of her that wished he would stay with her. As she turned to leave he hobbled over to her.

"When this is all over, I hope it will be alright if I come and find you," he said

Maggie's heart tightened. She was irrationally pleased at what he'd said, but knew that it was unlikely they would ever see each other again.

"I'd like that," she managed to say.

Peter squeezed her hand, then he turned and walked to the delivery truck. The old vehicle was powered from wood gasification. It usually delivered meat but today it was carrying men. Maggie gave the truck a wave and turned south. She had a long walk home in front of her.

Chapter Five: December 1942

The landing craft were disgorging their human cargo on the beach. Above them Commander James 'Pug' Southerland turned his F4F Wildcat in a wide arc. Off to the north clouds gathered, and he thought he saw a flash of lightning.

"Reaper Leader, this is Reaper Four. I can see planes coming in from the northwest, height fifteen thousand. At least twenty single-engine machines," said the voice of Ensign Palmer.

"I see them. Turn to compass bearing three fifteen and climb to twenty thousand feet," said Southerland.

The Wildcats climbed slowly but the American pilots had plenty of time. The enemy fighters also gained altitude but Southerland intended to ignore them. The Zero's controls stiffened at high speeds, something he was going to use to his advantage.

"Right, we dive on the bombers, then use the speed gained to climb again. Wingmen, stay with your section leader and if you do get into a dog fight with a Zero, remember your tactics," he said.

The Wildcats rolled over on their backs and headed down toward the bombers. Southerland felt his plane rattle and shake as it built up speed. He came in fast behind the trailing Betty bombers and aimed at their vulnerable fuel tanks. His first burst was high, so he dropped the nose of the Wildcat and raked the port wing of the last bomber. There was a small explosion and a tongue flame shot back from the engine.

"He is going down, Reaper Leader," said one of his pilots. Southerland was already climbing away from the formation of Japanese bombers, using his speed to gain altitude. When his flight had reached eighteen thousand feet he glanced over his shoulder and saw four Zeros trying to catch his aircraft.

"Time to dive again everyone," he ordered.

Southerland rolled his plane to starboard and pushed the nose of his aircraft down. For a split second he flashed through the sights of the enemy. Only one Japanese pilot managed to fire briefly, but his cannon shells missed. He flew swiftly down toward the bomber but noticed they had dropped their bombs and were heading north. Two damaged machines trailed the enemy formation and he headed toward them. A Betty limped on one engine, a thin grey line of smoke streaming from the machine. He dropped behind the bomber and gave it a long burst from his six machine guns. The entire Betty erupted in flames before exploding. Southerland had to turn sharply to avoid the debris. He saw that the second bomber was also burning, shot down by his wingman.

Below him the 1st Marine Division was storming ashore on Guadalcanal. The landings had been planned hurriedly to take advantage of the fact the Japanese had no operational carriers for the moment. Three were being repaired but wouldn't be available until February 1943. Meanwhile, the new light carrier Independence had joined the Enterprise. The Independence had been rushed into service and was still undertaking shake down operations when it was ordered to support the attack.

The whole landing was rushed. The code name of Operation Hurry reflected the speed in which the attack had been planned. There had been a struggle to gather the necessary landing craft and support vessels. Luckily, the assault took the Japanese by surprise and the fortifications around the island's airstrip were light. There was however the 4th Infantry Regiment from the 2nd Japanese Infantry Division based in the area, having recently arrived from the Philippines, via Rabaul. The unit wasn't well dug and suffered heavily from the bombardment from the battleships USS South Dakota and USS Colorado, and supporting cruisers.

The Japanese also had a single battalion on the island of Tulagi which inflicted heavy casualties on the four thousand New Zealand troops which landed there. The 8th Brigade of the 3rd NZ Division had to struggle over coral reefs to reach the landing beaches. If it weren't for the support of dive bombers from the Enterprise and the new B25 Mitchell gunships, the New Zealanders would have suffered even more deaths. The Japanese troops fought until they were wiped out.

Now the Marines were pushing past the airfield near Lungga point. The planes on the landing strip were either destroyed or had been moved to Rabaul. Enemy attempts to attack the US fleet or interfere with the landing had so far failed. The attempt by the Japanese bombers today was also a failure, with six Bettys being shot down and three Zeros destroyed for the loss of four Wildcats.

It felt good to be taking territory back from the Japanese. Since the Battle of Torres, the tide appeared to be turning. Now the Marines were ashore. Another operation was taking place on the even more lightly defended San Cristobal Island. Here the Americal Division, formed on New Caledonia had landed and taken the small emergency strip near the mouth of the Wango River near Tawasu Point. Only a single Japanese battalion defended this area and it was swiftly crushed. The airfield was already being expanded by the Seabees (United States Naval Construction Battalions). At least three damaged carrier planes had already landed there.

Southerland was exhausted. The rate of operations was tiring for all of the aircrew and there had been little chance to relax since the carrier battle two months ago. The air groups from the USS Enterprise had constantly supported attacks on the enemy bases in the Solomon area, while the rate of attacks on Japanese held Port Moresby and Milne Bay had increased. Indeed, the air battles over northern Australia increased in intensity with the RAAF now using Corsair fighters to supplement their aging Brumby interceptors. Losses on both sides were rumoured to be high. The effect of the twin air campaigns had been to keep the Japanese guessing the intentions of the Allies. A large scale misinformation campaign actually led enemy intelligence to expect an attack somewhere along Papua New Guinea's southern coast.

Constantly landing and taking off from a carrier deck was wearing Southerland down. One mistake could be your last, and some pilots had succumbed to exhaustion. The rate of deaths from accidents in the last week exceeded those from combat. He'd spoken to Captain Osborne Bennett directly about the issue. 'Ozzie

B' had told him that he hoped they'd all get a break in the New Year. The Enterprise was badly in need of a refit and the crew desperate for some leave. Still, while marines were dying and the Japanese were being forced back, the extra effort was worth it.

The deck loomed up in front of him and Southerland forced himself to concentrate. He watched the LSO signal with the batons to chop power. As his wheels hit the deck his left tire burst. Southerland hammered the right brake to compensate, but it was too late. The Wildcat lurched sideways. At the last second its tail hook caught one of the arrester wires, however the landing gear collapsed and the spinning propeller chopped into the wooden deck. The Wildcat stopped right on the edge of the landing platform. Southerland was disorientated. He felt the plane lurch. Then there was a man hammering on his cockpit. Looking to his right he could see other sailors and mechanics holding the wing. Southerland hauled open his canopy and felt the humid air hit him.

"Are you alright, sir?" yelled a mechanic who looked like he was fresh out of high school.

“I think so,” he answered.

“Then let’s get you out. I don’t think this bird is going to stay on deck much longer.”

The young mechanic helped him from the cockpit, and both men clambered along the wing as the Wildcat started to move. With a yelp Southerland sprang onto the deck with the sailor, just as his fighter fell off the side of the ship and into the sea. The man grinned at him and Southerland smiled back.

“I owe you a crate of beer, seaman,” said Southerland.

He glanced over the side of the ship and watched, as the tail of his fighter slipped beneath the waves.

V

Another winter was starting on the Eastern front and the Russians still hadn’t broken. Reichsmarschall Kesselring looked at the production figures and pulled out a map of the front in the area of Kamyshin. Of course the Soviets had attacked toward the Volga. The front here had swung like a door toward the river after the

Russian assault, trapping four divisions around the town and along the waterway to the south. Two Romanian Corps had been swept away, with another trapped in the pocket. A second offensive had pushed the German 1st Panzer army back toward Voronezh, with the Soviet 5th Tank Army and 21st Army throwing the Heer back thirty kilometres. Reinforcements looked like they'd help stop the Russians just outside the city and along the banks of the Don River, yet it was the other attack along the Volga that was causing the most concern.

Here the Russians had attacked to the southeast. The 65th and 51st Army advanced toward Stalingrad, with the 1st Guards Army reaching the Volga near Suvodskaya, cutting off the 14th Panzer, 60th Motorised, 44th and 76th Infantry Divisions. The Romanian VI Corps, or what was left of it, was also trapped in the long Volga pocket.

There had been intelligence reports indicating some Soviet units had been broken up to reinforce other divisions. All of the Russian 24th Army was rumoured to have been dissolved to strengthen other divisions. Prisoners continued to say the Soviet Union was still suffering from acute food shortages, with manpower probably being diverted to this area. Kesselring guessed this was also affecting Russian production levels too. Yet somehow Stalin had scraped together enough men to launch an offensive that had almost swept the Germans back to their positions of early September. The enemy had also trapped one hundred thousand German troops and twenty thousand Romanians.

The Führer wanted the trapped divisions rescued, and Generalfeldmarschall Manstein was ordered to launch an offensive along the Volga to reach the pocket. First the Germans had to halt the Russian advance on Stalingrad.

The supply situation was a mess. The Luftwaffe had lost over a hundred transport aircraft in the attack on Crete. The actual landings were only opposed by poorly armed Greek infantry, but long range allied fighters attacked the airstrips and intercepted Ju 52s and Me 323 aircraft, managing to shoot many down. Over eight hundred paratroopers and a similar number of mountain troops died in the air. Kesselring blamed himself for withdrawing some of his fighter units back to Germany after the fall of Athens, but he hadn't anticipated the American P38 fighters and F4U fighters appearing over Crete in large numbers.

Then there were the raids on Hamburg by Flying Fortress bombers. The US planes were based in Northumbria and attacked unescorted. The first raids by the heavy bombers were remarkably successful, as they found their targets almost unprotected. JG 1 was in Greece and most of the other fighter units protecting Germany were scattered. There had been little need to defend the skies over the homeland until now. A small number of 88mm or 105mm anti-aircraft guns defended German cities, but there weren't enough of them.

At least there weren't many American bombers. The last raid had been met by over forty Fw 190 A4s and fourteen Bf 109 G4s. Of the ninety Flying Fortresses, thirteen were shot down and another twenty damaged. The fighter force lost fourteen planes and Kesselring understood that his pilots were working out new tactics to attack the heavy bombers. Many of the German pilots had attacked from behind the formation of American planes, into a hail of defensive gun fire. He commended the bravery of his men and understood that some of the men were furious at the loss of civilian life, a new phenomena for Germany at this stage of the war.

Issues in Crete caused by the lack of escorts for the transport planes illustrated, yet again, how stretched the Luftwaffe was. Anyway, the losses meant the Luftwaffe lacked the machines to fly supplies to hard pressed German troops in Russia. From what he could understand, the railways were not functioning properly and there were bottle necks at Rostov, and as far back as Kiev.

Supplying a continued drive toward Georgia in the south by German forces was out of the question. There were ports in the area that could be used, but the roads around Sochi were heavily damaged and Soviet resistance among the coastal hills was fierce. The port of Poti was still held by German units and Georgian rebels, with the high ground to the east of the city being recaptured. However, to the north of the port, Russian troops had reached the Rioni River and even created a small bridgehead near the delta of the waterway. The airstrip was now being used to fly in supplies to the defenders of the port, with some of the new Ju252s bringing in food and flying out wounded.

His phone rang and he was told General Wagner was on the other end. What did that man want? He considered not taking the call. Kesselring took a deep breath and picked up the receiver.

"Yes, General," he said. "How can I help you?"

"Well, it's how I can assist you actually, or the Luftwaffe," said Wagner. The line was a little crackly and for a second Kesselring wondered of the Gestapo was listening in.

"Really?"

"Yes. A friend told me that the Herman Goering Panzer Division was having trouble finding certain resources. I know you have solved your artillery problem, and that the Skoda works are building a new panzer for you, but I believe the army hasn't supplied any mortars or anti-tank guns."

"True, to a certain extent. The division will have plenty of 88mm guns."

"But you need smaller, more portable and easily hidden pieces."

"I'm told they would be of great assistance to the unit's anti-tank capabilities."

"I have managed to get a number of Panzerwerfers. These are half-tracks mounting rocket artillery. They are new but the replacement army was to get thirty for training. I thought maybe a dozen could go to your division."

Kesselring was very happy with the offer, but wary. "And how could I assist you in return?"

There was a moment's hesitation on the other end of the line. "I want back in," said Wagner.

"You mean controlling supply."

"I hear it's not what it was. You could use me."

Kesselring knew this was true, but wasn't sure how the Führer felt about the pessimistic general. Since the death of Rhinehard Heydrich last month there was no chance of the Group of Four reforming. The problem was General Wagner had stood on many toes in order to increase production, and supply the troops at the front properly. Only Doctor Todt had survived the group's demise with his power intact. General Guderian was now Director of Panzer Troops and had responsibility for reforming the panzer divisions. An important role but not nearly as influential as being an army commander. Even Todt now worked with a minder, as Albert Speer watched his every move, though the two men still managed to work well together.

"You are needed and I'll see what I can do," said Kesselring.

"That's all I can ask for. I'll send over the details of how these Nebelwerfers will come your way."

Kesselring hung up and wondered how he would bring General Wagner up with the Führer. The supply situation was a mess and the troops were suffering. They needed the General back.

V

The fifteen Sherman tanks were parked under a canopy of bare trees. Roughton Moor Woods lay next to Horncastle Road. This high ground overlooked the town of Woodhall Spa. The 36th American Infantry Regiment occupied the town, while the Germans held the country on the other side of the River Witham. To the south, the enemy still occupied St. Helen's Wood and Coningsby, with the airstrip being behind German lines. Artillery fire had rendered it unusable and Sergeant Chuck Randel could still see the wrecked Italian fighters lying next to the grass strip.

The Bain River lay between the Americans and the Germans, though Hatham and its associated woods had recently fallen to US troops. The river in this area was more of a canal and operated as an anti-tank trench. There were numerous locks where infantry could cross, but getting armour to the other side required a bridge, and the two nearest had both been blown up. He moved back to his Sherman, Jumping Jack, and saw Private Olaf Magnusson staring at the turret.

"You still worrying?" Randel asked.

"Sarge, it's alright for you and the others. You've all got an escape hatch," said the big Dane.

"I know."

"I mean, what were they thinking? The German tanks have hatches for every crew member."

"Olaf, you've said all this before."

"Sarge, Jerry Caldwell burned to death the day before yesterday. The rest of his crew got out. We know how the Sherman burns quickly when hit. You have seconds to get out and I have a recoil guard blocking my path."

"What do you want me to do about it?"

"Cut me a hole and we'll rig something up. It won't be that hard to do."

"It's against regulations."

"I don't care, Sarge. This is life or death for me."

Randal considered the issue. There was no doubt that cutting a hole in the top of a turret would weaken its structure but not by a lot. The morale of his crew members was important, and Olaf had an excellent point. When a Sherman's ammunition ignited, the crew had to get out quickly. The small hatches didn't help, but not giving the loader his own door was a massive oversight.

"Okay, we'll do it, though we have to keep it quiet. Captain Stevens is a stickler for regulations. I'll get the cutting equipment but you'll need to find a hatch from one of the wrecks. It's going to be a very rough job."

"The captain won't see it unless he climbs on board," said Olaf.

"Or unless you stick your head out when he's around."

"I won't use it, except to escape."

"He'll probably see it if he drives up next to us."

"Sarge, if he sees it I'll take the rap."

"Yeah, it doesn't work like that Olaf. I'm the commander, it's me he will yell at. Still, you're right. The fact you don't have a door is insane."

Olaf found a hatch on a wrecked M3, and with a lot of experimentation the crew managed to cut a hole in the top of the turret and weld the makeshift door in place. Of course, all of the effort attracted the crews of the rest of his platoon. Soon they were all talking about making the field modification. Randel looked at Olaf and frowned. The big Dane shrugged and smiled. Luckily, Captain Stevens was away at Headquarters, and Lieutenant Kaminski had gone with him.

"God, the officers are going to kill me," muttered Randel.

"You've done the right thing, Sarge," said Corporal Freddy Spencer.

"I hope so," he muttered.

The following day the captain called all of the platoon commanders together. So far the modification of three Sherman's hadn't been discovered. Randel knew it was only a matter of time and he dreaded the tirade he'd have to endure. At the moment though, the captain was focused on the coming operation.

"Right, the infantry are going across the Witham River and take a bridgehead at Kirstead. The embankments on either side of the river will provide some protection for the attacking infantry, but as soon as the Krauts discover what's going on, they'll respond with mortar fire. Artillery and a spotter aircraft will help suppress the enemy. We have bulldozers to fill the river in. It's only fifty to sixty inches deep, however as you know, a Sherman without any wading equipment can only cope with forty inches of water. The other problem would of course be the mud and the steep banks. The river will back up quickly so we will need to get across fast. A proper bridge will be built later. One of our first jobs will be to protect the bulldozers," said the Captain.

The tanks rolled out and Randal was glad his platoon went first. He'd struggled to take in the details of the mission, as images of the doors cut into the top of the turrets of three tanks dominated his thoughts. An artillery barrage smothered the other side of the Witham River with high explosives. Sporadic mortar fire disrupted the American crossing, but the L-4 Grasshopper spotter plane redirected fire from American 105mm guns onto enemy positions. MG 42 fire from the upper storey windows of a few cottages cut down a few US troops as they pushed rubber rafts into the water. 75mm shells from the Sherman's main guns rapidly suppressed these positions, and soon the men from the 36th Infantry Regiment cleared the few German troops from the small village on the other side of the river. There was a brief firefight at an inn called the King's Arms before the infantry moved on.

Soon the bulldozers were pushing soil into the river. Randel could hear small arms fire from across the river but it seemed to be dropping off. The infantry then crossed open fields to take the only farmhouse in the area, before reaching a drainage ditch seven hundred yards from the river. The water here was shallow but at least the embankments provided the troops with some protection. Another ditch further south was deeper and wider, and stopped any

American tanks moving too far in that direction. The next high ground was over three miles to the west, and only rose above the surrounding landscape by seventy feet. Still, it and the village of Martin were the day's objectives.

The Captain drove past Randel's platoon standing in his turret. When he reached Jumping Jack he stopped his tank.

"What's the meaning of the monstrosity on the top of your turret, Randel?" the Captain yelled.

"Sir, my loader doesn't have a hatch," said Randel.

"That's the way it came. You don't get to cut holes in the tanks of the United States of America!"

"Sir, men are dying for want of a door."

The Captain's face became red. "We will discuss this later," he said. His Sherman then crossed the earthen causeway made by the bulldozers. Randel followed not far behind.

It was three and a half miles to the village of Martin. The company of Shermans didn't charge straight down the main road.

The countryside was extremely flat and open, with bare fields extending to distant windbreaks made up of thin lines of trees. The odd cottage sat by the road breaking up the landscape. Squads from the 36th Regiment scouted ahead and returned a few hours later. They reported Germans near a feature known as the Car Dyke. There was also movement on a hill named Martin Wood and in the village itself.

Captain Stevens called down artillery on the area and ordered the fifteen tanks forward. The infantry advanced with them. About a thousand yards from the village mortar shells started to fall around the Americans. MG 42 fire forced the infantry to take cover. The Shermans commenced firing HE rounds at the machine-gun positions, and slowly the US troops crawled forward. The flat crack of an 88mm gun shocked everyone. A Sherman stopped and caught fire. Men spilled from the vehicle, though Randel only saw three men escape.

"I've spotted a German panzer, Sarge," said Freddy Spencer. "God, it's bigger than any I've seen before."

"What's the range?" asked Randel.

"Seven hundred yards behind the dyke, so it's hull down," said Spencer.

Another Sherman was hit, but this one exploded. Randel felt his bladder tighten. There was no cover and the gun on this new tank sounded like an 88mm gun.

A voice crackled over the radio. "Sergeant Randel, take your platoon forward. That panzer has to be destroyed," said Captain Stevens.

"Can you hit it Freddy?" he asked.

"Yes," the little gunner replied.

"Fire," yelled Randel.

The first shell went high, but Olaf loaded another shell and this time Spencer hit the turret of the German panzer. It glanced off with a clang.

"It bounced," said Randel.

Another Sherman was hit, this time in the tracks. The crew abandoned the vehicle before a second shell caused it to catch fire.

"Again," screamed Randel.

Another shell hit in almost the same spot but this shell also bounced away.

"The armour on that monster is too thick," said Spencer.

"Destroy that panzer, Randel," ordered the Captain.

Randel keyed his microphone. "Sir, it's a new type of German tank. We can't penetrate its armour," he replied.

One of the Shermans from Randel's platoon had its turret ripped off by the next shell. The Panzer then drove over the dyke and stopped in the field.

"My God, look at that monster," said Spencer. The little gunner fired again hitting the Tiger I H1 on the hull. The shell broke up on impact. The turret of the enemy machine turned slightly and then Jumping Jack was hit. Smoke filled the turret and Randel was screaming for everyone to get out. He pulled himself from the hull as heat washed around his legs. Next to him Olaf was clambering from the rough door cut in the top of the turret. Both men tumbled onto the ground as the tank exploded in flames. Freddy was on the ground next to them but there was an ear piercing scream from inside the Sherman.

"Troy didn't get out," said Randel.

"Tom was killed by the hit," said Freddy.

Randel glanced at the little gunner and saw he was covered in blood.

"It's not mine, Sarge. This is what's left of Tom. The AP round cut him in two. It wasn't pretty," said Spencer. With that, the gunner started to shake. Randel pulled him to the ground and together they crawled away from the battlefield. Nearby, eight other Shermans were on fire. The American infantry also fell back toward the river and by night fall a bridgehead of about a mile from Kirkstead was established.

Captain Stevens visited him as they recrossed the river.

"You're going to get a new tank," said the older man.

"Yes sir," Randel answered.

"And you can't cut any holes in this one."

"Sir, Private Olaf Magnusson escaped today because of the door we cut. Without it he would have burned to death inside Jumping Jack."

"You don't get to modify tanks. Men smarter and better paid than you designed them and we don't get to chop them up."

"Yes sir," said Randel through gritted teeth. He'd already decided to disobey the order the first chance he got.

Chapter Six: January 1943

The snow lay deep around her yet Junior Sergeant Roza Shanina ignored any discomfort. She settled her sights on the German officer as he directed an anti-tank gun into position. The ruins of the railway yard surrounded her position. Wrecked locomotive engines, rolling stock that had been twisted, mangled, and destroyed, and warehouses dominated the landscape. And the dead. There were plenty of them to keep her company. The frozen corpses were covered in a white dusting of snow, as though someone had sprinkled them with flour.

Anna Adami, her spotter, was about fifty paces to her left, hidden under a train carriage that lay on its side. They had a third member of their little group these days. Nadia Smenko guarded the sniper from a position near a collapsed wheat silo. All of the women wore white baggy jump suits with hoods pulled tightly around their heads. They watched and waited, as the Germans struggled with the 50mm gun. The enemy seemed to be trying to set up a new defensive position near the railway yards, after falling back from their previous line near the park and the textiles factory.

The decision to let Nadia join the sniper team had been difficult. She was a valuable radio operator, but the Colonel had been talking about transferring her to another unit. The older man was now keen on placing a younger dark-haired girl in his bunker, and wanted Nadia to move on. The pretty radio operator wasn't worried about the rejection, she said she expected it from men like him. It was leaving her friends that troubled her. What concerned Roza was Nadia's lack of training. Sniper teams were masters of camouflage and patience. Nadia had little training in these areas, though she proved to be a quick learner and helped protect the sniper team from sudden surprises, however an extra member also increased their chances of being spotted. In the end, they decided it was worth taking a chance, especially as it meant the women could stay together. Getting the Colonel's permission proved easier than Roza thought. She thought he might not want to risk a well-trained radio operator on the front line but the idea didn't even seem to cross his mind.

The German officer squinted and pointed at something. Roza slowly squeezed the trigger of her Mosin-Nagant rifle and felt the slight thud as the weapon kicked back into her shoulder. The Nazi jerked backwards and fell next to the anti-tank gun. His men scattered, except for one who jumped behind the gun shield. She heard the Germans yelling, then their weapon turned slightly and fired. There was an explosion to her left which threw shrapnel, rocks, and ice into the air. A corpse that had lain half hidden under the metal bogies of a locomotive disintegrated. The German gunner must have believed the dead body had been the sniper. She tried to get her sights on the enemy gunner but he stayed hidden. The enemy gun traversed again and this time a round struck the cab of the train engine near where she was hiding. It didn't explode but punched a hole through the metal structure. Roza wondered why the enemy was using armour piercing shells and then realised the Nazis were probably running low on ammunition. Finally she managed to get the crosshairs of her scope on the slit in the 50mm gun shield. She couldn't see the German but knew this was what he'd be peering through as he attempted to aim.

Roza squeezed the trigger and saw the gun muzzle of the enemy anti-tank gun flash. Her bullet went through the narrow gap in the gun shield and hit the German in the right eye, killing him instantly. The 50mm round he'd fired as his life ended smashed into the earth in front of her, throwing rocks and bricks in her direction. One of the flying projectiles struck her rifle, smashing the stock and a rock hit her helmet, which sent her sprawling. For a moment she lay stunned. The round had also stripped away her camouflage and now the Nazis could see her.

Bullets ripped up the ground around her. Anna fired at the enemy with her SVT-40 automatic rifle, and Nadia started shooting at the Germans with her submachine gun, even though they were out of effective range. Her friends were trying to distract the enemy and give her a chance to reach cover. Roza rolled behind a pile of rocks. She heard the tearing sound of an MG 42 and then, after a moment, the firing stopped. The three women slowly crept away from the enemy lines, meeting at a prearranged location near the wrecked silo.

Nadia hugged Roza, making her smile.

“I thought they’d hit you,” said the pretty radio operator.

“It was close. If the German gunner had used HE instead of an armour piercing round, I’d be dead,” said Roza.

“Why do you think he did that?” asked Anna.

“The Nazis are running low on everything. Those units trapped inside the Kamyshin pocket are hungrier than we are,” said Nadia.

“You are probably right,” said Roza.

They made their way back to their own lines and reported to the company commander. He commended Roza for killing two Germans, then wrote her a note so she could get a new rifle.

“I’m going to get an SVT- 40 like yours,” Roza said to Anna.

"What about the sights?" her spotter asked.

"It comes with the standard 3.5," said Roza.

"You have to treat the SVT carefully," said Anna. "The weapon has its problems."

Later, the three women ate boiled potatoes rubbed in a little pig fat and sprinkled with a pinch of salt. Then they shared what was left of a bottle of vodka. They listened to music on the radio, which was followed by a broadcast exhorting everyone to throw back the Nazi invaders.

"I heard from a friend at divisional headquarters that our forces have reached the Don River and are trying to hold off a Nazi thrust down near Stalingrad," said Nadia.

"Yeah, the Fascists are trying to reach their forces trapped on the Volga," said Anna.

"They won't save them," said Roza.

The Russians had forced the Heer back to the line roughly equating to the Don River, though the frozen river wasn't a barrier, it just highlighted were the Soviet advance stopped. Stalingrad hadn't been recaptured but Field Marshal Manstein had managed to advance fourteen kilometres toward the trapped Panzer Corps. Then his army was struck in the flank and he had to retreat, or risk being cut off. Russian forces were also fighting at Voronezh, where infantry had reached the river of the same name.

"The Nazis can't hold out much longer. The only airstrip they hold inside the pocket fell yesterday. The Luftwaffe won't be able to fly in any more supplies. It's too far for their helicopters to go and they'll have to drop stuff with parachutes," said Roza.

"Then we will win the war?" asked Nadia.

"We will at least have a victory worth celebrating. This time we didn't just stop the Germans or throw them back a few kilometres. We will capture part of one of their armies," said Anna.

"Maybe we should have a party?" said Nadia.

"When the Nazis in the pocket surrender, we will," said Roza.

V

Winter sleet turned to snow, carpeting Berlin in a white blanket. Reichsmarschall Kesselring watched a plough clear the capital city's roads before turning back to the maps that lined his walls. At least it was warm in his office.

The surrender of the Volga pocket had come as a shock. The XXIV Panzer Corps and the VIII Army Corps had surrendered two days ago, and Germany was still recovering from the news. Just under half the 6th Army had been lost. The Führer wasn't speaking to anyone and blamed the defeat on General Paulus, whom he'd promptly sacked. Field Marshal Manstein received some of the blame, as had Kesselring himself. He'd told the German leader he couldn't supply the pocket from the air but the Führer refused to listen. There was only one airstrip and the Luftwaffe was struggling to replace the transport planes lost in Crete. Then the last airfield had been lost to a Russian assault.

At least Manstein had been left to his own devices since the surrender, and had managed to stabilise the situation. Russian losses were very heavy and though they'd captured one hundred and twenty thousand German troops, their armies were exhausted. All Soviet efforts now seemed to be on taking Voronezh. There were signs of another impending attack on the German lines west of Moscow, and the XLVII Panzer Corps had been moved to the area to counter any thrust. These units were almost at full strength. The 502nd Heavy Panzer Battalion equipped with new Tiger 1 tanks was also in the area and ready to fight. It had twenty of the massive panzers as well as sixteen Panzer IIIs equipped with short 75mm guns.

Still, he wasn't concerned about the Heer. The Luftwaffe was his domain and it was now facing enemies on multiple fronts. The Allies had just taken Tobruk and were growing in strength in the Middle East and Cyprus. American and British fighter aircrafts had proved to be dangerous opponents over Crete. Attacks by medium level bombers in and around the Eastern Mediterranean were becoming a nuisance. Over England Kesselring felt the German Air Force was losing control of the skies. JG 77, 26 and 2 were being worn down by constant attacks and three Kampfgeschwaders (KG) of bombers needed to be withdrawn and reequipped. Schnellkampfgeschwader 10 had been sent with its sixty Fw 190 fighter bombers to the area, as well as a large force of Ju 88C5s with KG 30. These eighty planes were extremely fast, and provided the Luftwaffe in England with renewed striking power. Yet even these units were already taking heavy losses.

The problem was the American numbers were having an impact. A new fighter had also been met over Liverpool. These were supposedly called the P-47, or Thunderbolt, by the Americans. The new plane reportedly dived quickly, had a good rate of roll and was fast. It also packed a tremendous punch, with eight heavy machine guns. Some of the German aces in Britain said it was easy to out maneuver, especially at lower altitudes, but it was an improvement on the P-40. What concerned Kesselring was that the enemy were introducing new types that seemed to perform well above six kilometres. He really needed the Fw 190 C to work. The Luftwaffe had placed a lot of hope in that particular aircraft.

A new type of plane had come into service in the German Air Force. Thirty Ju 252 transport planes were about to fly east. Of course they were too late to help the troops trapped on the Volga, but at least they could supply troops along the Don River. Maybe they'd fly south to help the army trying to fight its way to Georgia.

The pilot schools had to be expanded again. Kesselring was sure of this. He wouldn't raid them again, not even in emergency situations, because a number of valuable instructors had been deployed by the Luftwaffe and killed in attacks on Greece and Yugoslavia. It mustn't happen again. It had taken eighteen months to make good the losses from the first invasion of England, though by speeding up the training process, qualified single-engine pilots were reaching German units just before the attack on the Soviet Union. Again, Kesselring hadn't liked taking short cuts but the Russian pilots had proved to be under trained, so the risk had paid off. This wasn't the case with the Americans. Their pilots were extremely well trained, and if their aircraft continued to improve then the Luftwaffe would be challenged.

Over Crete the Luftwaffe had already faced another difficult opponent. The F4U Corsair seemed to be the equivalent of the Fw 190 A4, and it could fly five hundred kilometres and fight. Those flown from Libya were responsible, with a group of P-38s, of shooting down many German transport aircraft. The American gull-winged aircraft was highly effective at altitudes between one thousand and four thousand metres. This was where most of the combat occurred at this time, with only a small amount occurring above five kilometres.

The Fw 190 C wouldn't help the Luftwaffe gain its technological superiority and the Fw 190 D wasn't supposed to be ready until the spring of 1944. The second fighter (the D) would perform well at all altitudes.

Meanwhile, the situation in England seemed to have stabilized. The line had barely moved, with only small scale attacks and counterattacks occurring. All of Rommel's attempts to take Liverpool had become grinding battles of attrition, in which towns like Stoke-on-Trent and Chesterfield were destroyed. The lower area of Lincoln had been devastated but the historic precinct on the top of the escarpment wasn't as badly damaged. Lincoln had been the high-water mark of the German advance on the eastern side of England, and since reaching the city the Heer had retreated about fifteen kilometres to the village of Navenby.

There were worrying stories of new American units arriving at Liverpool and Glasgow. The promises of the Kriegsmarine to stop the flow of reinforcements and supplies across the Atlantic hadn't been kept. After early successes in the first months of 1942, the Canadians and US Navy managed to turn the tide against the U-boat attacks. Heavy Kriegsmarine units were kept close to home in order to protect the sea routes to England. The Channel and the southern half of the North Sea were controlled by the German Navy, but further afield the Allied forces dominated. There were areas of ocean which remained contested. These included the seas off the eastern Scottish coast and the Bristol and St. George's Channel between Wales and Ireland.

Irish aircraft had shot down three British fighters that had strayed over their territory. To prove they were going to be even handed, four Spitfire Mark IIs from the Irish Air Force shot down a pair of German Arado AR 196s. These Spitfires were the same machines that had been used by American volunteer pilots in 1940, and flown across the Irish Sea when the British government sued for peace. Two days prior Luftwaffe Fw 190 A4s had deliberately provoked the Irish Air Force by flying over Rosslare. Hurricanes had tried to intercept the German fighters and four Irish planes were shot down. This mission had been ordered by the Führer to show the government of Ireland not to attack Luftwaffe aircraft, even if they violated Eire's territory. Kesselring didn't like the idea. He thought the Luftwaffe had enough enemies.

Intelligence reports suggested that the US 2nd Armoured Division was gathering north of Harrogate in the woods along the Skell River. Fighter bombers from the Luftwaffe tried to raid the area and had been met by a hail of anti-aircraft fire. An American division had taken over garrison duties on Iceland and there were bound to be other US and Canadian units in Northern Ireland. Some of the Americans were undertrained, yet the sheer weight of numbers and equipment would concern the German Army in England. This army had received little in the way of reinforcements. Indeed, the 7th Panzer Division had been withdrawn to Poland where it was in the process of reequipping. Now, only the 22nd, 23rd, 24th and 25th Panzer Divisions remained. All of these units were below their established strength. The 503rd Heavy Panzer Battalion with its Tigers had been sent to England, but Kesselring thought more was needed to reinforce Rommel's Army. As it was, that unit had only received twelve of the massive machines.

Africa was going to fall. The allied advance under Heathcote Hammer had stopped at Benghazi, while Commonwealth forces cleaned up Italian forces trapped in the upper Sudan, and those still based in Ethiopia. The Commonwealth Navy and Air Force ruled the Eastern Mediterranean, with the exception of the Aegean Sea. Even the waters off the Southern Peloponnese were no longer safe.

There was no doubt that the axis powers had suffered reverses of late, especially in Russia.

However, Kesselring reminded himself that Germany still held territory from Stalingrad to southern France. The majority of the English were controlled by his country and mainland Europe was occupied. Now if the Heer and Luftwaffe could finish the Soviet Union in the summer of 1943, then maybe the Americans and British would be forced to the negotiating table. He remained hopeful.

V

The 130th or Panzer Lehr Division wasn't supposed to be ready for action. It had been thrown together in an emergency. The unit had only been an idea in mid-1942 but now it was part of the German Army. Major Lang was glad the division was undertaking more training. Most of its parts hadn't worked together before charging into Yugoslavia. Now it was engaged in training and occupation duties. It was based in Thessaly, within the expanded German occupation zone in Greece, and Major Lang had enjoyed a much milder winter than he had the previous year. The Italians held the south of the country, and Lang wished his unit had been moved to Crete or perhaps one of the other picturesque Greek islands.

The beaches of Volos overlooked the Pagasetic Gulf. Overhead, the sky was blue and only a cold breeze from the mountains forced Lang to wear his jacket. Hauptmann Scholler sat next to him sipping on a beer and frowning.

“What’s the matter? This is a celebration of your promotion! You should be smiling,” said Lang.

“See those truck sir, they are carrying olives to the port. From there they will send them to Thessalonica. Then the produce goes on a train to Germany. We are looting this country from top to bottom. It’s a race with the Italians on who can take more,” said Scholler.

“That is always the fate of the conquered.”

“I know, but I wish our government would stop working so hard at making people hate us.”

"Cheer up. Later there is going to be party, with women!"

"Most of the locals spit at us."

"Not all. There are going to be Greek women and some German girls from the local Kriegsmarine base at the party. I think they're telephonists."

"The Greeks, they're not being forced to come are they?"

"Scholler, you know I wouldn't permit such a thing. No, they are related to the local Reich appointed government officials. I must admit there is a group of working girls coming as well, though it is their choice to attend."

"Those three different groups of women in the one room together will be interesting," said Scholler.

Lang laughed and sipped his drink. The beer, Fix, was alright but it was a little sweet for his taste. He preferred the Dortmund beers from Prussia. The German beer had a slightly bitter edge he enjoyed. Still, it was beer and not the local wine or Ouzo, which were both terrible. He hated the latter with its strange liquorice flavour.

"Alright, we better go and meet the headquarters' boys," Lang announced as he drained his glass. "We have a bit of a drive to the hotel."

"You managed to get the fuel we need?"

"As you will discover Scholler, rank has its privileges."

The drive in the Kubelwagen took them over a small hill where they picked up two NCOs and a young Leutnant. They then continued over the headland and back down to the beach. One of the last remaining British trucks taken as war reparations sat in front of the hotel. Lang remembered when the trucks could be seen everywhere, now they were a rare sight. Music and laughter drifted from the front of a two storey hotel.

"Looks like they started without us," said Scholler.

Beer flowed freely, as did wine. Lang sang with his men and danced with both the German girls and the working women. The other Greek women kept their distance, only dancing occasionally with the men from his battalion. After his fourth beer, Lang slowed his drinking. He was pleasantly lightheaded and buzzing slightly from the alcohol. Smiling, he approached the Greek girls who were from the collaborationist government families. He tried speaking English.

"Welcome to the party and thank you for coming," he said.

All of the women looked to a dark-haired beauty who stood a little taller than most of her friends. She wore a plain dress which couldn't hide her perfect form. Lang tried to stop his eyes from wandering, but probably failed. She frowned at him.

"You are hospitable, but most of us are not here by choice, and your accent is terrible," said the woman.

Lang judged that she was probably no more than twenty to twenty-two years old and had honey-colored skin.

"I understand. We only put out the invitations. Let your friends know they are free to leave, and if they do so there will be no repercussions."

The woman turned and spoke briefly to the other Greek girls. One rolled her eyes, while the rest looked away.

"It is not that simple, however I thank you for your offer."

"I'm Major Kurt Lang, may I know your name?"

"Sophia Alexakis. My father is now the Minister for Agriculture. We have a villa nearby, though father is in Athens. Mother said I had to come."

"And if you arrive home early you will be in trouble with her, and then your father?"

"Exactly."

"Well then, be assured that none of my men will harass you. I will make sure of that."

"Thank you, Major." She then turned and translated to her friends.

"I gather our presence here is unwelcome?" said Lang.

Sophia bit her lip and glanced away, then shrugged. "Not you personally. You seem quite nice, for a German, but you are uninvited guests here."

"Your attitude is understandable."

"Why did Germany invade?" she asked suddenly.

Lang was still tipsy. "Because we can?" he quipped.

"A joke? About the rape of my country?"

Lang blushed. "I'm sorry. I can give you the official reason, but I think it's because the leaders in Germany thought your country was becoming too friendly with the Allies. I have no idea if that's true or not, though your troops were using a lot of American guns."

"We probably were becoming closer with the Americans. Father was against us forming a relationship with them and warned anyone who would listen, that Hitler would become angry. He also said that Germany treated Greece with contempt. Why do you think we turned to the Allies?"

"I don't know."

"Because Hitler kept breaking his promises. Our country was on the verge of starvation. Father says Greece imported grain in peace time. When the war started, that supply slowly diminished, and after your country declared war on America it stopped completely. Greece was going hungry. The Americans offered us food."

"What about the weapons?"

"The same reason. Germany promised us artillery and planes, but the Italians protested, and later when we asked again, we were told that panzers and guns would be sold to us. It never happened. It was a similar situation with oil."

Lang was unfamiliar with some of the words Sophia was using. Her English was much better than his but he was understanding enough to work out most of the conversation.

"I see," he mumbled.

"Father said we should tighten our belts and plant out every inch of the country with grain. He said not to make Germany angry. The Allies were in no position to assist us yet, if we were invaded."

"Their aircraft helped your people over Crete," he said.

"I didn't know that," said Sophia. "Anyway, it doesn't matter now. My country will starve. Our granaries were emptied after Germany won, with most of their contents being taken to Italy, Bulgaria or your country. Our factories have been looted and our economy destroyed."

"So what will you do?"

"Me? Pray that you win. My father is a collaborator. If Germany loses the war, my family will be killed. The average Greek hates you and soon partisan movements will spring up. It will be dangerous but I won't starve."

"You need an escape plan," said Lang.

Sophia's eyes went wide. Around her most of the other Greek women drifted away. "Do you think Germany may lose the war?" she asked.

Lang sighed. This party wasn't fun anymore. "I don't know what I think. I've had too much to drink. The actions of my country make me feel embarrassed. I feel strongly toward the men in my battalion and probably even toward the division, but beyond that? Shame, no worse, disgust. I've seen things..." he trailed off.

"You are strange for a Nazi."

Lang's eyes blazed and his fist clenched in anger. "I'm not a Nazi," he spat.

Sophia took a step back in shock but then she peered at his face. "I will dance with you Major, if you want," she said.

"Why?"

"Because you interest me, and you are handsome, in that pale Nordic sort of way."

"Thank you, I think."

Sophia laughed and glided out onto the dance floor with him. Later they spoke of their lives before the war and their dreams of what they'd like to do after it.

"I want to study in England," said Sophia. "I love reading the novels of the Bronte sisters and even Dickens."

Lang hadn't heard of these writers but spoke of his love for Goethe and his play 'Faust'.

"Part one or part two?" asked Sophia.

"You know the plays?"

"I've read them in English. They are very depressing."

"It is a reflection of what my country has done to itself."

Sophia covered her mouth in shock. "You believe Germany sold its soul to the Devil?"

"I saw what we did in Russia. The Jews are supposed to be the enemy, but I don't believe that any more. How can children and old women really be a threat to Germany? Our leaders push a policy of butchery. I know if I said this to most of my comrades they would think I was a traitor."

"How do they feel about the Jews?"

"Many are uncomfortable about what's happening, others are in denial, while many more believe killing them all to be a necessary evil."

"And what will you do about your Germany?"

"What can I do? Already I've been in trouble for fighting against what is happening." He told her the story of standing up to the SS officers in England and Russia.

She took his hand. "You poor man. When I first saw you I thought, 'he looks sad.' Now I know why."

"You think I look sad?"

"Yes. It covers you like a cloak. Your men, I can see they like you and your friend, Scholler?"

"Yes."

"He doesn't look sad. With him there is a sort of worry that hovers close by."

"I didn't know."

"Most people don't see this and think I'm crazy when I speak this way. Yet I believe I'm right."

"What should I do?"

"That's easy. Right now you are going upstairs with me."

His eyes went wide and he stared at her.

"I think the sadness just disappeared," said Sophia with a smile.

V

He saw Sophia four more times after that night and each time the experience was bittersweet. Lang could easily fall in love with this amazing woman but he knew any relationship with her would be impossible. Instead, he worked at keeping their time together secret, and they even discussed possible ways of her staying safe if Germany did lose the war. There was a chance she could go with her father on a diplomatic trip to Turkey as a translator. Then she would slip away and, using some gold and silver she had, buy her way into allied controlled territory. Lang hoped she would succeed.

The 130th Panzer Division moved further north to Thessaloniki toward the end of the month. Lang managed to send Sophia a message of farewell and he never saw her again. She did escape to Turkey, then to allied territory in Iraq, and later immigrated to America.

Lang watched as his half-tracks were removed from a series of flat cars. As he did he noticed a group of men walking along the line of vehicles waiting to be unloaded. A small hawk-faced general strode slightly ahead of the small entourage, before stopping near him. He gave the old salute, which was acknowledged by the man.

"General Wagner, sir?"

"Correct Major. Have we meet?"

"I saw you in the distance once. In Russia, sir. You were boarding a helicopter after sorting out a supply issue. You seemed to be everywhere in those days, sir."

"Thank you. I tried my best but in the end..." the man stopped. "You didn't give me the Nazi salute?"

Lang's face wrinkled as though he had smelt something off. "No sir, I didn't."

The General waved the other officers off, waiting until they were a distance away before speaking again. "It offends you?"

"Sir, I fight for Germany."

"As do I. Though our oath requires us to be loyal to the Führer."

"I'm painfully aware of that, sir."

"Painfully?"

Lang went silent and stared into space.

“Relax Major. I understand how you feel. The last two years have been difficult. I fear for our country.”

Lang glanced at the hawk-faced man and noted he was being examined. He felt as though he was a bug under a microscope.

“Major, I would like your details please.”

“Sir, am I in trouble?”

“No, no, nothing like that. As I said, relax.”

Major Lang gave the required details and the general wrote them down in a small notebook. Wagner then gave him a pat on the shoulder and strode off. Lang stared at the general as he re-joined his entourage, not understanding what had just occurred.

Chapter Seven: February 1943

The new Shermans were painted with a rough whitewash over their original olive colour. Sergeant Randal looked at the line of tanks and wished they had doors for the loaders. Major General George S. Patton was inspecting their company today before they were sent to the front line. At the moment everything was quiet. There was still the odd local counterattack and people died but not in the numbers they would during an offensive.

Private Olaf Magnusson walked over and stood next to him.

“You’ve done all you can, Sarge,” said the big man.

“Have I? Maybe I should just ignore the Captain. I mean, what will he do if I make the hatch while he isn’t around?” said Randel.

“He will have you thrown in the stockade, and I’d prefer to have you in charge of the tank than anyone else.”

"Thanks Olaf, I appreciate that. Still, this is such an easy fix and people's lives are at risk."

"The Captain has warned everybody what will happen if they mess with their tanks. He won't have anyone defacing the property of the US Army, blah, blah, blah."

"There has to be a way," growled Randel.

The big man shrugged and walked off to find some coffee.

A few hours later the tanks were all lined up and the men in clean uniforms. It was a bit of a rush getting everything ready for General Patton, as he was renowned to have high standards. At least he seemed like a half decent leader, thought Randel.

Later, three jeeps pulled up and the battalion commander walked out to greet General Patton. A, B and C Companies were all present but the light tank company was located further south. Fifty-one tanks were ready for inspection, as well as twelve trucks and fourteen half-tracks. Patton stepped forward, saluted, then shook hands. He was a tall man, powerfully built, and was rumoured to have been an Olympic athlete. The general walked among the men, pumping hands, and peering at the tanks. As he approached Randel made a snap decision.

"General you need to know that the Sherman is a death trap for the loader," he called out loudly.

"Who said that?" yelled the Major Bradley, the battalion commander.

"I did, sir and the general needs to know of the easily fixed design flaw."

General Patton turned and was staring right at him. Randel felt his bladder loosen at the look.

"You are out of line, Sergeant. Captain, control your man!" yelled the Major.

"As the crew with the highest number of kills in the division, I should be heard, sir," said Randel.

He could see Military Police striding toward him and knew his chance of speaking with General Patton was slipping away.

"Stop," said General Patton. Randel noted the man's voice was strangely high pitched, however everybody froze.

Patton turned to the Major. "Is the Sergeant the leader of the highest scoring crew in the division?"

"Yes General, he is. I believe Randel and his crew have destroyed six enemy tanks or assault guns," answered the major.

Patton took long strides toward Randel stopping just in front of him. The Sergeant struggled not to take a step backwards. The General stood eye to eye with him and stared for a moment before speaking in his squeaky voice.

"Son, you are embarrassing your commanding officer," said Patton.

"Something I would never do sir, if the issues wasn't so urgent."

"Have you really destroyed six enemy machines?"

"Sir, I don't count the truck so I make it five armoured vehicles."

"Good enough. Well, what do you want to say?"

"General, this is a problem best seen up close. Have you been inside a Sherman, sir?"

"No, other tanks yes, but not the Sherman."

"Sir, the issue can be best examined from the loader's seat."

"You better not be wasting my time son, however I'm intrigued. Lead on."

Randel lead the general and a group of officers to his tank, Raising Hell, and watched as Patton clambered aboard. He didn't offer any assistance and when one of the junior officers did, the general glared at the man. "I'm no invalid," Patton snapped.

The big man did seem fit for his age as he climbed down into the tank.

Randel asked the general to take a seat in the gunner's position. Patton climbed under the recoil protector and sat.

"Now look up, sir," said Randel.

Patton did so and frowned. “There’s no door,” he said.

“Correct, sir. So if a Sherman is hit, the loader has to climb under the recoil protector and leave via my hatch. If I’m dead he is trapped. There is also the problem that, though a good tank, the Sherman tends to burn if hit. The ammo is stored in easy to reach locations but unfortunately this means it also catches fire quickly. This tank burns fast if the crew area is struck. You have seconds to escape. Already boys have died horribly because they can’t get out.”

“I see the problem and I think you will present me with a solution?”

“Sir, I’ve already done it once and it saved my loader’s life. We were hit by that new Kraut tank, the Tiger, outside Martin Wood. The Sherman burned quick and hard. I lost two friends. Olaf would have died as well without the hatch we made.”

“Let me guess, you’ve been told not to cut open any more tanks that are US property?”

"That's correct, General."

Patton nodded. "Yeah, I might have played it safe if I was in your captain's position, maybe."

"Sir, can you help?"

"Son, it's my duty to help. Anything that gives you boys more confidence when fighting the enemy is a good thing. I've approved of extra armour plating being added to some hulls and seen a few field modifications already. This one is a bit larger than most, and it does mean cutting a hole in your tank but hell son, I think it's necessary. You go right ahead and make your hole."

Randel felt his shoulders sag in relief. He could tell Olaf that his chance of surviving the war had just increased.

"Now, I'm interested in this German monster you fought. The Tiger. Our intelligence boys say there are more on the way. Any ideas on how to fight them?"

"I've thought about that, sir. The best way might be to draw the enemy crew's attention, then flank the Tiger. Or, using our faster rate of fire we could pound it into submission, even with high explosives. Taking the Tiger on in single combat would be extremely difficult. You'd need to ambush it from the flank to have a chance."

Patton sat in the loader's position and cradled his chin in his hands. He glanced around the interior of the tank and pointed at the ready rack of ammunition.

"So the shells are handy to reach, but ignite easily if the Sherman is hit?'

"That's right, sir."

"What would you do about that?" Would you prefer them moved to a safer location?"

Randel thought for a moment. "I don't think we need as many shells at the ready. If there were fewer in that location then it would help somewhat, sir," he said. "Sir, do we have something in development that can match the new Kraut tank? If they have this monster, they'll be working on other types."

"Son, we fight with what we have, but it's an interesting question and one I will look into. For now I'll put out an order allowing modifications to the Sherman but your captain isn't going to be a happy man. The 2nd Armoured Division has just arrived but it lacks experience and to be honest with you, the unit probably needs more training. I'm going to move you and your crew to the new division. I've decided to make you a second lieutenant and give you your own platoon on a permanent basis. I'll find a company commander who'll listen to your advice, not someone with a stick up their arse. How does that sound?"

"Me, an officer, sir?"

"It's not as big a deal as you think. The US army has been giving out battlefield commissions for a long time. In World War One we did it six thousand times."

"Thank you, sir."

"I'll get someone to draw up the papers. Pack your stuff. A jeep will be picking you up tonight. Now I better get back to the inspection. Still, I'm mighty proud of what you boys are doing and pleased that I can now say I've had a good look around inside a Sherman."

The two men climbed from the tank and Patton stood on the turret and gave the crowd a thumbs up. A nearby photographer took a few pictures, then the General went and spoke to Randel's commanding officers. Both men nodded and the major spoke briefly. Patton's chest puffed out and he pointed at the major and the man saluted. Patton turned and waved. He climbed into his jeep with his entourage and drove away.

Major Bradley strode over to him. "Randel pack your things. You are leaving as soon as the jeep from the 2nd Armoured arrives. The General also said you are to paint your kills on your next tank. He doesn't want rings on the barrels like the Krauts do, but something on the hull. Everyone in the corps is going to be told to do it. You better scrub up Randel because I think a few photographers are going to be sent your way," said the officer.

Randel walked back to his tank and found Olaf and Freddy. "You got your door," he said to the loader.

"And?" asked Freddy Spencer.

"We are being shifted to the 2nd Armoured. Oh, and Patton is making me an officer."

Both men glanced at each other and grinned.

"Laugh it up boys. The press are probably coming to take photos of me and I'm going to have you two right by my side."

V

"He would be a snug fit in the cockpit," said Commander James Southerland.

"Caldwell's not much taller than me," said Lieutenant Stanley W. Vejtasa.

Both men stood under the shade of a palm tree and watched as the Australian wing commander stepped from the B24 Liberator.

"What's he here for?" asked Vejtasa.

"I don't know but I mean to speak with him."

"Why?"

"The man's a legend! Forty-six kills against the Italians, Germans and Japanese. He has experience flying the Brumby fighter but now flies Corsairs. His last six kills have been over Cairns and the northern part of Australia."

"So why is he here?"

"At a guess, to share some of his knowledge, at least that's what I'm hoping."

"Do we need the Aussies to tell us how to shoot down Japs?"

"Swede, don't be an idiot."

The wing commander disappeared and Southerland checked on the repairs to his Wildcat. Overhead, thunder rumbled and by the time he was satisfied with the work it had started to rain. As he ran back across to the mess hall he wondered how long his squadron would be based here. The Enterprise had been hit by a single torpedo off Fiji and rather than leave with all her planes, a fighter and dive bomber squadron had been transferred to Guadalcanal. Before the air base had been taken by the Marines, the Japanese had built a number of huts. Most of these had been captured intact and gave some relief to the terrible conditions usually faced by air crew on the island.

In the distance artillery rumbled, reminding Southerland of the fighting still going on between the marines and Japanese to the northwest. There were at least two enemy brigades on the island and they were still fighting stubbornly, despite lacking supplies. The rain started to fall and it became difficult to hear the 105mm guns anymore. He managed to make it to the balcony surrounding the mess hut the main down pour hit pour. It came down in big heavy drops unlike any he'd seen in Pennsylvania. The green fields and the forests of the Appalachian Mountains never experienced rain like this.

He stepped from the balcony into a long open room where the folding tables were stacked against the wall. A rough bar lined one wall and a covered walkway led to a tent where food was cooked. Clive Caldwell sat with Swede and Brigadier General Roy Geiger. The commanding officer of all air units on Guadalcanal waved him over.

"Our guest has brought Australian beer with him," said Geiger.

"It's a Tasmanian brew called Boags and it's a bit stronger than what you are used to," said the tall Australian.

Everybody filled their glasses with the cold beer that had been chilled in one of the few refrigerator units on the island. These units were normally used to keep blood plasma cool. The local Themo-King unit had been patched up twice due to shrapnel hits from Japanese bombs, but it still worked.

Everyone sighed appreciatively after their first sip.

"It's crisp like our beer but the hop flavour is stronger," said the General.

"Its cold beer on a warm day," said Caldwell, the man's eyes shining. "There's nothing better."

"This rain might cool things down," said Swede.

General Geiger finished his drink then excused himself, explaining to Caldwell that they'd speak again.

"The wing commander is here to exchange and gather info on the Japs," said Swede.

"Yes, this is one of the hottest locations for fighting the enemy right now. Darwin still gets the odd raid but the fighting there has fallen away. Even the attacks on Cairns and Townsville have decreased. The Japs grabbed Thursday Island in the Torres Straight and made a strip there last December. That's five hundred miles from Cairns. By comparison, you are over six hundred miles from Rabaul. The difference is you are the first hole in the Jap perimeter. They don't really need to attack Northern Australia."

"Sir, I don't know what we can tell you? Our planes are vastly different to your Brumbies and we haven't been fighting here that long," said Southerland.

"Please, call me Clive, and you've been fighting the Japs just as long as us. The intensity of operation here is what interests me. Yes, our planes are different but we both face a fighter that can easily out turn us, especially at lower speeds."

"Clive, the Brumby is faster than a Wildcat and it climbs almost as well as a Zero," said Swede.

"We are all aces and have tactics to share. Your Thatch Weave is something we Aussies haven't done. The teamwork used to pull off such a maneuver is new to me. And yes, a Brumby can outrun a Zero. The Australian fighter is a bit faster than the Jap machine but it can't take the same amount of punishment as the Wildcat. It also has two fewer guns."

"We use the dive and swoop tactics, same as you," said Southerland.

"Yeah, the Flying Tigers first came up with that move over China I believe, but you came up with the mutual support idea. You've both used it?"

Southerland and Swede nodded.

"Can you explain how it works?" asked Caldwell.

Later, feeling a little disoriented from the beer, Southerland shook his head at the conversation. He and Swede had spent the evening explaining air warfare to a pilot who'd shot down forty-six enemy machines. This man had fought against the best the Luftwaffe could put in the air and won. Caldwell was also a legend in the Pacific Theatre. His leadership over Darwin was an example not just to the Australians under his command, but to other pilots fighting the Japanese.

Caldwell had spoken of his belief that the Australians should drive the Japanese off Thursday Island. It was a slight on the country's national pride; the only time Australia had been invaded and lost some of its territory. He also thought the enemy needed to be driven from at least the southern coast of New Guinea. Southerland didn't know what the grand strategy of the Allies should be. He believed new carriers were being built. Stories were rife about a new flat top named the Essex training off the coast of Hawaii, and the HMAS Tasman was supposed to have been repaired. A new light carrier, the USS Princeton, had already been participating in small scale attacks in the Solomon's area.

In the meantime, surface fleet actions had occurred between cruisers and battleships. So far the US navy had lost a battleship, three heavy cruisers, two light cruisers, and four destroyers. The Japanese had lost about the same number of ships but three of these had been to air attacks. In the night actions the Japanese held the upper hand. This was until the last battle when the US Navy finally used its radar effectively.

Southerland hadn't been on Henderson Field when it was bombarded by Japanese battleships but the Marines told him the experience was terrifying. Nearly every plane in the area had been destroyed or damaged that night, and it was two days before replacements were flown in from the New Hebrides. While there was no air cover, the enemy landed two brigades of troops and twenty tanks, as well as light artillery. 75mm mountain guns were manhandled into position, and assisted an attack by over six thousand Japanese troops and twenty type 95 Ha-Go light tanks. The enemy hacked tracks through the jungle by hand so the tanks could move, creating trails lined with the trunks of fallen trees.

The American perimeter at this time was just over five miles from the airstrip on the Matanikau River and at Mount Austin. These two features were furiously attacked by the enemy but the Japanese were thrown back with terrible losses. Wrecked tanks lay bogged or burn out along the riverbank. The marines had destroyed most of the machines with fire from 37mm guns, though some were disabled with satchel charges or grenades.

More enemy reinforcements arrived and further enemy attacks were attempted, however the results were the same. A night attack by the 35th Infantry Brigade supported by mortars and mountain guns, as well as ten type 97 Chi-Ha medium tanks, penetrated the marine lines. Only a counterattack by the 1st Marine Parachute Battalion restored the situation, though the unit involved suffered very heavy casualties including their commander. Now it looked as though the Marines were preparing to advance.

Randel listened to the rain falling, not knowing that another battle was about to erupt out to sea. He didn't even hear the shell fire as the fighting took place near Buena Vista Island, over thirty-five miles from where he slept. Six enemy destroyers were sunk and another four retreated, virtually halting the enemy's plans for another offensive on Guadalcanal. Three thousand Japanese troops drowned. Two American cruisers were sunk by torpedoes and the battle now moved into another phase.

Chapter Eight: March 1943

The ground was drying after the last rains. Here and there new patches of fresh green grass poked out of the earth. Second Lieutenant Randel smiled at the hatch his crew had finished working on yesterday. It was rough, but it would do the job. Olaf would now have a door through which he could escape if the Sherman were hit.

The last two weeks had been a whirlwind. His crew had moved to the 2nd US Armoured Division near the small village of Clay Cross, to the southeast of the Peak District. He and his crew had been allocated to the 1st Battalion of the famous 66th Armoured Regiment. This was part of Combat Command A. His new tank was named Mother Magee and he commanded a platoon of five Shermans. Randel barely had time to meet his company commander, Captain Black, before he was told to prepare his unit to attack.

Overhead air activity was intense. There were battles every day with both Luftwaffe and US planes frequently being shot down. A P-38 had crashed into a patch of forest near the village of Stretton the previous day and a Ju 88 was destroyed by flak over Morton, eventually exploding by the railroad track further north. Even now aircraft fought overhead. Randel had no idea who was getting the better of these engagements but he had seen formations of B-25s heading south to bomb the Germans. The Americans ground forces were only being occasionally attacked by enemy planes, and Randel was extremely grateful for this. He had a fear of being attacked from the air.

Randel slept that night next to his tank, waking at three a.m. to prepare his men. At four thirty American artillery opened up with a tremendous barrage. 105mm guns and 155mm 'Long Tom' guns pounded the enemy for thirty minutes. Then the order came for the Shermans to move. It took an hour to drive to the jumping off point and become organised. Further to the west, the high ground between Ashover and Critch was being attacked by the 1st US infantry division, while the Combat Command B attacked south from Heath to Hilcote. The Canadians had the job of advancing into the built-up area around Mansfield. They were also to keep the Germans off the flank of Patton's attack.

Randel knew the objective for the first day was four miles away. This was the crust of the enemy defence and it was believed that once the Allies had broken this, the advance could move faster. He didn't know the US 1st Armoured Division would attack from Macclesfield to Burton on Trent. While the 36th National Guard

Division advanced into Stoke-on-Trent, a new British division would try and take Whitchurch and Market Drayton. The aim of Patton's offensive was for the two US armoured spearheads to link up near Derby and trap the 384th and 385th German Infantry Divisions. Patton didn't believe it would be that easy and expected the panzer divisions to make an appearance at some stage. For that reason he kept his most recent arrival from America, the 9th Infantry Division in reserve. Though this unit had no armour it was still fully motorised and the 601st Tank Destroyer Battalion with its M10s had been attached to it.

Light was creeping into the sky when the company was ordered forward. The line of advance was along a low ridge, and Randel was concerned at first about flanking fire from across the valley. The village of Wooley, however, was under assault from US infantry and if there were any Germans in that area, they had their hands full. The first mile was covered without difficulty, as mortars and artillery dropped shells on any enemy soldier who moved. The lead platoon blasted its way through Hallfield gate but struck trouble just after it crossed the bridge over the Alferton Brook. The creek wasn't an obstacle, however the woods dominating the next low ridge and in the valley itself were swarming with Germans. Luckily, the heaviest weapon the enemy seemed to have available were 20mm anti-aircraft guns and a battery of 50mm Pak 38s. One Sherman was disabled and then artillery fire was called down on the woodlands. Soon the Germans were withdrawing and the advance continued.

After a quick stop to eat and refuel, the company pushed on. Supported by infantry Combat Command A (CCA), moved through Sommercotes, pas the iron works and drove on to Riddings. Further west another column from CCA was held up by a Luftwaffe attack while advancing through Swanwick. Eighteen Fw 190 fighter bombers attacked the American column forcing it to disperse. Only two half-tracks and a tank were lost and eight men wounded, but it cost time. A smaller force made up of troops from the 1st US Infantry Division were moving along the railway line in the valley when they ran into a local counterattack by two battalions from the

554th Regiment of the 389th German Infantry Division. Fire from mortars and MG 42 machine guns forced the Americans to take cover and two assaults failed to move the enemy.

The high ground around the village of Crich was furiously defended by the 546th Regiment from the same German division. Around St Mary's Church the fighting ebbed and flowed, with the enemy eventually being forced back to the Old Black Swan Inn. An enemy platoon held out in a series of thick-walled stone cottages near the corner of Roes Lane and didn't surrender until the following day. Further east the 23rd Panzer Division had created a Kampfgruppe from the 2nd Battalion of the 201st Panzer Battalion and a battalion of soldiers from the 126th Panzer Grenadier Regiment. Forty Panzer IVs attacked after another Luftwaffe raid, this time by twelve Ju 88s. Combat Command B (CCB) took the full force of this attack which stopped the American unit in its tracks.

Meanwhile Randel and his company moved into Riddings. The windmills that had dominated the area had both been destroyed by a B-25 raid. The 23rd Panzer Division had sent in a battalion of infantry and a platoon of Panzerjagers. Six turretless T-34s had been armed with 50mm or 75mm Pak guns. The Germans called the turretless vehicles Cockroaches, but the new combination was later known as a Jagdhund, or Hunting Dog. This unit arrived in Riddings from the southeast, as Randel's company drove in from the north.

An MG 42 opened up on the US infantry who were accompanying the lead Sherman, leaving a man dead and scattering the soldiers. The tank stopped as its front left drive sprocket was hit by an anti-tank round. A German assault gun sat further down the road. The Sherman's track came off and it swerved sideways into a wall. The road was duel carriageway so the second Sherman drove around the wreck. It was also hit but the 50mm round bounced from the American tank's gun shield, luckily the thickest armour on the vehicle. Big Betty was commanded by Sergeant Jim Childers. As the range was only one hundred yards, the shell fired from his tank punched straight through the 47mm of sloped steel, killing the driver and starting a small fire which quickly destroyed the German vehicle.

Big Betty charged down the road firing its machine guns. It reached an inn called the Red Lion when a bundle of grenades thrown by a German officer landed on the engine compartment. There was a large explosion and the Sherman ground to halt, its engine damaged. Randle looked at the advancing German infantry and radioed a warning.

"Spray the windows and doors with machine-gun fire," he ordered. "And close all doors."

He knew this last order would rob the tank crews of their visibility, however there were just too many enemy troops around. It would be very easy for a German to drop a grenade inside a Sherman. Ahead, the wrecked Cockroach blocked the road as it was jammed next to a damaged double decker bus. Randel took a turn to the left along West Street. Two hundred yards further on he saw a group of German infantry advancing.

"Load HE. Target enemy troops. Shoot them Freddy," he said

The little gunner fired the main gun and the explosive shell burst on the side wall of a house, showering the Germans with shrapnel and bricks. Two men fell and the others took cover. A German vehicle appeared from around the corner. The assault gun mounted a 50mm weapon.

"German vehicle straight ahead gunner," yelled Randel.

"I've only got HE up the spout," said Spencer.

"Fire at the gun," ordered Randel.

The 75mm fired with its shell hitting the top of the gun shield on the enemy vehicle. The explosion killed the crew of four and left the Cockroach driving up the street at twenty miles an hour until it went over a hedge and into a garage. It crashed into the building and came to a stop. More German vehicles appeared and Randel screamed at his driver to reverse. Danny Fredrick was new to combat. He went backwards at full speed but at an angle and the

Sherman crashed into the front of a two storey cottage. The tank went over a low stone wall and through a large window before becoming wedged in the lounge room of the house. Overhead the ceiling sagged dangerously. Then the Sherman stalled. Mother Magee was stuck.

"Grab a weapon and get out," yelled Randel. All five men clambered out and went through a hole in the wall into the next building. Randel looked around and saw that only he and Olaf had decent weapons. The other men carried Colt M1911s in shaking hands. Randel grabbed a bag of grenades and tossed one of the bombs to Olaf. Then they heard German voices. Randel could see movement through an open doorway to his left. Without thinking he pulled the pin on a grenade and tossed it into the next room. There was a flat crack and dust filled the air. Randel heard Olaf coughing and a voice screaming. He charged, firing from the hip with his Thompson machine gun. Shooting at anything that moved he kept his finger on the trigger until the firing pin clicked on an empty chamber.

His crew followed him in and Freddy Spencer whistled.

"God, boss, you got' em all," said Danny.

Olaf went straight to an MG42 which was leaning against the window. He picked it up and smiled. "Undamaged," he said.

"Six boxes of ammo for it near the door," said Private Dave Russo, the radio operator and bow gunner. The dark-haired man turned over one of the dead Germans and wiped off a ZK-383 submachine gun. "Never seen one of these before," he said.

Randel was surprised at how calmly his crew took the carnage in the room. He'd just killed five men. Usually he blew up enemy soldiers at long range. Randel had seen dead Germans but never those he'd killed. This was more personal. He leaned into the next room and vomited. His crew said nothing and continued to loot the dead.

Rifle fire smashed the plaster in the walls and everyone dropped to the floor. Randel heard American's yelling and screamed back.

"Stop shooting you idiots," he yelled.

"Who are you?" someone called.

"The crew from that Sherman stuck in the wall," said Randel.

"Password?"

Randel thought frantically. "Salmon?"

"That was yesterday," said the voice. "Who won the Major League last year?"

Randel didn't know. He was a football fan. "The Red Skins won the NFL last year. Does that help?"

"The Cardinals won," yelled Freddy Spencer.

There was some talking outside and then a voice called out. "Alright we're coming forward," said a man in a New York accent.

A head poked into the room. "The Yankees were robbed in that game," said a tall captain.

"Two to zero sir, it was close," said Freddy.

The captain glanced around the room. "You boys have been busy. I'm Captain Phillips, 41st infantry Regiment."

Randel introduced his crew.

"You boys better tag along with us. Maybe, since you have one of Hitler's Buzz Saws, you can act as fire support?"

Randel glanced at Olaf and the big Dane shrugged.

"Sure, we aren't doing anything else," Randel said.

Part of him wanted to curl up in a ball and hide after what he'd just done but everybody was watching him. His crew grabbed all the ammunition they could carry and then followed the infantry captain back out onto the street.

The sound of automatic fire came from close by and a group of American soldiers ran past. One carried a strange tube like object.

"What's that?" Randel asked Captain Phillips.

"A bazooka. It fires a rocket which can punch through three inches of armour, however the rockets aren't always reliable," said the infantry officer.

"I know where there might be some targets," said Randel.

Phillips peered at him then whistled at the men. They stopped and he called them to him.

"We are going tank hunting, boys," he said to the squad.

"Sir, these rockets don't always go where they are supposed to," said a red-headed soldier. "If they leave the tube at all."

"Then reload quickly and try again," said the captain.

The squad grew to about thirty as soldiers gravitated to the two officers. By the time the men infiltrated through the ruined buildings onto West Street near the park, another ten had joined them. Here the street changed its name to Church Street on the small map the officer carried. There were more trees in this area. A red-bricked primary school sat on the corner, while on the other side of the road a white-walled cottage hid behind a low stone wall and a line of trees. The roof was on fire and occasionally smoke drifted across the road. The group could see two assault guns further up the street, surrounded by enemy soldiers. Captain Phillips signalled his men to move through the trees in the school yard until they were closer. The Germans remained unaware of the Americans until a Soldat spotted movement in thin scrub on the northern side of the road. The man yelled a warning and Phillips ordered his soldiers to open fire. At least four of the enemy including an officer were cut down in the first exchange of shots. Then Olaf opened up with the MG 42. Randel could hear the Dane counting to four as he fired, before repeating a little mantra about stopping to rest. Then he fired again. The short, well directed bursts kept the enemy pinned down as Phillips sent ten men through buildings to the south to flank the Germans. He told them to circle back to the road where there was a break between buildings.

This group ran into a squad of Germans with the same idea, and another deadly close range battle erupted in the backyards of cottages, among veggie gardens and greenhouses.

Meanwhile Randel directed the bazooka team.

"Hit it before it runs," he said to the private holding the weapon.

"Better stand clear, sir. The back blast of these things will burn you face off," said the red-headed man.

The distance to the assault gun was probably seventy yards, well within the weapon's range. The first shot didn't leave the tube. Randel heard the operator yell 'misfire' and the rocket was carefully removed, before being tossed through a window. There was an explosion inside the house and both men glanced at each other before reloading. The second shot left the bazooka and hit the Jadghund as it turned into the narrow street. The shaped charge punched into the engine compartment of the converted T-34, severing fuel lines, and causing a small fire. An explosion made smoke billow from the vehicle and the crew jumped out of the assault gun, running for cover. Two of them didn't make it as Olaf's MG 42 cut them down.

American fire was heavy and the Germans were outnumbered. The crew of the second cockroach panicked and abandoned their vehicle. Americans were in front of them and behind them. Olaf and his gun supported the forty US soldiers who swept the enemy away in a storm of grenades and bullets. Twelve Germans surrendered and the rest scattered. Fourteen lay dead in the street and another six were taken to aid stations with wounds of varying severity.

Randel waited by his tank as a second Sherman fixed a tow cable to the front of his vehicle. The enemy had been pushed south and CCA were across the railway line and the Cromford Canal. Other assaults by the US Army had been stopped but the success of the attack on Riddings allowed the Americans to outflank German defences further west and take the large town of Ripley almost uncontested. To the east, the 1st US Armoured Division had also been halted though General Harmon did everything he could to keep the formation moving. He had previously commanded the 2nd

Armoured until Patton moved him due to the poor performance of General Orlando Ward.

The commander of the 2nd Armoured Division pushed the unit forward into the night, only allowing the troops to stop when vehicles were short on fuel. Later, Patton congratulated the decision. This allowed the Americans to capture the twin towns of Heanor and Eastwood in the early hours of the morning. Further to the east US units only managed to move as far as Heage. The following day Rommel launched a full scale counterattack against the flank of the American advance. CCA waited for the orders to renew the advance but were kept in reserve in case CCB couldn't hold the attacks of the 23rd Panzer Division. The two forces fought a bloody brawl along the high ground marked by the Derby Road and Annesley Forest. Places such as the Ice House Woods, Annesley Hall and Target Hill changed hands many times. The area was soon littered with wrecked Shermans, half-tracks and panzers. Newstead Village was destroyed as was the nearby abbey. At the end of the day the line had only moved a few hundred yards. Both sides stopped and licked their wounds. Further west the 22nd Panzer Division also attacked with similar results. Air battles raged overhead. The weather remained remarkably dry and mild as CCA was fed back into the meat grinder. Eventually the Americans took Derby and Nottingham, the advance stopping at the River Derwent. As Newmarket and Stoke-on-Trent were yet to fall to the Allies, a bulge formed in the line with the tip of it pointing at Leicester.

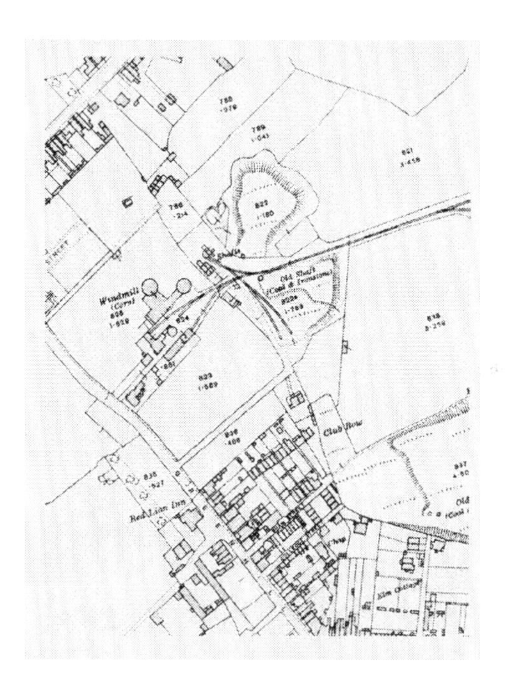

Red Lion Inn and area of Randel's battle.

Randel stood by the side of the tank and smiled. He posed next to the seven swastikas painted on the side of his Sherman. If he weren't being interviewed by Kathleen Harriman then he'd be trying to escape this situation. The female correspondent had told him she was supposed to have gone to Russia, but the fighting there had diverted her to England. She smiled at Randel and his heart clenched. God she was beautiful.

"I want to capture something of the man who has destroyed so many German tanks. Do you have a wife or sweetheart?"

"Ah, no," Randel stammered.

The young woman turned and winked at her camera man. "He'll be a heart throb back home, Stan," she said.

The older man nodded and snapped more pictures.

"I'm just a farm boy out of Maine," he said.

"Nothing wrong with that. The ladies will love it."

He wondered if he had a chance with the polished and urban reporter. Even though she flirted with him, Miss Harriman disappeared with a swirl of her skirt, leaving Randel with only a whiff of her very expensive perfume. Randel sighed and endured the teasing of the other crews. A day later his unit was ready to attack once more.

V

The situation reports from the Eastern Front indicated that all offensive action had stopped. Reichsmarschall Kesselring understood that Russia was deep in 'Rasputitsa'. The front was a sea of mud. The same couldn't be said about England, where warm weather had allowed the Allies to attack relentlessly for two weeks. Stoke-on-Trent had fallen. Many Germans were dead but the most important casualty was Field Marshal Rommel. The famous general had been wounded by long range American artillery and was recovering at a hospital in Ulm. This, at least, put him in close proximity to his wife and son.

Field Marshal Ernst Busch had been moved from Army Group North in Russia to England. With him went General Model, who would directly command the ground forces in England.

Kesselring was concerned about the appointment. Busch showed little independent thought and often deferred to the Führer's judgement, and Model was extremely temperamental. There had been little action in northern Russia since the fall of Leningrad, except for one Soviet offensive. That attack had shown that Busch wasn't capable of making a move without checking with Berlin first. The Russian assault made it as far as the Neva but didn't reach the Baltic Sea. A counterattack by local forces recaptured a small amount of the lost territory, and since then the area had become a backwater.

The first US offensive in England seemed to have run its course but there were signs that Patton was already getting the US 7th Army ready for another attack. The Commonwealth 1st Army was licking its wounds near Lincoln, while the British 8th Army continued small scale assaults in Wales. The Allies would move again soon.

At least German replacements were flowing across the English Channel. Units like the 23rd and 22nd Panzer Divisions had received over one hundred tanks and assault guns. The infantry divisions had also been brought up to their regular strength. Well, that wasn't strictly true as some units were still waiting for men who were in transit. An SS division was on its way to England, though Kesselring didn't know which one. The Italians had also moved replacements to England, despite their situation in Africa.

An offensive by the Italians to retake Benghazi had failed, though Commonwealth forces in the area took heavy casualties holding the assault. Kesselring believed it would be at least two months before the Allies attempted to renew their advance on Tripoli. Work was being done to get the French to support the Italians in North Africa, but so far the Vichy Regime had shown little interest in helping. The French authorities in Tunisia did allow use of ports in the colony to resupply the Italian forces, but that was as far as they would go with their support.

Kesselring's biggest concern were the losses the Luftwaffe had taken over England in the last two weeks. JG 2, JG 26, and JG 77 were shadows of their former selves. All three fighter units had borne the brunt of the allied air offensive, losing one hundred and thirty-six planes in the air with another twenty-one being destroyed on the ground. The Italian air contingent lost twenty-two planes with another eight blown up at their airstrips. This was in addition to the sixty-three aircraft destroyed in February and thirty-nine the previous month. Added to these losses were those in Greece and Russia. The Ju 88 Gruppen had been decimated and Kesselring was forced to withdraw these units. All were shells and needed to be rebuilt from scratch. It didn't matter that four hundred allied aircraft had been destroyed in the same time period. A loss ratio of one point five to one was something the Axis powers couldn't afford. The allied losses were actually twenty percent lower than Kesselring thought, making the actual figures two hundred and ninety German and Italian planes against three hundred and forty-three allied machines.

JG 77 had been withdrawn and replaced by JG 1, while JG 26 was in the process of being swapped with JG 5. A new fighter unit, JG 11 was forming and Kesselring hoped they would soon be ready to take the place of JG 2. All the original fighter gruppen needed to be withdrawn, for rest and re-equipment. Then there were the bomber units. Kesselring knew that Kampfgeschwaders (KG) 30, 54, 76, and 77 had been virtually destroyed. KG 6 was forming in Germany but this was an inexperienced unit that he wanted to send to a quiet sector in Russia. There was only KG 100 to replace the losses. Zerstorergeschwader (ZG)1 had just finished reequipping with Ju 88 R1. These planes were using the powerful BMW 801 A engines and could now reach three hundred and fifty miles an hour. This still wasn't fast enough to escape American fighters but at least it gave the attacking aircraft a chance and they still often outran older allied P40s.

He would send KG 100 over to England and also KG 55. The second unit was equipped with He 111s so it would have to operate at night. It was the best he could do until more of the Fw 190 fighter bombers became available. At least production of this aircraft and all other types was increasing. It helped that the Luftwaffe was producing fewer types of planes. This allowed the factories to concentrate on the successful models. Production on the Bf 110 had ended, and proposed models such as the He 117, Me 210, and Me 410 never started. Dornier were only making sea planes, and Heinkel the 111. Production had narrowed to only two fighters. The Ju 88 filled the role of heavy fighter and fighter bomber, while the Ju 290 was both a transport aircraft and long range reconnaissance platform. Transport was now mainly being done by the Ju 252 and Me 323. Bf 109 Gs were being exported to Hungary and Finland, as the Spitfires used by those countries wore out, and older Bf 110s were sent to Spain and Romania. The only new plane on the horizon was the Me 155 which would replace the aging He 112s on Germany's carriers. This aircraft would come into service in June with a non-naval version being sold to Bulgaria.

Kesselring was still thinking about production figures and the output of the pilot training courses when he was interrupted by a knock at his office door.

"Yes?" he said.

"Sir, General Wagner is here," answered his adjutant Oberst Martin Fiebig.

He'd been dreading this moment.

"Send him in," he sighed.

When the sharp-faced man appeared he looked calm, less intense than he usually did.

"You have received my news then?" Kesselring said without preamble. If he remembered correctly, Wagner liked to get straight to the point.

"That I have to stay with the replacement army? Yes," said the general. "My reason for visiting you today is to find out why. The supply situation in the east hasn't improved according to my sources."

"The fact nothing is moving has helped ease the fuel situation but otherwise you are correct."

"So why haven't I been reinstated?"

"Everyone who matters spoke against you. Himmler doesn't trust you and Bormann hates you. Goebbels didn't care but Keitel was against it, though I think he was just saying what the Führer wanted to hear. Our leader doesn't want you anywhere near the front line. He says you are too valuable doing what you're doing."

"That isn't true. I don't command the replacement army, Fromm does."

"Still, it's a force of over a million men."

"It's about 1.6 million at the moment and growing."

"That's my point. Somebody needs to equip it and you're the perfect man for the job."

Wagner shook his head. "In the east I had clout. My orders overrode most other commanders and generals. Not anymore. I have to fight for every scrap of equipment I can find. This is understandable, as the best panzers and guns are needed at the front. Still, a soldier needs experience driving a Tiger before he has to steer one toward the enemy. I have four of the heavy panzers to work with and only two of them work."

"I see your problem," said Kesselring.

The general shrugged. "I will get my hands on a few more soon. Your generosity at letting me have forty of the new Skoda panzers has helped. The Wolfe is fast and heavily armed."

"That's what they are calling it, eh? Well, you delivered on your promise to outfit the Herman Goering Division with artillery and I failed to hold up my end of the bargain. It was the least I could do."

"You tried. It's a shame, as the situation at the front is not looking as good as it did when I asked."

"What do you mean? The Russian are still stuck on the Volga and the Don rivers, and we hold most of England."

"North Africa will fall, the Allies are piling on the pressure across the Channel and Russia fights on. There is no end to the war in sight."

"We will win. The Allies will become exhausted."

"They hate us for what we have done, and what we are doing in the camps," said Wagner quietly.

"I'm only concerned with the Luftwaffe. Politics is nothing to do with me," said Kesselring quickly.

"Don't get me wrong. I'm no friend of the Jews but it's not just them. We treat the Slavs the same way. The Americans see us an aggressive, expansionist nation who will never stop. I can't see an end to this. This is a war that will never end, one our grandchildren may fight in."

"You're wrong, Wagner. Eventually we will win. Now, if you will excuse me, I have meetings to attend."

The general sighed, saluted and left the office. Kesselring shook his head. The man was such a pessimist. Germany had experienced a few setbacks but held nearly all of Europe. Wagner was an idiot and Kesselring decided to cut all ties with him.

Chapter Nine: April 1943

The 87th Rifle Division was being brought up to strength. Fresh recruits and men from disbanded units flooded into the division, filling out platoons and companies which had been depleted to a few soldiers. Junior Sergeant Roza Shanina was just relieved to have a rest. The fighting along the Volga had exhausted her, and she was happy to sleep and gather food. She stared down at the English writing on the can. American C rations were keeping the Soviet Army alive. She had heard from someone that their Allies didn't like the cans of processed meat, but to Roza they were delicious.

Spring was in the air. However, what was known as the 'green famine' was in full swing. The growing season had started but there would be nothing to eat for another two months. At least the area where the 87th Division was reforming was renowned for its hunting. The town of Yaroslavl held about three hundred thousand people. It was positioned two hundred and fifty kilometres northeast of Moscow. Despite being well behind the line, the local railway bridge made it a constant target for Luftwaffe raids. Recently the local tire factory had been completely destroyed. Luckily for the 87th Division they were based twenty-five kilometres northeast of the town.

The mighty Volga River was still over eight hundred metres wide. This was despite the fact the unit was well over a thousand kilometres upstream from where her unit had been fighting the Nazis.

Today her company was going to celebrate. Yesterday, Roza had put her hunting skills to good use by hiking with her companions into the local forest, camping overnight, and shooting a two young male moose the following morning. Lieutenant Sergei Ivanov knew the area, and had led the group in the hope they'd find something to eat. The officer's family lived in town and were struggling to find enough food. His wife, brother, and father had all died in Leningrad but his mother and children escaped. Recently, his dead wife's younger sister had also arrived.

Roza could understand the man was very worried about his family and had broken regulations. Sergei had found a jeep and enough fuel to transport some of the meat back to town. He'd also caught a sturgeon in the river. After drying the large fish, he promised his men meat if they let him take some food to his family. With the killing of the moose, he would now take the offal back to town, as well as the head. The drive only took half an hour so the officer was expected to return in time to participate in the feast and celebrations. What he didn't know was after he left, Roza had also shot two wolves. Another company had participated in a successful fishing trip, which also added to the booty.

Her battalion had been incredibly lucky. It only consisted of five hundred soldiers at the moment, and the game that had been caught would be enough to give each of them a kilo of fresh meat. As one of the hunters, she might even get a little more. The very thought made her mouth water.

Russia was starving. If it weren't for the food coming from America, the country would have been paralysed. The mud and ice floes on the rivers made it difficult to transport supplies, and people in rural villages were dying of hunger every day. Roza believed the situation in Moscow wasn't much better. It was the same story everywhere, people desperately tried to find food anywhere they could. There wasn't even a cat or dog left alive in the capital, so now people were catching and eating rats.

The success of the hunting trip was unlikely to ever be repeated. With so many soldiers in the area, all of the game would be frightened away. It might still be possible to shoot something if Roza could find a vehicle to take her further afield, but petrol was strictly rationed. Maybe the lieutenant would be able to find a jeep with a tank of fuel. If he did, Roza was confident she could bring down a few deer, as she was a sniper after all. There were supposed to be bear to the north, and if her team could just manage to drive one hundred kilometres or so away from civilization, then maybe she would be able to feed more than just her company.

The smell of cooking meat almost drove Roza mad. Eventually she took her cut from the shoulder of one of the moose, sprinkled it with a pinch of salt, and started eating. It was delicious. A line of men, mixed with a few women, lined up for their cut. Everyone was well behaved and there was even a little left over. Lieutenant Ivanov returned in time for his portion. He was beaming after delivering food to his family. His children were well, and the meat he'd given them would help them stay that way. More importantly, the lieutenant brought twenty bottles of vodka back with him.

After eating Roza found herself sitting with her two friends, the lieutenant, and his two sergeants. Everyone shared a bottle of vodka, and Roza found herself looking at her commanding officer in a new light. It was dusk and everybody sat around fires as the temperature dropped. It had been a mild day, reaching about twelve degrees celsius, but it would drop to zero overnight.

"Your family is well?" she asked the officer.

"Yes comrade, and now their stomachs are full. My youngest son has a sling, and has added to the cooking pot with the odd duck and even a woodcock," said Ivanov.

"That is good. I have heard they have suffered."

The man's eyes lost their focus. "We have lost our home, the cradle of the revolution, to the Nazis. Their mother was killed by a bomb. Uncles and aunts died from shelling or illness. Some have just disappeared. My brother wrote to me from Finland where he escaped from the Germans but is now a prisoner of war. I received one letter from him, but was warned not to write back by the regimental commander."

"Because he is a prisoner?"

"Yes. He said the Finns treated him well. Maybe that's true. The stories all say they aren't as bad as the Nazis but there's no way of knowing for sure."

"I don't know what I'd do if I was faced with certain death," said Roza softly. "Maybe I'd surrender."

"I don't judge my brother but I would deny that to the security services." He glanced at Roza and she smiled at him.

"It would be wrong to judge him. Being shot at is terrifying."

"Anyway, I'll fight until the enemy are driven from our country or until I die. There is no choice in this. The Nazis believe we are less than human. Some of the stories coming from the occupied territories are horrific. The Germans let many of the people left in Leningrad starve. That much at least was in my brother's letter. I've met other men who have escaped east to continue the fight and they talk of villages being destroyed, mass executions and the killing of the Jews. They seek to exterminate us so we must fight."

"I know," said Roza. "I've been lucky. My village is north of here, near Arkhangelsk, well within a few hundred kilometres. It had been untouched by the war."

"Nowhere is untouched in Russia. Young people like yourself will have died. Your village will be struggling to feed itself, just like everywhere else. This fight has affected everyone. That's why I hate them."

"The Nazis?"

"The Germans."

Roza thought of the young man she'd rescued from execution and wondered if she should hate the Germans.

"You are good to your family," she said, trying to move away from uncomfortable thoughts.

"I try. I'm all they have left in some ways. My mother is old and my wife's sister is only sixteen. I send my pay to them and have told them to save as much money as they can. If I die or worse, if I'm crippled, then they will need every last Rouble."

Roza reached and touched the man's army. She felt sorry for the officer and the vodka was starting to take effect.

"I'm here comrade," she said.

He looked at her and his face softened. "Roza, you've just turned eighteen. You shouldn't even be here."

She snatched her hand away. "I'm one of the regiment's best snipers."

"I meant no offense. You are very attractive but I'm seven years older than you."

“I don’t care. I want to know what it feels like.”

Across the fire Nadia was already leading one of the sergeants to a tent. Anna was kissing the other man. It looked as if full stomachs and vodka were having a similar effect on everyone. Or maybe it was because it was spring. Sergei kissed her and then took her by the hand.

“Come with me,” he said.

She woke the following day next to her officer. The night had been everything she’d expected. Roza was lucky as her lover was experienced, tender and attentive to her needs. Unfortunately he didn’t have a condom, as Russian troops weren’t issued them. Sergei took what precautions he could but there was still a danger that Roza may fall pregnant. She would have to talk with Nadia and find out what she could do to make sure that didn’t happen.

Above her was the canvas roof of an M5 half-track. The company only had two of these, which were mostly used to carry casualties. For Roza it was private and warm.

Outside, a misty drizzle had started to fall. She knew very little in the way of American equipment had arrived in Russia, so her regiment was fortunate to have a few jeeps and half-tracks. Most of the supplies sent by the Allies to the Soviet Union were food, clothing, fuel, and boots. Roza had a pair of the boots herself, and she had to admit that the workmanship was better than any of her previous ones.

Slowly she untangled herself from Sergei and dressed quietly. The rest of her squad was gathered around a fire near the river. The three women all smiled shyly at each other.

"Quite a night," said Nadia.

"My head hurts," added Anna.

"I'm alright," said Roza.

"Better than alright I'd say," said Nadia.

They all laughed. Roza then dangled a set of keys from her fingers and shook them at her friends.

“For the Jeep. I believe its tank is still half full. Time to do a little more hunting?” she said.

“Does the lieutenant know?” asked Anna.

“He’s not going to object after last night,” said Nadia.

“I’m not his campaign wife,” snapped Roza.

Nadia’s face fell and Roza realized what she had said. “I’m sorry. I didn’t mean it like that. It’s just, what happened is a once off. I don’t have permission but if we bring back a deer we’ll be fine.”

Nadia nodded though she still looked pale.

They brought back a boar, a hare, and a fox. Nobody in the company objected that the jeep was almost out of fuel by the time they returned the following evening. Everybody was too busy eating. Roza found herself alongside Sergei that night. In the morning she decided an apology to Nadia was in order. And she definitely needed some advice on how to stop herself from getting pregnant.

V

Spring in Devon was busy. Maggie stretched and wiped the dirt from her face. There was little fuel for the tractor so most tasks had to be done by hand. Fields had to be ploughed by old Nellie, a cart horse that used to pull a milk cart but was now being shared among half a dozen different farms to plough their fields. This in itself was difficult, as Nellie had worked as a cart horse for the last ten years. Luckily though, when the animal was younger, she had pulled a plough.

At the moment Maggie had the unenviable job of collecting all the manure from the chicken pen and the pigsty, and moving it to the cart. Later it would be spread in the fields as there was no artificial fertiliser. She wore a scarf over her mouth to protect her from the stench. The scent of the chicken pen wasn't too bad but the pig manure was disgusting.

"It's a tough job, lass," said Uncle Peter.

"It has to be done," she answered. Turning, she saw a man in a German uniform standing next to her uncle.

"This is Feldwebel Grunwald. He is here to take a couple of the piglets," said Uncle Peter.

"Exchange!" said the overweight German in English.

"True. Exchange. He takes a couple of piglets and we get barley to keep the rest of the animals going."

Maggie frowned but nodded. It made sense to do business with the German supply apparatus but she didn't have to like it. The two men walked away talking, and later a cart carrying sacks of barley and lupins arrived, driven by a skinny German missing an arm from the elbow down. The man smiled at her and she scowled back. He looked away and the Feldwebel came and spoke to him. She left the man to unload the sacks, not caring it was an awkward job with only one arm. She spotted the older German having a beer with her uncle, and tried to contain her anger. The need to find food for the pigs didn't mean her family had to enjoy a drink with the enemy.

Later the two men went to help the one-armed German, and soon after lunch the enemy left the farm.

She finished filling the wagon with manure and washed up. Uncle Peter met her in the kitchen.

"After a bite we'll take the wagon and spread the slop over the field," he said.

She ignored him and cut a loaf of bread with vigour. She didn't see the glance that passed between her uncle and Aunt Mary.

"Our friendly Feldwebel had a few interesting things to say. He likes to talk, especially after he's had a beer or three," said Peter.

Maggie stopped slicing a block of cheese and turned around. She raised an eyebrow at the older man.

"You didn't think I was entertaining the German because I was bored, did you?" he asked.

"I wasn't sure what was going on," she said.

"Grunwald's not a bad man. He fought in the first war and doesn't like the fact that we are fighting a second one."

"He's still a German," said Maggie.

"And he likes the fact that his country seems to be winning. Still, his son has just been sent to the Eastern Front so he's worried."

"But that's not why you were talking to him?"

"No, you see the piglets are for the Gestapo leadership in Exeter. It seems they want to throw a bit of a party for Oberführer Muller's brother. The Gestapo chief's brother is a Luftwaffe gruppen leader. KG 100 is landing in England to replace some other bomber unit that has taken heavy losses."

Maggie stood a little straighter. "Do you have a time and location for the unit's arrival?"

Her uncle smiled. "I do. They will land at the Exeter strip in six to seven days. It won't be the whole unit but part of it. I don't understand the structure of the Luftwaffe."

"It's probably a gruppen of twenty to thirty planes," said Maggie.

"If you radio this to the Allies, won't they work out where the information came from?" said Aunt Mary.

"Probably not, but there are ways to make that even less likely. The allied air force can start sending reconnaissance flights to lots of different axis airfields. Anyway, they might think hearsay isn't enough to mount a major raid, or they might double-check the information with other sources. Our little operation here is part of a much larger picture," said Maggie.

"Is that what they taught you in Scotland?" asked Mary.

"That, and other things. I'll have to use the Paraset radio," she said.

After spreading the manure on the fields with her uncle, Maggie walked down through the woods at the end of the driveway. There was a small hut near a tiny brook, in which timber was kept. Maggie unlocked an old padlock and went inside. Along one wall hung an oiled two-man saw and an axe. On a bench was a sharpening stone and a skinning knife. She knew that the hut was sometimes used by her uncle after he trapped rabbits in the area.

She unpacked the radio from its hidden location and checked that it worked. Then she began the hike to the moors to get a decent signal. Maggie felt fairly relaxed at the moment. Since the Germans had arrested and hung four black market operatives in the Torquay area, everything had quietened down. There had been a ferocious manhunt by the Gestapo for the two men Maggie had killed on the moors. Luckily, the larger German was linked to the black market and the theory was that he'd cheated his contacts. The British side of the operation was run by Billy Hill out of London. His men weren't gentle and at least one murder was linked to them. All it took was for Maggie to arrange for a bullet from an MP 40 be left in a shed associated with one of the black market operatives, and the Germans were satisfied. Of course, she needed to leave clues at quite a few locations before the Gestapo found the trail. The inefficiency of the Germans in some ways was reassuring. The personnel of the enemy security force was undermanned and relied almost entirely on collaborators to track down those suspected of working for the Allies.

They did have other ways of tracking the resistance movement and Maggie wasn't to know that one of those techniques was in the area. She hiked the one mile to Bel Tor, the summit of the hill giving her the elevation she needed to send her message. The wind picked up as she placed the aerial at the top of a low tree. Maggie pulled her coat around her. It had almost been dark when she'd left the shed and she had used her torch intermittently to guide her. Even though she knew the way, it was a difficult walk at night.

She tuned the two lights on the set until they glowed. When they both shone brightly, Maggie knew she had maximum resonance. Maggie didn't know she was contacting another agent near Hull. After waiting for a coded acknowledgement she sent her message, received conformation, and packed up to leave. Unfortunately, a German vehicle was using VHF directional-finding equipment in the area. This Very Close Unit consisted of only two men and they were only testing their equipment in one of the most elevated areas in Devon. The team immediately picked up the direction and strength of the signal, though they couldn't triangulate it. It was however enough for the two man team to contact their headquarters in Exeter. From here a message was sent by radio to the closest patrol in the area. This happened to be a squad of five men crammed into a Kubelwagen near Two Bridges.

They were only a distance of five miles from Maggie's location. However, the Germans could have easily driven northeast in the direction of Postbridge instead. Unfortunately for Maggie they didn't. The Feldwebel in charge of the group thought that any radio transmissions would probably come from an area closer to population centres. Postbridge was a tiny community and you didn't hit another village driving in that direction until you reach Lettaford. According to the radio intercept boys, the signal was south of that area. The message to look out for a resistance radio operator took a while to get to the patrol and that allowed Maggie to almost reach Higher Uppacott before they found her.

It was windy and she didn't hear the vehicle until it was coming around the corner one hundred yards behind her. She tried to dive off the road, but high hedges and a low stone wall fenced her. She cursed herself for using the road. It was late and dark, and the area was usually deserted at this time. Maggie had wanted to use the road to speed her trip home. Now she was going to pay for that decision.

The vehicle came to a stop as she finally managed to scramble into the hedge. German voices yelled, and a burst of automatic fire tore into the foliage around her. By climbing into the hedge the strap around the radio had become tangled. Maggie tried to pull it free, however it was firmly wedged. In the dark she couldn't see where the strap was caught. The sound of pounding feet alerted her to how close the Germans were. All she had to defend herself was the Welrod silenced pistol and two grenades. She had to abandon the radio but didn't want the enemy to capture it intact. Pulling the pin from her grenade, she dropped it next to the radio. Rolling to the other side of a stone wall, Maggie placed her hands over her ears.

After the flat crack of the grenade, the Germans fired at the hedge for a few seconds before advancing. Rifle fire and the bursts from the MP 40 sent pieces of rock flying around her and she waited for the impact of a bullet. When the firing ceased, she was up and running. The field in front of her was split by a hedge. A small gap in the foliage allowed animals to move around. Maggie vaulted the low gate but almost fell as her feet skidded in the mud. She could hardly see. The advantage was, neither could the Germans.

Following the hedge, she ran away from the road. Suddenly there was a hiss and a light shot into the sky before exploding in a plume brightly above the hills. The enemy patrol had fired a flare. Ahead, Maggie saw a different hedge fifty yards in front of her. The Germans were still finding their own way through to the field, and she ran until she saw an opening in the trees. Maggie had just made it into the next field when she heard a yell and the crack of a rifle. The bullet snapped a branch only a pace to her left. She took off again into the next field. Maggie ran alongside the hedge until the land became even steeper. After jumping a low stone wall, she found herself in an area of waist high bracken which was cut by various tracks.

Maggie knew where she was. The road to the Leusdon Village Hall was nearby. After crossing that track there was the upper plantation behind Spitwitch Manor. If she could get that far, there was a chance she would escape. Another flare burst overhead and Maggie crouched low. Behind her the MP 40 barked again. The flashing of the muzzle allowed her to pinpoint the German patrol. The Feldwebel was firing blind. She started running again.

Eventually Maggie reached the road. Stumbling to the other side she plunged into a line of alder and oak trees. It was dark here and she had to move forward slowly, feeling her way through the scrub. Maggie didn't dare use her flashlight. She knew that the manor was downhill and eventually Maggie broke through into a wide field. Not daring to cross the open ground, she followed the edge of the tree line until she hit the Newbridge Road. Taking a risk, she followed the road for two hundred yards until she heard the sound of an engine. Ahead was a thatched-roof cottage, hugging the track. She dived back over a stone fence and crouched low as the Germans drove by. They stopped eighty yards further on and started to shine torches into the bushes. She could see a man in the back seat trying to tune a radio set.

She was only five hundred yards from home now. Maggie knew every inch of the surrounding country and decided to head toward the valley. This low ground was thickly wooded, and would eventually allow her to reach the driveway to the farm. Maggie was exhausted by now and the adrenalin that had kept her going was starting to dissipate. Staggering through the woodlands, Maggie reached the track. Following it took her to uncle's land. She ran up the driveway to the house with the silenced pistol in her hand. Bursting through the back door of the cottage she was greeted by the sight of Uncle Peter, standing in the hallway in his dressing gown. His white knuckles gripped an ancient shot gun.

"It's alright. I lost them," said Maggie.

Aunt Mary appeared, wrapped in a long woollen shawl.

"Get out of those boot," said the older lady. "Peter, clean her footwear. Maggie you need to get changed and give the dirty clothes to your uncle. Everything, including the gun, needs to be well hidden."

"I've got just the place," said Uncle Peter.

"I had to blow up the radio," Maggie gasped.

"Can't be helped. Now get changed quickly," said Aunt Mary.

Maggie went to her room and pulled off her dirty clothing. She was surprised at the amount of mud and leaf litter caught in her hair. Then she found the bullet hole in the hood of her coat. She put her finger through it, staring with wonder. Her aunt found her like that. The older woman saw the hole and immediately understood how close her niece had been to dying.

"Oh," the older woman gasped.

She turned and tears welled up in her eyes. Aunt Mary wrapped her in a hug and Maggie started to sob.

Later, when her hair had been combed and all suspicious items hidden by her uncle, Maggie sat down to a bowl of chicken soup with thick slices of bread. Her uncle reappeared and nodded at his wife.

"There are lights and the sound of engines up in the village," he said.

"They'll be the Germans based in Ashburton. I think they have a company there," said Maggie.

"Did they see you?" asked Aunt Mary.

"I'm almost sure they didn't. They probably saw nothing more than a vague shape in the darkness. At least that's what I think," she answered.

"So not enough to know it was a woman?" said Peter.

"I believe they wouldn't have seen enough to know that."

"They will be here soon. Do you think you can hold it together when they arrive?" asked her uncle.

"I was trained for what's to come. How will you two be?"

The older couple glanced at each other. "We'll be alright," said Aunt Mary.

"I didn't injure or kill any of them, so hopefully there will be no hostages taken. They will tear the area apart looking for me though," said Maggie.

"The Germans are still thin on the ground and your precautions were very good. If everything is as well hidden as you think, then all they can do is huff and puff," said Uncle Peter.

Two hours later a truck drove up the driveway. Uncle Peter met the Germans in his dressing gown and escorted them inside. He gave the Feldwebel leading the group a lantern to use in his search, as the patrol was short on torches. The enemy searched thoroughly but they were respectful. Nothing was broken and the non-commissioned officer even apologised for the interruption. A few of the patrol eyed Maggie up and down. She kept her face neutral and endured the examination. Uncle Peter gave the Germans a dozen eggs and a wheel of cheese, and the patrol left with smiling faces.

"Now we just have to hope they didn't find anything at any of the other resistance member's houses," said Maggie.

The enemy didn't, but they did establish a permanent presence in the area. Ten men and a vehicle were based in a house near the inn. The Gestapo threatened to take hostages, but in the end nothing came of it. Maggie wasn't sure if the village would be as lucky if there was another incident. She was also concerned about the enemy who were based only five hundred yards away. Maggie wondered what to do however she couldn't even ask for advice. She didn't have a radio.

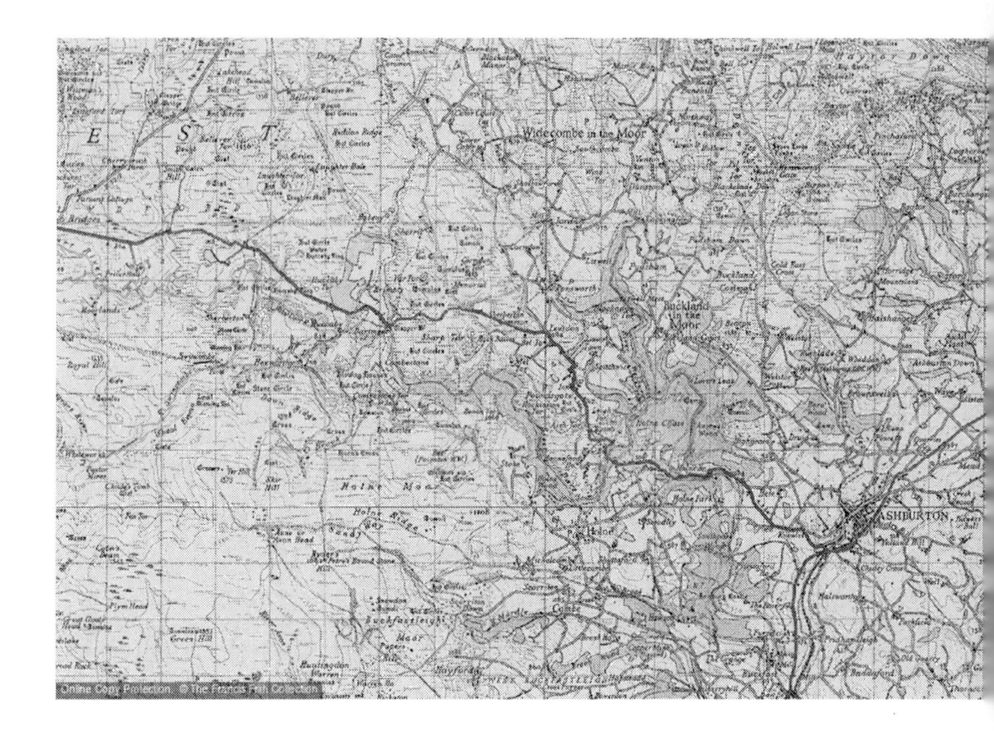
Widecombe in the Moor
Buckland in the Moor
Holne Moor
Holne
ASHBURTON

Chapter Ten: May 1943

Finally the squadron returned to the Enterprise. Commander James Southerland really missed life on the carrier, but he only be had another two days at Henderson Field. In the meantime there were still enemy planes to shoot down. The Japanese had evacuated the island, but that didn't mean they weren't still attacking American shipping in the area. The US 43rd Division had landed on the Russell Islands and taken them unopposed. The new airstrip at Yadina would allow the Wildcats to refuel after any flight over New Georgia. This was an improvement that allowed the US fighters to roam further than earlier.

His squadron took off with eight Grumman TBF Avenger torpedo planes carrying bombs. Fourteen Douglas Dauntless SBD dive bombers made up the rest of the attack force. Japanese destroyers had been spotted near Kula Gul. These ships dropped off supplies and men on Kolombangara Island, where a single airfield had recently been built on the southern end of the volcanic island.

The peak stood four thousand three hundred feet above the surrounding ocean. Today they would try to intercept a group of barges that had been spotted by a Catalina float plane, heading southwest toward the island.

The flight was longer than Southerland was used to. The aircraft was sluggish on its ascent due to the drop tanks, but once the fuel in these had been used and the tanks dispensed with, the plane became easier to handle. Below Southerland, the Pacific was a brilliant blue. In the distance tall clouds towered like white columns over the Russell Islands. Here his squadron met the bombers, and the formation headed north. Over the island of New Georgia he could make out hills of dark green. There seemed to be no breaks in the canopy except near the higher peaks.

The twin peaks of Kolombangara Island were clearly visible now, though there was no sign of the barges. The formation leader, Captain Lennard, ordered the aircraft to head toward the Japanese airstrip. Then they spotted three barges unloading at a pier, just inside a large inlet. At the same time Lieutenant Commander Stanley Vejtasa (Swede) yelled a warning.

"Fourteen fighters, four o'clock low," radioed the fighter pilot. "What are they?"

"They look like Bf 109s," said Southerland.

"Stow the chatter," said the captain. "Escort, do your job. Attack aircraft get ready."

The dive bombers were soon in position but the torpedo planes found this difficult. Lining up on the barges inside the lagoon was extremely hard for the Avengers, as they needed to attack at a shallow angle. Meanwhile, the Wildcats dived on the new Japanese fighter.

These machines were Kawasaki Ki-61s, the 'Tony' of the Japanese Army. The new plane had been introduced a few months earlier and still suffered from many mechanical issues. The 78th Sentai had flown from Truk to Rabual losing fourteen of their thirty fighters on the way. Another twenty had been shipped in crates to the area with spare parts. Despite having forty Ki-61s at Kolombangara, the enemy could only get less than half that number into the air. Still, these planes were faster and more maneuverable than the Wildcat. They also had self-sealing fuel tanks, meaning they didn't catch fire as easily as the Zero.

At this time, the fuel used by the Japanese Army was of good quality, though it wasn't going to last. Poor maintenance and lack of trained mechanics, led to a very high unserviceability rate. At this time the 78th Sentai had enough fighters to challenge the US formation, but that wouldn't always be the case.

Having the advantage of height allowed the Wildcats an initial advantage. In his first head-on attack Southerland managed to hit a Tony in the wings. The fighter fell away trailing smoke, with the pilot bailing out over the coast. When the Wildcats tried to dive away they found the new Japanese fighters on their tail. The enemy machine could follow them through all their maneuvers and even the Thatch Weave had limited success. The factor that saved the US navy pilots was the light armament of the Tony. Each of the

Japanese planes only had four heavy machine guns, although later versions would change two of these guns for a 20mm cannon.

Southerland had lost his wingman and two of the Ki-61s were on his tail. His squadron had absorbed nearly all of the attention of the Japanese fighters, allowing the bombers to do their job. All three barges were destroyed as was half the material they were carrying. Three enemy planes were then blown up on the airstrip. Only a pair of Tonys managed to attack the retreating dive bombers, shooting one down. None of this helped Southerland who was in the fight of his life.

He was now low and slow, flying above the many streams which ran down the flank of the dormant volcano. His controls were sluggish and Southerland could see the holes in his wings. Two of his wing guns had been smashed, and one of the ailerons was completely missing. It was only a matter of time before his plane would catch fire or explode. Climbing for a little altitude Southerland checked his parachute and pulled back his canopy. Breathing a sigh of relief, he pulled it completely open.

A stream of 12.7mm bullets came from behind the Wildcat. Southerland tried to turn to throw the enemy pilot off his aim. Either he was too slow or the plane's responses were damaged. The glass in his cockpit shattered and the instrument board exploded in front of him. He felt the control stick go sloppy in his hands, and the fighter started to roll to port of its own accord. Southerland looked down and realized he could see the jungle through the floor of his cockpit. Smoke poured from the engine and he decided it was time to go.

Launching himself free of the plane, Southerland only counted to two before pulling the cord on his parachute. He was too low to wait. With a snap the canopy opened above his head. He only had a few seconds to look around at the trees. His plane hit the ground and exploded only two hundred yards away. Southerland crashed through a tangle of branches and leaves. He had only come down five miles from the enemy airstrip and was hung up in the tree, hanging above the Vila River. Below, the stream tumbled over boulders before slowing to form a pool beneath him.

Southerland checked his body for injuries and groaned when he touched his shoulder. His body was battered and bruised, and his face cut by flying glass, however his shoulder was extremely painful. He guessed he had probably broken a bone, or dislocated the joint. Trying to move was painful but he couldn't stay here. The Japanese weren't known for their kind treatment of prisoners. Southerland had a hunting knife in his boot, and a Colt revolver. His emergency backpack contained many other items but it had been torn off in the canopy.

Looking down he tried to judge the depth of the pool below. In the end Southerland decided that didn't matter, as he couldn't stay where he was. Pulling the release straps, he fell down into the pool. The fall was probably twenty feet and he hit the bottom before pushing off and swimming upwards. His heavy jacket was an encumbrance, but he couldn't shrug it off as his left arm dangled uselessly. He struggled to break the surface of the water. The pool was probably only eight feet deep and thirty across, yet swimming to the bank almost exhausted Southerland.

After regaining his breath he discovered his first aid kit intact, hanging from the front of his vest. He sprinkled disinfectant powder on his many cuts and abrasions. Southerland then used the bandage to support his shoulder. He looked at the water and wondered if it was safe to drink. His pocket contained water purification tablets and his salt tablets, but he didn't want to use them yet. Deciding to take the risk, he drank deeply. If he moved away from the river then he'd become dehydrated very quickly. The heat was already noticeable, despite having just left a pool of cool water.

The Japanese base was downstream, so Southerland decided to try and push further up the volcano. He hadn't gone more than a mile before he was fatigued. There was no track to follow and the land was steep and slippery. Insects buzzed around him and Southerland was forced to stop and apply a thick layer of insect repellent from his first aid kit, which was proving to be a treasure trove.

After some time Southerland needed to move away from the stream and strike out at an angle across the slope. Here it was possible to follow a thin winding track. Above him the forest canopy blotted out the sky. The air felt almost too think to breathe, such was the humidity. Sweat poured from Southerland and he wondered how long it would be before he would need water again. Pushing hard, he tried to continue upward, but found the track descended. By now Southerland was exhausted and confused. Not knowing what to do he staggered on and was relieved to find another track which climbed at a forty-five degree angle toward the summit. He'd only gone a few hundred paces in this direction before two shadows stepped from the path and pointed weapons at him.

Both of the men were natives. Buiku Gasa and Eroni Kumana carried Japanese weapons. One held a Type 38 short rifle while the other man carried a Type 100 submachine gun. The two men stared at the pilot, then one signalled with his hand.

"Come," said the taller man. The natives took positions behind and in front of Southerland. They didn't ask for his weapons or answer any of his questions. In the end he wasn't sure how well they spoke English. Eventually, with Southerland swaying on his feet, they reached a small hut in the jungle. A white man wearing a slouch hat, shorts, and an old shirt greeted him in a small clearing.

"You look all in mate," said the suntanned man.

He handed Southerland a canteen of water and led him into the hut. From the window there was a clear view through the trees of the surrounding ocean and one could just make out the distant Japanese airstrip.

"Name's Arthur Evans. I'm a lieutenant in the Royal Australian Navy. They sent me here to spy on the Japs, report their movements and such. Knew the area when I was younger so they sent me back," said the man in a thick Australian accent.

"You're a Coastwatcher?" asked Southerland. He handed back the now empty water container and introduced himself.

"I saw your plane come down. Those new Jap fighters are a handful by the look of them."

"Are they a German make?"

"Na, the KI-61 is homebrew. I've sent some pictures of them to your boys to help with identification, but I don't think they've reached Guadalcanal yet."

"I saw some of the natives. They were heavily armed."

"Those boys know the jungle. I manage to keep 'em fed and they don't like the Japs."

"You're carrying a Jap pistol yourself?"

"The Type 14 was better than the revolver they sent me here with. I've got an Owen gun around here somewhere."

"Can you get me out of here and back to my people?" asked Southerland.

"You need a little rest, and I better have a look at your shoulder. We will also have to move very soon as the Japs will be looking for you. We've left them a couple of presents near your chute and that will make them cautious. Still, we need to go soon."

"Presents?"

"Booby traps and a couple of land mines. Doubt if we will hear them when they go bang, but you never know."

Southerland's shoulder was dislocated and Evans popped it back into place. The pain when he did was excruciating. Southerland sat, ate, and drank, while around him natives packed up. Evan took apart a large radio, and stowing it carefully before sending it with a group of men, along the trail into the jungle.

"Right mate, time we got movin'," said Evans. Southerland hauled himself to his feet and wondered if it would ever cool down.

"Is it always this hot here?" he asked.

Evans laughed. "No. It's a little better where we are going. The higher we get, the cooler it becomes. It's just making the climb is back breaking."

"Great," said Southerland.

They walked until well into the evening, finding their way through the forest by touch. The natives never seemed to place a foot wrong, yet Southerland must have fallen at least a dozen times. Every time he did pain shot through his shoulder. When they finally reached a group of huts near one of the two high peaks on the island, Southerland collapsed into a rough bed. Evans was correct. At four thousand feet it was a lot cooler.

The following morning he woke late. Though Southerland's shoulder hurt, he felt relatively rested. He'd slept under a mosquito net, and the cooler temperature allowed him to be comfortable. Evans woke him with a cup of tea and a slice of coconut. Later, he ate some cooked fish and drank cold water.

"The Japs are on the move," said Evans pointing.

From their location high on the side of the volcano they could see the Kula Gulf. Southerland could see ships in the distance moving toward the coast.

"Cruisers?" asked Southerland.

"Nah, only destroyers. There's one of the bigger types, probably a Shimakaze, the others are smaller varieties, maybe a Hatsuharu destroyer. It's hard to tell from this far."

The Australian adjusted his binoculars and Southerland noticed they were a Japanese naval variety, mounted on a tripod. Made by Nikkon, they were extremely powerful.

"Their decks are crowded with crates, though the big one carries troops. They're coming this way," said Evans. "I better radio it in."

Southerland went and looked through the eye piece, and after adjusting the focus he found the enemy ships. He was amazed at the detail he could see. The six 12.7cm guns on the largest destroyer were clearly visible. There were at least four hundred men sitting on the deck, and probably another two hundred on one of the smaller vessels. That was almost a battalion of men coming to New Georgia.

Soon Evans was back by his side. “This island and the local airstrip aren’t as important as the Munda field further south. That’s about fifteen miles from here across the strait,” said the Australian. “You’re going down the mountain tomorrow. We are taking you to a US sub in a few days. It’s all arranged.”

“Thanks. I’d be dead without you guys,” said Southerland.

Evans waved the comment away and went back to peering through the binoculars.

A week later Southerland was aboard the USS Growler, a Gato class submarine that had been patrolling the area. He immediately noted the air-conditioning, and was later given a cool flask of water from the refrigeration unit.

“We’ll soon have you back at Henderson,” said Commander Schade.

Southerland collapsed into a bunk and slept. Two weeks later he was back on board the USS Enterprise.

V

Reich's Marshal Kesselring stood with his Führer and Field Marshal Wilhelm Keitel, staring at the map on the table. The conference room at the Wolf's Lair was dominated by a huge table. At the moment only the three men were in the room.

Kesselring was spending more and more time at the Führer's headquarters and he wasn't enjoying the experience. The forest in which the base lay was cold in winter and bug-ridden in summer. It was important he stayed here as much as he could, as the Wolf's Lair was where all the important decisions were now being made.

"It must succeed," said the Führer in his rich, deep voice.

"It will. We will take Moscow and the Soviet Union will collapse," said Keitel.

Kesselring rolled his eyes at the comment. Keitel was embarrassing at times. He often grovelled when he was with the Führer, disgusting Kesselring.

"We are certainly gathering enough divisions," Kesselring added.

"Yes, thirteen of them and many of them elite formations," said the Führer.

"How many panzers will we have available?" asked Kesselring.

"In the first attack there will be two thousand with another five hundred in reserve," said the Führer.

"That leaves very little in the way of reserves for other theatres," said Kesselring.

"Don't you think I know that?" snapped the Führer. "The main front is two thousand kilometres long, without even counting the line along the Caucasus Mountains. We have to finish this, then the British and Americans will sue for peace. What are the final numbers on the aircraft you are sending to support the attack?"

"We will have two thousand eight hundred planes ready. With the US bomber raids from northern England we have been forced to strengthen our defences in Germany, and there is the attack to retake Nottingham coming up in a few days, so we have sent another gruppen of fighter bombers in support."

"Moscow has to be the main focus," growled the Führer.

"I know, and I've stripped planes from Greece and Italy. I found a gruppen of Ju88s and one of Bf 109s in these areas."

"Are our Romanian oilfields still safe?" asked the Führer.

"There has been no sight of heavy US bombers in Africa or the Middle East. We have also strengthened the Romanian air force with the delivery of sixty modern fighters."

The Führer nodded, seemingly satisfied. "And the Hungarians? What are they contributing?"

"All their British equipment is worn out, so once again we had to supply them with aircraft. They received twenty fighters from us but they also brought fifty of the new Italian Macchi 205s."

"Is it a good plane?" asked the Führer.

"About the same as the 109G, with maybe a slightly better turning circle."

"And these planes will be present at the battle?" asked Keitel.

"The Macchis will be, the others will cover the Don Front. We have some Romanian fighters watching the mountains and Georgia."

"And we have nothing in reserve," said the Führer.

"That is almost correct. There is a fighter bomber unit forming in Bavaria and JG 302 is almost ready to defend the air space over the Reich."

"That is good," said the Führer. "I am also interested in the new types of aircraft the Luftwaffe is developing."

Kesselring drew a deep breath. "The Fw 190 C is ready for combat in very limited numbers but still has overheating problems. The first Do 335 has just flown and the aircraft shows great promise. There are still many problems to be fixed so the plane won't be ready for at least a year. The Fw 190 D will be an all-round fighter and is progressing well, and will also be ready in spring of next year."

"What about bombers and jets?" said the Führer.

"The Do 335 is fast and can drop one thousand kilos of bombs. The jets are having problems with their engines. I can't see them being ready until 1945," answered Kesselring. "I'm putting a lot of effort into them but I think these very promising piston engine machines will be ready first."

"And this flying rocket bomb? Are you still developing that?"

"It is a low priority. They are a weapon with a range of two hundred kilometres and are extremely inaccurate. I'm focusing on the radar guided bombs that can hit enemy ships. They'll be dropped from Ju 290s and He 111s. I'm hopeful they'll slow the rate at which the USA is reinforcing their army in England."

The Führer stroked his chin. "Don't give up on the big rocket bombs. We might be able to launch them at Moscow, if we don't take it ...... However, I agree with your allocation of resources and hopefully, we won't need the weapon."

"I'm very confident that we won't even need the piston driven planes, but I'm not sure how long it will be after we defeat Russia that the USA and the Commonwealth realize they can't win," said Kesselring.

"Churchill is behind all this. I would love to put him on trial, then hang him. However, you are probably right. It will be necessary to deal with the west at some stage and make peace."

"Do you have any idea of what we'd accept from them, my Führer?" asked Kesselring.

"There would need to be a cap on the size of the Royal Navy. I'd expect areas of occupation on the Isle of Wight again, but this time I would also want land around Dover or maybe Exeter. The USA would have to withdraw all its forces from the area and hand Iceland and other islands in the Atlantic to us. The Allies would eventually see they have no choice. Of course, we need to totally destroy Russia first."

Kesselring was shocked. There was no chance the USA would give up territory in the Atlantic, especially if it allowed the Luftwaffe to reach their shores. It would take a great victory to convince the Americans to accept such humiliating terms.

"It would be best to occupy Britain completely, but I would settle for weakening the country to a point it could never threaten us again," the German leader continued.

Again, Kesselring considered this very unlikely.

"We would need to dominate the sea to force such a peace deal on them," he said.

"Well, Russia first, then we will see," said the Führer.

"Do you see us negotiating a deal with Stalin at any point?" Kesselring asked.

"At the moment, no. My aim is to destroy the Slav nation completely, to drive them beyond the Ural Mountains. We will repopulate their lands with good German folk. If I were forced to deal with Stalin it would only be for short term convenience. One of us would break the treaty. There can never be a lasting peace with the Communists."

"Those lands are our birthright," added Keitel.

So the war would continue for the foreseeable future. Kesselring left the meeting feeling deeply disturbed. For the first time his optimistic outlook had cracked. The USA was keeping Russia in the war and Germany was bleeding. His country didn't have enough oil, rare minerals, or food. Even if the Heer took Moscow, what then? Russia was starving but US food supplies allowed Stalin to keep his army and factories going, just. They had weakened the Soviet Union but the knockout blow was as elusive as ever. Unless they took the Baku region and found a way to deliver the oil from there to Germany, then finishing off Russia was impossible. Even if they took the oilfields, it would take years to repair them and build the infrastructure needed to take advantage of the resource. That meant the war would drag on. Kesselring could see it would go for at least another two years, maybe longer. He decided to push the Luftwaffe's aircraft development. If the fighting were going to drag on for that long, they would be needed.

V

The German counterattack had caught the Allies by surprise. It was known that shipments of panzers had increased and that an SS division had crossed the Channel, but there were also signs that the enemy was digging in. General Model's attack would later become known as the Battle of Nottingham, even though most of the fighting took place in the twenty-five miles between the city, and Lincoln to the east. The industrial area around Colwick was devastated but the centre of the city itself wasn't as badly damaged. Model sent the 23rd, 24th and 2nd SS Panzer Divisions to attack the US positions along the line of the A46. The enemy burst through the front held by the 9th US Infantry Division and the 27th National Guard Infantry Division. In two days the SS and the 23rd Panzer had advanced ten miles to reach Tuxford, and the Sherwood Pines Reserve. The 24th had only made it as far as Eagle Moor and

Girton, as attacks by the 1st US Armoured Division had slowed the enemies' progress.

Further west the 22nd Panzer Division attacked north across a road known as the Long Lane, but were stopped by Canadian armour and anti-tank guns along the Ashbourne Road. This was the first time seventeen pounder guns were used and their effectiveness shocked the enemy tank crews. The 389th German Infantry division assaulted the east area of Nottingham. First, the enemy infantry had to take West Brigford and the locks over the canal. Then they stormed across the Trent River, into the racecourse, and north to the suburb of Carlton. Here, they were stopped by determined defence from the 9th US Division's 47th Infantry Regiment. The battle along the railway at Netherfields turned into a contest of wills, where neither side would give an inch. Eventually the US troops gave ground, retiring in good order to Gedling, only having surrendered a few hundred yards.

V

The Sherman sat just back from the edge of the forest, the town of Mansfield only about four miles to the southwest. Lieutenant Randel watched the open fields leading down to the river, with satisfaction. The SS tanks and half-tracks were advancing into the village of Edwinstowe to the west, while another battle group looked as though they were about to cross the River Maun near the Clip Stone Inn. Through his binoculars he could see the ruins of King John's Palace and the railway line.

"Any second now," he whispered to himself.

The US 2nd Armoured Division had moved forward during the night and nobody had much sleep. The area to the east of Mansfield contained many patches of forest, and General Patton had directed the division there, to hit the 2nd SS das Reich Division and throw it back toward the Trent River. Combat Command A (CCA) was to strike into the Edwinstowe, and then down to Rufford. From here they were to advance due south down the A614, until they reached the rail line to Newark on Trent, at which point they'd turn east.

Randal heard the rumble of distant guns, then the whistle as the shells passed over his position. The first rounds landed in the village. He could see the flashes among the dust and the small fires that broke out in the houses. Directly to his south another barrage dropped on the Germans about to cross the small river. Being slightly elevated, Randel could see over the railway embankment and into the tiny hamlet.

"We will wait for this to finish, then advance," said Randel to his crew.

Around the tanks, nestled among the trees, were hundreds of American soldiers. All peered through the scrub at the explosions, as the shells ripped houses and trees apart. After ten minutes the barrage rolled back to the enemy's rear areas.

"Right, the local bridge won't take the weight of a Sherman so we're going through the river. Its only three feet deep, so it shouldn't be a problem and the banks aren't steep," he told his driver Private Danny Fredrick. Fifteen Shermans moved from the forest, as well as six hundred men. They fanned out and crossed the river without too much difficulty. One Sherman became bogged and was towed from the mud later in the day. They stormed the small village, overwhelming the dazed SS men. After rounding up one hundred prisoners CCA moved along the A611 until they could turn into the Rufford road and advance to an area known as the Wilderness. This small forest had just been flattened by sixty B-25 bombers and there was little opposition. CCB was moving over a series of low ridges toward Kneesall.

For the time being this column had been stopped by a battery of Pak 40 anti-tank guns and a battalion from the 4th SS Panzer Grenadier Regiment 'Der Führer'.

Randel could see one of the M3 scout tanks parked by the road just where the forest ended. The commander of the vehicle stood by the road while another man vomited. Randel peered into the woodland and saw lines of bodies lying among the trees. All were wearing American uniforms and appeared scattered across a clearing like rag dolls. He ordered his driver to pull over next to the M3.

"What happened here, Sergeant?" Randel asked.

"The Krauts, they shot them all. They just mowed 'em down and left them there," said the man. The M3 commander wiped his eyes before replacing his spectacles. "There aren't any weapons. The men were from the 9th Division. They just shot them."

"Are you sure? How do you know they were prisoners?"

"You just have to look at how they are lying. Also we found a survivor. He hid under the bodies and crawled away later. The SS walked among the men shooting them with their submachine guns. First, they set up a machine gun and then closed in. Our survivor was lucky as he has bullet holes in both legs."

"The SS did this?" asked Randel.

"That's what he said."

"The bastards."

Randel and the crews of his platoon pulled their tanks off the road and parked in the forest. He knew they should continue forward but Randel felt he should see this.

"Who has a camera?" he asked.

His men all looked at each other shocked.

"This is a war crime. We need evidence of what happened here. There needs to be photos and we are some of the first Americans here," said Randel.

The men nodded and Sergeant McCoy from Leaping Lizard brought him a Kodak Vigilant Junior. The man took pictures of the field from a variety of different positions. Randel could see the man was pale and shaking by the time he'd finished.

"I count one hundred and two dead, Skipper," said Freddy Spencer.

"Jesus. Why would they do this?" said Randel.

"The SS have a bad reputation. Story is they are worse in Russia. Remember how that British Corporal told us about something that happened in France," said Freddy.

"Yeah, that was the 3rd SS wasn't it?" asked Olaf.

"I think so. They were supposed to have murdered a similar number of soldiers. After Britain signed the peace deal two of the survivors came home and told the army what had happened. They were told to keep their mouths shut, but instead took their story to 'The Daily Express'," said Freddy.

"What happened to the men?" asked Olaf.

"There's a few stories, but the Corporal wasn't sure which one was true. Some thought they immigrated to Canada or Australia. They were thrown out of the army and lost their pensions."

"For speaking out about the murder of their mates. That's so unfair," said Randel. "And now Britain is back fighting the Nazis and those men are probably in the good books."

"What are we going to do about this, Skipper?" said Olaf.

"I'll radio it in and give the pictures to whoever asks for them. Not much else we can do."

"We can shoot every SS man we capture," said Freddy.

Randel didn't answer. For some reason he was uncomfortable with idea.

"Maybe that's what the officer who ordered this wants," he said.

"What do you mean, Skipper?" asked Olaf.

"Well, the SS boys won't give up now will they? They'll expect a bullet in the back of the head. Maybe this was done to make it harder for them to surrender," said Randel.

The big Dane looked thoughtful.

"I don't care. If I get hold of them, that's exactly what will happen," said Freddy. "The rest of their army don't do this."

Randel grimaced. That much was true. The rest of the German Army didn't have the same reputation as the SS, at least not in the west, and there had to be a reason for that. He was sure it happened occasionally, but the stories about the SS now seemed to be proven correct.

The company was directed to turn east earlier than planned. There was heavy fighting to the south along the line of the railway line, and his men, as well as a company of infantry, drove toward the village of Earkring. To the north Randel could see smoke. As they approached the village he saw the lane in that direction was dotted with the wrecks of Shermans.

"Off the road, follow me," he ordered.

The tanks veered south behind a thick line of trees. In front of Randel the land sloped gently upward to a bare ridge.

"What's up Skipper?" radioed Sergeant McCoy from his Sherman.

"There's either one or more powerful anti-tank weapons in the village," he answered. "I'd radio for artillery but they haven't caught up. I could try for an air strike but I haven't seen a target yet."

He crawled up to the tree line and looked through his binoculars. For a while he stared at different patches of trees and scrub, searching for movement or something out of place. He watched for ten minutes and then he saw it.

"Oh no," he said.

Lying next to him in the long grass were two of the sergeants commanding other Shermans.

"What is it, Skipper?" asked McCoy.

"A Tiger at the end of the lane. See that hill in front of us. It is marked as Malt Hill on the map, and behind it is the village we want to take. There's a lane which runs over the ridge to the south. It has the usual hedge and trees running alongside it. The Tiger is hidden right at the end.

"Then it won't be able to see the road into the village," said Sergeant Findlay.

"The Krauts will have something covering it as well. My guess is there's a platoon of Tigers covering the village and they will be watching every angle of approach. One of them has already destroyed at least eight Shermans to the north of the village," he said.

The Tiger platoon was commanded by Hauptsturmführer Zimmermann. It was all that remained of the heavy company of fifteen tanks that operated with the division at this time. Two others had been destroyed and the rest were being repaired due to breakdowns or battle damage. The five vehicles covered the village, along with a company of infantry from the 3rd SS Panzer Grenadier Regiment 'Deutschland'. This unit participated in the initial breakthrough, but then had been held in reserve. It was waiting for the repair workshop in Grantham to return extra heavy panzers to the unit before returning to the front line. Due to the sudden US counterattack the five Tigers had rushed forward to help stop the Americans.

"We need to sneak forward for a better look. I'll talk to the Lieutenant commanding the infantry we have with us, and see if his boys are up for the job. Also, we need the rest of the company here. I'm not taking on a handful of Tigers with one platoon of Shermans," said Randel.

The officer in charge of the thirty men sent two squads forward with instructions not to engage the enemy. In the meantime, Randel poured over the map. He could see that if the unit fell back behind the colliery, his platoon might be able to make its way to the Earkring woods just south of the village. He was sure the Germans would have observers on the hill, so he needed to divert the attention of these men.

"We need to shell the top of the hill. It doesn't need to be accurate, just enough to make the enemy keep their heads down. Smoke would be even better. It would blind them, and with the lack of breeze it should hang around for a while," he said to his tank commanders. Just then the rest of the 2nd Platoon drove up. Quickly, Randel explained the situation to Lieutenant Jefferies.

"I've a couple of half-tracks with me carrying mortars," said the red-headed man.

"Good, they can hit the top of the hill," said Randel.

The other platoon stayed further back as Randel explained his idea. His platoon would circle to the south of town, while the other two from the company would approach from the west. He'd tried to find out which unit was attacking from the north of the village and eventually received a reply. A captain from the 701st Tank Destroyer Battalion answered Randel, but refused to do more than attack the village from long range. He hoped it was enough. This unit would have a dozen or more M10 Tank Destroyers. The 3-inch gun on these vehicles could, perhaps, defeat the armour on a Tiger at close range. Still, Randel didn't blame the Captain for being cautious. Assaulting a village held by enemy tanks was not how the M10 was supposed to be deployed.

The mortars started to drop a mixture of smoke and high-explosive rounds on top of the hill. Randel waited five minutes and led his platoon along a dip in the ground to where the woods started. Then he turned east and tried to find a way through the small forest. It was his intention to sneak up on the Tiger guarding the side of the hill and drive quickly into the town. Hopefully, the Germans would retreat or, with the help of the rest of the company, they'd destroy the enemy heavy armour. Thirty soldiers rode on the five Shermans and Randel hoped this would be enough to protect his platoon from any Germany infantry in the town.

The Earkring Woods weren't held by the enemy. A couple of jeeps had established this earlier. This squad had also marked a logging track which took the Shermans through to the other side. The area was actually a little higher than Mill Hill and gave Randel a good view of the southern part of Earkring. He crawled to the edge of a hedge and watched with his other tank commanders. To the north, shells landed near some of the cottages.

"At least the tank destroyers are doing something," he whispered.

"The Tiger's gone from the hill," said Sergeant McCoy.

"I can't see it. Hopefully it's not watching the south of the village," said Randel. "Alright, there's no cover, but I don't think they know we are here and I'm hopeful they don't have more than a squad guarding the southern approach. We'll charge across the open ground and move into the streets of the village. From there, it will be a game of cat and mouse with the Tigers. Hit them in the side and if you can't, run. I'll have a word with the infantry. They'll need to watch our backs."

Five Shermans drove down the slight incline at thirty miles an hour. They crossed the field in a minute. An MG 42 started firing when they were just over halfway and two men were shot from the side of Randel's tank. Then they were in Earkring. The infantry leapt from the tanks, while Sergeant McCoy's Sherman blasted the machine-gun position. The five Shermans shot at cottages and fired into buildings, as they drove at high speed toward the centre of the village.

"Right we'll split into two groups as planned. The rest of the company are on the way," said Randel over the radio.

McCoy and Randel turned into a paddock, drove through the backyard of a small residential house, then scattered a group of Germans gathered by a Kubelwagen. The bow gunner on McCoy's tank shot two soldiers down and accidently ran over a wounded man. Randel looked away as the German screamed briefly. His own Sherman crashed into the back of the enemy vehicle and drove over the top of it, crushing the German car and grinding it beneath the tank's tracks.

The delay caused Mc Coy to pull ahead. Randel saw the Sherman fire at something at the end of the lane, then the Sherman burst into flames. The burning tank careered through a hedge, before smashing into a cottage and exploding.

A Tiger sat with its turret turned, facing down the lane.

"Freddy, that monster is side on. Hit it!" yelled Randel.

The range was only one hundred yards and the little gunner didn't hesitate. Side armour on a Tiger averages about 60mm whereas the penetration of the Sherman's main gun at this range was roughly 80mm. Freddy hit the Tiger right above the rear drive sprocket. The armour-piercing round punched through and struck the Maybach engine, cracking the engine block and severing fuel lines. A small fire started and smoke began to fill the fighting compartment of the massive tank. Olaf reloaded the gun and Freddy fired again, as the SS crew tried to gather their wits. This round hit the middle of the Tiger and penetrated the crew compartment. It was only partially successful, causing steel to fly from inside the tank and around the interior, wounding some of the crew. This was enough for the men inside and they hastily bailed out. Freddy hadn't finished though. He fired again and the 75mm round slammed into the gap between the turret and the hull, jamming it in place. The mighty 88mm gun could no longer move. Not that it mattered. Its crew were now lying on the ground, on the far side of the vehicle.

Randel halted the tank while they fired three more shells into the Tiger. Smoke was now pouring from the open commander's hatch and it was obvious it was out of the fight.

"We did it, boys," he said.

Any celebrations were cut short by the crack of another 88mm gun. This was followed by an explosion.

"Skipper, Wendel's tank has just been hit," said Sergeant Mcklosky, commander of Wild Wendy.

"Where did it happen?" Randel asked.

"Near the church," said the Sergeant.

Randel ordered the tank forward but was met by a hail of machine-gun fire. A grenade exploded on the rear deck and he saw German infantry trying to hide behind the Sherman.

"Into the field and then across to the main road," he ordered.

The tank accelerated quickly, throwing up mud and dirt as it crossed the open area, before crashing through a hedge and emerging near the Wendel's burning Sherman. An American machine-gun crew was firing at the church and Randel took the risk of opening his hatch and yelling down to them.

"Where are the Tigers?"

"There's one without a track just to the north of here, between two houses. The Krauts have abandoned it. Another three just left town to the east, sir. It looks like the Germans are leaving."

From the west and north the Americans advanced into the village. Two SS companies tried to disengage, but one platoon was trapped in the church and the priest's residence. After three Shermans sat back and fired a dozen HE rounds into the building, the SS men came forward with their hands in the air. They wore the distinctive camouflage patterned jackets and helmets, with lightning flashes on their collars. Some of the enemy were wounded, while others had soot-covered faces.

The Americans roughly pushed the SS men toward a red brick wall across from the church. One of the US soldiers lifted his rifle and shot one of the prisoners in the head. Then a Corporal lifted his Thompson machine gun and gunned down two men, who were assisting a third, wounded comrade. Randel saw it all. A Lieutenant stood by and did nothing as other men cocked their weapons. A young SS man started praying, while an older soldier yelled in German.

Randel jumped from the back of his tank and fired his pistol in the air.

"You men stand down," he ordered.

The American infantry turned and stared at him.

"This isn't going to happen," he said.

"Sir, these bastards murdered our boys," said one of the men.

"Do you know that? The SS did, but was it these men? Anyway, this is why we are fighting them. I'm not in this war to turn into my enemy. There will be an investigation and maybe some of these prisoners have information on what happened to our boys. We don't murder prisoners! We aren't like them!"

The SS men stayed against the wall. One of them was still praying. The rest just looked at the angry Americans.

"Do any of you speak English?" Randel asked.

"A little," said a young man with a bloody bandage around his wrist.

"You are to stay with my tank until I can hand you over to our military police. These men would like to kill you for what happened in the forest."

The man nodded. "We weren't there, but we heard," said the blond soldier.

"Good, you will need to answer questions about the massacre."

The German nodded but then another voice yelled out. "Tell them nothing Steiner."

Randel pushed forward and found an older man lying against the wall with his hand clutching a bloody wound on his shoulder. He wore an Iron Cross and appeared to be an officer.

"It would be in your interest if you cooperated," said Randel. "I'm not asking for military information. We just want to know who killed those men."

The man smiled but the expression held no warmth. "Your degenerate people cannot win," said the officer in accented English. "You are too weak. You are a mongrel race ruled by the Jews. In the end we will destroy you."

Freddy Spencer had walked up next to him. The little gunner held his strange submachine gun over his shoulder. Randel looked at the gunner and sighed. Freddy brought the gun around and fired a quick burst. The SS officer jerked and then slumped sideways.

"Sorry sir, but that one had it coming," said Freddy.

"I don't want to kill them. That's an order," said Randel.

The little gunner frowned, then nodded.

"These aren't your men," said the lieutenant.

"You stood by and were going to let these *soldiers* commit murder," said Randel spinning toward the man.

"The boys are feelin' a might angry," said the dark-haired officer in a southern drawl. "And they're my unit."

"Well, I'm taking the Germans into *my* custody and if there's any more killing of prisoners, I'll make a report."

The dark-haired man stared at him for a moment, then spat on the grass. "Alright boys, let's move out," he said.

The American infantry walked away muttering, leaving Randel with forty prisoners. Freddy kept his gun on them while Randel watched the soldiers go. Then he turned.

"And what the hell am I supposed to do with you lot?" he muttered.

Chapter Eleven: June 1943

The offensive in England had taken little ground and the casualties had been heavy. To begin with it had gone well, but the American counteroffensive had thrown Model's assault back. Reichsmarschall Kesselring looked at the losses his Luftwaffe units had suffered and shook his head. Even worse, with the coming offensive in the east, he couldn't rebuild the shattered gruppen. The Reich had to take Moscow this summer or it would never happen. Russia was growing stronger. It was Kesselring's opinion that the Soviet Union had been teetering on the edge of collapse over winter and perhaps into early spring. American food supplies had kept Russia going.

There was no doubt the crisis that Germany's enemy had suffered would have slowed weapons' production and inhibited the growth of the Soviet Army. It would also mean that America would mainly send food and not weapons or trucks to Russia. This would continue to be the case, as long as Germany held the Soviet Union's grain growing areas. The attack on Moscow was hoped to take the capital and probably advance as far as Vladimir, another one hundred and twenty kilometres further east. At the moment the Heer was two hundred and twenty kilometres from Moscow. The winter offensive by the Soviets had pushed the Heer back another thirty kilometres. Kesselring couldn't see the German Army advancing more than three hundred kilometres. He would be happy if they managed to take the capital city and hold it. Moscow was a hub for rail transport and its fall would massively disrupt Russian communication. The loss of the city would also be a huge blow to the enemy's morale.

The Luftwaffe was gathering as many planes and all the supplies it could shift to the battlefront. Oil was still a problem, but an increase in synth fuel meant that fifty-seven percent of Germany's fuel came from coal to oil plants, and that figure was even higher for the Luftwaffe. The Russian fields only added nine percent to the Reich's overall total. Reich minister Todt and Reich Minister Speer had informed him that they doubted they could increase the supply of fuel by more than another couple of percentage points. The two men warned that if the Allies ever started to bomb fuel production facilities or oilfields, then production would probably drop, not increase. So far that hadn't happened. Indeed, the lull in the east had allowed for a small reserve to have been created behind the lines.

The situation in England wasn't good. Supplies were low after the failed offensive and reinforcements would be slow to arrive. Over a hundred and fifty panzers were lost permanently. Thousands of men had been killed or wounded and in the end the line was back where it had started. None of the objectives had been taken and even the much vaunted Tiger units had taken heavy losses. Surprisingly, the Führer wasn't troubled by the failed attack. He believed the Americans had also taken severe casualties (and indeed they had), and bleeding the US Army would weaken their resolve to fight. He thought the Americans lacked the will to accept heavy losses. The Führer told anyone who would listen, that in the end they'd come to the negotiating table, especially if more of their soldiers died in battle. Kesselring wasn't so sure.

He wondered how the offensive would have gone if Rommel had been in charge. The man was a great tactician, most of the time, though his temperament was questionable. Many of his subordinates hated working with him and he was known to have a quick temper. Still, he had the knack of knowing how to crack a frontline, and advance quickly and decisively. Maybe he was being unfair. From his information it seemed as though the enemy general, someone called Patton, had organised a quick response to General Model's offensive and unleashed his armour at just the right time.

The Luftwaffe struggled to support the attack and the army blamed the air force for its failure. On the first day the bomber and fighters had mounted just over one thousand sorties. They had been met by a wall of enemy-fighter aircraft of all types. P-40s, P-38s, Canadian Spitfires IXs, Corsairs and new P-47s fought Ju 88s, Fw 190s and Bf 109s across the Midlands from Liverpool to Hull, and Birmingham to Peterborough. Air combat raged for the five days of the offensive. Luftwaffe bases were repeatedly attacked and by the third day German fighter units were on the defensive. Bomber attacks switched to only occurring after dark, due to the strong enemy defences. The Luftwaffe ended up losing one hundred and fifty-five aircraft, and the Italians had another twenty-eight destroyed. Over four hundred enemy planes had been claimed shot down by Flak and fighters, but Kesselring suspected this was an exaggeration. Actual allied losses amounted to two hundred and twenty planes.

Most of the German bomber units, or what was left of them, had been moved to the south coast of England. The fighter gruppen were dispersed and ordered to conserve their strength. Many staffel now flew from small, camouflaged airfields that were heavily defended by light Flak guns. The only replacements Kesselring had managed to get to these units was thirty Fw 190 A5s and twelve Bf 109 G6s. These he pulled from training schools. He also sent replacement parts which allowed another fourteen fighters to be rebuilt.

At least at sea the Luftwaffe had experienced some success. Flying from Land's End near the very tip of Cornwell, four Ju 290s equipped with the new Fritz X flying bomb had found a troop convoy heading for Liverpool. The allied navy had cleared the sea of U-boats and many convoys travelled with escort carriers. This one didn't, and three of the guided bombs struck. The USS light cruiser Nashville was hit between its two funnels and a twenty foot hole was blown in the bottom of the ship. With great difficulty the damaged vessel limped into Belfast. A tanker was also sunk, but the real success was the destruction of the HMT Rohna which sank quickly after being hit on the port side, near the after end of her engine room. This vessel was a troop transport. Three hundred and twenty men were rescued. Strong winds were blowing making any attempt at picking up survivors difficult. Then night fell, making the task even harder. One thousand five hundred and fifty-two men died, making it the largest single loss at sea so far for the Allies.

All of the news coming from the Pacific was worrying as well. The Japanese were in retreat, though there were indications that they were about to take the battle to the enemy. Long-range bombing attacks from Midway on Hawaii were costing Germany's ally dearly, but it seemed their carrier fleet was ready to renter the battle. Information from the Japanese embassy pointed toward an attempt at fighting the American carriers before too many were built. At the moment, intelligence had the Americans with three heavy carriers and two light carriers. To this could be added a Commonwealth heavy carrier and one light one. The intelligence estimates were close - one of the heavy US carriers had damaged itself on a reef and the HMAS Tasman, the Commonwealth heavy carrier, was still being repaired. If the Japanese brought the enemy to battle soon with their two heavy and single light carrier, then they'd have a chance, especially if the Allies split their forces.

For the moment, all fronts remained quiet. Kesselring was glad of this but he thought the attack on Moscow should be launched as soon as possible. The enemy would expect an assault, and hiding so many panzers and planes was difficult. He believed the Soviet Army would be waiting for them. It would be wise not to let them build up their defences. Still, the Führer wanted to get the new Panthers to the front to participate in the battle. The development of these new panzers had been rushed and Kesselring hoped the wait would be worth it.

Chapter Twelve: July 1943

Last month had been gloriously quiet. There was more food, plenty of vodka, and many nights lying under the stars with Sergei. Even when the 1382nd Regiment of the 87th Rifle Division moved into the lines to the west of the town of Tula, there was still little action. They were only twenty-five kilometres from the town. The area had already seen battle over the previous two years. From Junior Sergeant Roza Shanina's trench she could see a wrecked Panzer III, two destroyed Russian armoured cars, and the mangled remains of an aircraft she couldn't identify.

Her relationship with the Lieutenant was something Roza relished. She was careful not to treat him as anything but an officer when around other soldiers, but in private it was a different matter. They never spoke about what they might do after the war and Roza treasured every moment they had together. Sergei was a caring man and much loved by his troops. He wasn't a natural soldier and relied on his sergeants for tactical suggestions, often including her.

At the moment the Germans trenches were almost a kilometre a way. The area was mostly flat with only the slightest rise or dip breaking up the countryside. There was a small patch of forest to the east. Otherwise, the area was covered in fields of wheat, many of which were bordered by lines of alder or elm trees. The village of Lukino, or what was left of it, lay two kilometres to the northwest with the German lines cutting through the land to the south. Roza could see it was great tank country with few rivers or other barriers to slow a force of panzers. About twenty kilometres further north there was a thick band of forest that ran for over one hundred kilometres. It started just east of Tula and snaked across Russia, all the way to the Oka River.

The regiment had marched through this forest to reach the front line. Roza noticed the fortifications among the trees. There were both log and concrete bunkers, as well as extensive minefields. Indeed, the countryside between the woods and the frontline was crisscrossed with barbed wire and trenches. There were hidden anti-tank guns everywhere and the area was pockmarked with bunkers of different sizes. Roza couldn't remember seeing anywhere in Russia that had been so heavily fortified.

The Germans were up to something. All of the signs were they would attack here soon, and the preparations by the Soviet Army indicated they knew the Nazis would attack toward Tula. Roza knew the large town stood on the road to Moscow. The previous winter's offensives that had followed the German defeat on the Volga had recaptured Rzhev and Vyazma. The attacks to the west of Tula had been less successful. In the end the Russian Army had exhausted itself, but now the closest Nazi positions were one hundred and eighty kilometres from the capital. In this area, the line was just over two hundred kilometres from Moscow.

"Are they making tea?" asked Nadia as Roza crept toward her friend's observation point. The camouflaged position was reached via a short communication trench. Nadia was observing the Nazi lines through a simple trench periscope. Next to her was a small notebook in which she wrote her observations.

"They just started. It should be ready by the time you finish here," said Roza.

It was almost dawn and first light was creeping into the sky. There were no clouds and only a light breeze ruffled her friend's dark hair.

The whistle of the approaching shells overhead took them both by surprise. Roza huddled next to Nadia. She knew that if you could hear shells, they weren't going to land on top of you. The scream of the Nebelwerfer rockets however, sent them diving to the bottom of the trench. The earth shook around them and the shock waves permeated the ground. Roza felt the pressure waves buffet her and kept her mouth open so her eardrums wouldn't rupture. Behind her the trench collapsed, forcing her and Nadia to crawl to a new location.

She could see the fear in her friend's eyes. They clung to each other while the rockets tore the world apart. Over the impact they could hear the screaming and yelling of Russian troops. Dust made it difficult to breathe and dirt matted their hair and uniforms. Roza clutched at Nadia and both of them buried their heads in each other's shoulders. Her friend was muttering under her breath and it took Roza a while to work out Nadia was reciting a prayer. Religion was frowned upon in the Soviet Union, however Nadia recalled it from her childhood as her grandmother used to whisper it softly to her at bedtime.

They clung to each other until the rockets stopped falling. The explosions also ceased but Roza could still hear the screaming of the wounded. She grabbed Nadia.

'We are too exposed here. The Germans will attack soon and we must be with the company," she said.

Nadia appeared stunned, and Roza needed to shake her slightly.

"Yes, yes," her friend said.

The two of them stumbled into the main trench, after clambering over shattered positions and destroyed anti-tank guns until they found Sergei and a few other men yelling instructions. Roza felt a surge of relief that the young officer was still alive.

"Where's Anna?" she yelled out.

Sergei turned and frowned. With some effort he resisted a rebuke at her disrespect for military protocol in front of others. "She was wounded, Comrade Sergeant. I don't know how badly. The stretcher bearers took her to an aid station. Hopefully she'll be alright," he said.

"I'm sorry, Comrade Lieutenant. Where would you like me to position myself?" she said, acknowledging her slip.

His lip curled in a slight smile. "You know best, I trust your judgement," he said. She would always remember him like that.

A blinding flash of an explosion lifted him and the soldier standing next to him off their feet, sending everyone diving for cover. When Roza looked, all she could see of Sergei was a bloody body. She tried to crawl in his direction but heavy mortar shells were dropping all around them. 120mm rounds were landing along the trench line, with many dropping near strong points. It was obvious that the enemy had pinpointed many of the Russian positions, including the position of the company headquarters. Roza almost screamed. Sergei was dead. Their commander was dead. A senior sergeant looked around and realised he was now probably in command.

"Get to your trenches. Junior Sergeant, take your spotter and try and pick off the Nazi commanders. The enemy will be on their way," he yelled.

It took Roza a moment to realize he was speaking to her. She wiped her face and stood, her knees shaking. "Yes, Senior Sergeant,' she said.

Wiping the tears from her face, she pulled Nadia to her feet. The two of them stumbled along until Roza found a shell crater at the edge of the trench. The explosion had made a small gap in the planks, so she slipped into the gap and found rubble and a ripped tarp to camouflage her new position. Mortar rounds were still falling but the rate of explosions had decreased. Smoke and dust drifted across the battlefield.

"Nadia, take a spot near the wrecked bunker. It looks like there's plenty of cover," she said woodenly.

Her friend stood in the middle of the trench, her face wet. She sobbed silently and stared into space. Roza went to her.

"We need to fight. The Nazis are coming and we must defend Russia," she said.

"Are we going to die?" Nadia asked.

Roza hesitated. "I don't know," she whispered. "But we must try to save our country. We know what the Nazis will do to it if they win."

"I'm so tired. Sometimes I wish this would all end and I could go back to Rostov and find my family."

"Maybe you will, but today we have to kill Nazis."

Nadia nodded and walked slowly to the shattered bunker.

The sound of tank tracks were clear. Roza couldn't see the squat armoured vehicles at first, but soon they emerged from the dust and smoke. Tanks with short barrels moved forward, next to giant vehicles with guns like telegraph poles. Panzer IIIs churned through the low wheat next to Tiger Tanks and half-tracks. Men in spotted camouflage uniforms trotted towards the Russian trenches carrying machine guns or rifles.

It was the Soviet 89th Rifle Division's misfortune that day to be directly in front of the main assault from the 1st SS Panzer Division. Twelve Tigers led sixteen Panzer IIIs and dozens of Panzer IVs. The enemy were driving toward the road junction a few kilometres north of Lukino. From here, the German thrust was to continue along the main road to Tula. To the west of the Leibstandarte Division, the Grossdeutschland Division assaulted the Russian lines. To the east, the new Herman Goering Panzer Division with its Wolfe tanks attacked. Though this unit was well trained, this was its first taste of battle and it struggled to penetrate the front line. Bringing its Tiger tanks out of reserve, it broke through in the evening and the fast moving Wolfe panzers from the Skoda works in Czechoslovakia quickly reached Rzhavo.

Roza stared at the advancing panzers and tried to pick a target. When the Soviet anti-tank guns began to fire and a Panzer III caught fire, she felt a moment's relief. Then she watched as a shell glanced from the front of the massive German Tiger tank. Twice more the tank was hit, but the heavy panzer shrugged off the blows. Coming to a halt, its giant gun turned and fired. The flat, heavy crack of the 88mm drowned out all other noise. One of the 76mm anti-tank guns disintegrated, its Russian crew tossed into the air. The German tanks continued forward. One hit a mine and lost a track in what was left of the minefield, but many of the explosive devices had been disabled by the enemy bombardment.

A Nazi commander popped his head out of his turret, then disappeared before Roza could shoot him. She looked and saw the advancing infantry was only a few hundred metres away. A man carrying an MG 42 trotted next to another man, carrying boxes of ammunition. Roza shot the soldier in the chest and he toppled to the ground.

"Enemy officer, six hundred metres, standing near the panzer with the broken track. He is peering through binoculars," yelled Nadia.

Roza ran her telescopic sights across the battlefield and found the man. “Got him,” she replied.

Her shot hit the officer in the shoulder, making her curse. She didn’t like the SVT-40, finding it less accurate than her old bolt-action Mosin Nagant. She picked out another man carrying a submachine gun. She’d heard the German squad leaders carried MP 40s. This time her bullet hit the man in the chest, wounding him critically. Bullets threw up dirt around her position and she slid back into the trench. The enemy was only a couple of hundred paces away and had probably spotted her location. Nadia started firing her own automatic rifle at the Germans. A German half-track sprayed her friend with machine-gun fire. Roza heard a grunt of pain and started running along the trench to where Nadia lay. She was calling her friend’s name and trying to ignore the pounding of her heart. Bullets were ripping up the sandbags along the top of the trench as she crawled up next to Nadia.

Grabbing her friend’s leg, she pulled. Nadia rolled over and landed on her feet. Her eyes were open and staring. Above the bridge of her nose was a red hole. Through her tears Roza saw that most of the back of her friend's head was missing. She staggered and fell to her knees. Around her, parts of the trench blew apart as German shells killed her comrades. The enemy were now only a hundred metres from the Russian positions. Tanks fired their main guns at Soviet bunkers or machine gun nests. In the wheat field, at least half a dozen German panzers smouldered or burned. A whistle blew three times, signalling that the battalion should fall back. Russian soldiers began to run. The Germans surged across the trench and broke through the second and third line of defences. Roza struggled to understand the mayhem. Around her vehicles caught fire and soldiers died. Explosions kicked up so much dust it became difficult to breathe. Roza thought she had died and was in hell. A T-34 with flames pouring from the turret drove past her. Somehow the tank was still going even though its crew had long since perished. Bullets whizzed by and anti-tank guns fired at the enemy. The noise, the smell, and the likelihood of her death, threatened to destroy Roza's sanity. At some point she lost her rifle, but had enough presence of mind to pick up a submachine gun.

Eventually, toward the late afternoon, Roza pulled herself onto a truck that was fleeing the area. With twenty other men she travelled to Rvy, over eighteen kilometres from the front line. Here, the truck ran out of fuel and everyone dispersed into the village. Roza was exhausted and thirsty. She managed to get some water to drink from the local well, finishing what remained in the bucket by pouring it over her head. Then she ate a crust of bread and a hard piece of cheese before curling up next to the road and falling asleep.

Upon waking up in the morning, she tried to decide what to do. Her shock at losing two of the most important people in her life was profound. Anna might be dead as well, there was no way of knowing. She also felt ashamed. Roza knew she'd fled the battle. Many others had as well, but that didn't make it right. The power of the Nazi assault had destroyed her company and probably her battalion. She needed to avenge her friends and continue the fight to protect her country. Nothing else mattered. Finding herself a bolt-action rifle, Roza boarded a supply truck heading toward the front. Jumping in the back, she sat among bags of flour and crates of ammunition. In the distance she could see smoke. A low rumble of guns reached her ears. Roza dreaded going back to that hell and at one point she almost leaped from the truck. Shutting down part of herself, she decided that from now on her main goal would be to serve her country. Nothing else would distract her. Roza moved toward the sound of the guns.

V

Giant ships cut through the Pacific Ocean. From Commander Southerland's position high in the superstructure, he could see both the Essex and the smaller vessel, the Independence. Somewhere to the south, the HMAS Melbourne cruised through the sea.

Southerland hadn't seen so many allied carriers together before. Nearby, probably seventy to eighty miles away, sailed a second fleet. This one was made up of transports carrying Australian and American troops. Recently, the Commonwealth had taken back Thursday Island. This campaign took the Japanese by surprise and though the garrison fought fiercely, there had been little in the way of naval or air interference. The Japanese Army tried to attack the landing fleet but it only had about eighty serviceable planes. These were overwhelmed by the aircraft on the supporting carriers.

Southerland hadn't flown during those operations. His shoulder needed time to recover, so he'd been confined to a supporting role. Now, finally, the medical staff believed he was fit to fly a Wildcat.

Taking Thursday Island back from the enemy had been necessary, but it did indicate where the focus of the next landing would be. The allied fleet was sailing for Port Moresby. Reconnaissance flights showed that the Japanese had recently reinforced the area, so the 51st Infantry Division were moved there. Naval guns had been placed in dug-in positions near the harbour, and the 5th Naval Landing Unit were designated as a counterattack force. The one thousand men of this formation were supported by a dozen tanks.

The Japanese Navy decided it would take a stand in the area, so they surged planes and personnel to Buna on the northern coast. The enemy High Command realised it was time to halt the Allies before their material strength became overwhelming. They needed another victory to buy more time and build up their own forces. Over one hundred Japanese naval aircraft waited for the order to fly to Port Moresby, to strike at any invasion force.

At the same time, the Imperial Japanese Navy (IJN) had three carriers on standby ready to strike at any allied fleet that dared approach the coast of New Guinea. The Kaga and Zuikaku were the only heavy carriers available, and they were supported by the lighter Ryujo. This gave the IJN a strength of one hundred and ninety planes, plus those that would be rushed into Port Moresby.

The Allies also had support from aircraft that were land based. Lightning P-38s and B-25 Mitchells were operating from Thursday Island, and the carrier fleet had two hundred and forty planes at its disposal. The 90th Bombardment group armed with the latest B-25s also stood ready. These planes started as medium bombers but had now transitioned to gunships. The crews that flew them were trained to attack enemy shipping at very low level. They also strafed their targets with as many as eight .50 caliber Browning machine guns mounted in the nose. Later, a 75mm gun would be fitted. The RAAF also moved two squadrons of Corsairs to Thursday Island.

As soon as the allied fleet sailed north from Brisbane, the Japanese started to move aircraft to Port Moresby. Their long range float planes spotted the fleet when it was about four hundred miles east of Townsville. Zeros, Val dive bombers and Kate torpedo planes then flew to the Kila Kila airstrip near Moresby. US reconnaissance aircraft picked up the move and attacked immediately. A furious air battle occurred, in which the Allies lost twenty-two machines, and the Japanese twenty. More importantly, facilities at the landing ground were heavily damaged, making it difficult for the enemy to use the area.

Japanese carriers immediately moved south, passing around the chain of reefs that ended at Rossel Island, the eastern tip of New Guinea. Here the enemy fleet was spotted by the Gato class submarine, the USS Harder. By this time, Japanese land-based airpower had been defeated and the landings around Port Moresby were already taking place. The enemy attacks on the US and Commonwealth fleet had only managed to damage a light cruiser and sink a transport vessel carrying food and medical supplies. There had been some losses among the defending US and Australian fighters, but not many.

Southerland missed out on the action, but his friend 'Swede' Vejtasa had shot down another four aircraft, taking his overall score to twenty-eight, well above Southerland's score of twelve. Finally, he was ready to fight again and hopefully today would be the day. He'd already flown three patrols and his shoulder was fine. There was no way of knowing how it would stand up to combat, but there was only one way of finding out.

With the death of General MacArthur, General Walter Krueger was given the command of all US forces in Australia. MacArthur and his family had been killed when PT-41 was destroyed by a Japanese cruiser on March 12th while fleeing the Philippines. The new general had proven to be both intelligent and diplomatic. He managed to soothe Commonwealth fears of being sidelined from the Pacific war, while setting reasonable objectives with sensible timelines. The invasion of Papua New Guinea was however the biggest risk he had taken.

The Second Battle of the Coral Sea started the following day. Both fleets discovered the location of the other early in the day and sent air groups out to hit the enemy fleet. The actual battle zone was about one hundred miles south of Milne Bay, and the two fleets never managed to get closer than one hundred and fifty miles from the other.

Southerland led his flight of Wildcats as they flew above the Avenger torpedo planes. Off to the south, Japanese naval aircraft travelled in the opposite direction. When the enemy attack force reached the allied fleet, they found it protected by forty Wildcats and twelves P-38s. Squadrons from Thursday Island were taking turns at reinforcing the Combat Air Patrols (CAP) over the allied fleet. Unfortunately, the P-38s were almost about to depart. They stayed and fought, before most ditched next to US ships after the battle. Three crash-landed on carriers after all of the navy aircraft had been retrieved.

The Combat Air Patrol fought off the enemy attack. The Vals managed to mount attacks against the HMAS Melbourne, hitting the light Commonwealth carrier twice. Fires started in the Pri-fly. Smoke poured from the tower area as men tried to douse the flames. A single torpedo struck the USS Independence, allowing water to flood parts of the machine space. Pumps mainly kept up with the flooding, but the ship developed a slight tilt to starboard. The Japanese strike force was decimated. The second attack wouldn't achieve any results except a hit on the battleship South Dakota with a single bomb, which knocked out A turret.

Southerland saw the Zeros at three o'clock low.

"All fighters, protect the attack aircraft. Reaper Squadron, intercept the Zeros below. VF-9 hold your position," ordered Commander Vejtasa.

Southerland dived toward the Zeros, that were trying to break through to the Avengers. The heavy fighter quickly built up speed and was soon only four hundred yards from the last of the enemy fighters. Suddenly, the Zero attempted a turn to the left. The problem with Zeros was that when they were flying at high speeds, they became hard to maneuver. The pilot had seen Southerland's flight and panicked. Southerland didn't have to allow a lot of deflection on his burst. He aimed slightly ahead of the Zero and it flew straight through the cone of heavy machine-gun fire. The enemy fighter blew up immediately when its fuel tank was ruptured.

Another group of Zeros came straight at Southerland's flight, and soon fighters were twisting and turning all over the sky. There was a slight twinge in his shoulder but he ignored it as a Zero flashed by. Ensign Davis stayed with Southerland as he kept the

Japanese fighters away from the bombers. A few managed to break through and the Dauntless dive bombers took heavy losses. However, today was the day of the Avenger. The torpedo planes managed to attack, virtually unscathed. These aircraft obtained twelve hits, five of them on the Hiryu and four on the Ryujo. Both these carriers sunk quickly. Other torpedoes struck the fast battleship Kongo and the heavy cruiser Nachi. Two bombs also hit the battleship, causing it catch fire. A second strike later finished it off. This raid would also cripple the Zuikaku.

Southerland landed back on the Enterprise with two more kills. His shoulder ached and he realised he probably shouldn't fly for a while. The US and Commonwealth fleet had both of its light carriers damaged, but they were repairable. All three enemy carriers had been sunk. The Japanese plan to support their ships from Port Moresby had been undone by allied land-based air power. The enemy was overwhelmed by more experienced American and Australian pilots, as well as a greater number of machines. The Japanese carrier fleet had been knocked out of the war for the next twelve months.

On land, the invasion came ashore near Kila Kila and the beaches around Joyce Bay. The airfield was taken and the nearby hills assaulted. Casualties were very heavy, with the enemy fighting until every last soldier was killed. Sentinel tanks armed with short twenty-five pounder guns blasted the Japanese from their bunkers. These vehicles then thwarted a counterattack by Type 97 Chi-Ha medium tanks. The low velocity 57mm guns on the Japanese vehicles couldn't penetrate the Australian armour, and soon twenty of the enemy tanks had been knocked out. Port Moresby fell a week later.

V

The Sherman tank eased forward toward the hedge. Overhead, the sun bleached the English countryside light green. Lieutenant Randel surveyed the area from his open cupola. To the southeast he could hear the distant rumble of guns. The 2nd Armoured Division had been in reserve until yesterday. An offensive by the Canadians and British had thrown back the Italian 8th Army. In the space of three days the spearhead of the assault had advanced to Ely in the county of Cambridgeshire. Fifty miles had been covered in that time. Attacking alongside the Commonwealth divisions was the US II corps, made up of the 1st US Armoured Division and the 1st US Infantry Division. These two formations had taken Cambridge unopposed. To the south of the city they had been stopped by Italian 90mm guns operating in an anti-tank role, and by fierce counterattacks from newly arrived P26/40 tanks. Forty of these slammed into the 1st US Infantry Division with a brigade of fresh infantry. These attacks were supported by three batteries of 100mm guns, which was enough to stop the advance of the Americans.

The Germans hadn't been idle. They gathered two panzer divisions and the 2nd SS Division, and struck the long allied flank which ran from Nottingham to Cambridge. General Patton had been waiting for this. He'd kept the 2nd Armoured and 9th Infantry Divisions ready to meet these units. The arrival of the 3rd US

Armoured Division substantially increased the strength of the forces waiting for the Germans.

On the high ground to the west of Kettering, the Germans gathered. Near the ancient Civil War battleground of Naseby the 22nd Panzer Division attacked toward Kelmarsh, while the 2nd SS Division advanced northwest from Holcot. The 23rd Panzer Division was trying its luck further north, where it crashed into the nearly arrived 3rd US Armoured Division.

The hills and woods around Kelmarsh ran almost north-south, with a spur of land running west. None of these hills or ridges were very steep or high, but they did allow well-placed American observers to survey the surrounding countryside. Lieutenant Randal's company, however, were refuelling in the woodlands, around the tiny village. CCA was spread along woodlands called the Dales. M3 Gun Motor Carriages were also sitting near the top of a ridge, which was covered in trees. His own platoon had just finished topping up their tanks and had driven to a position overlooking the fields to the west of the River Ise. The waterway wasn't much more than a brook at this point, and he'd jumped across it to pace out the distance to the nearest farm track.

The low valley to the northwest was wide and open, with the nearest cover being about a mile away. Randel spotted the armoured cars first. These eight-wheeled vehicles travelled with two half-tracks. There were only six German armoured cars and they stopped frequently. In the distance Randel thought he could see tanks, but it was hard to tell. He raced back to his tank, but before he arrived the 75mm guns on the M3s had opened fire. Two of his own tanks also joined in.

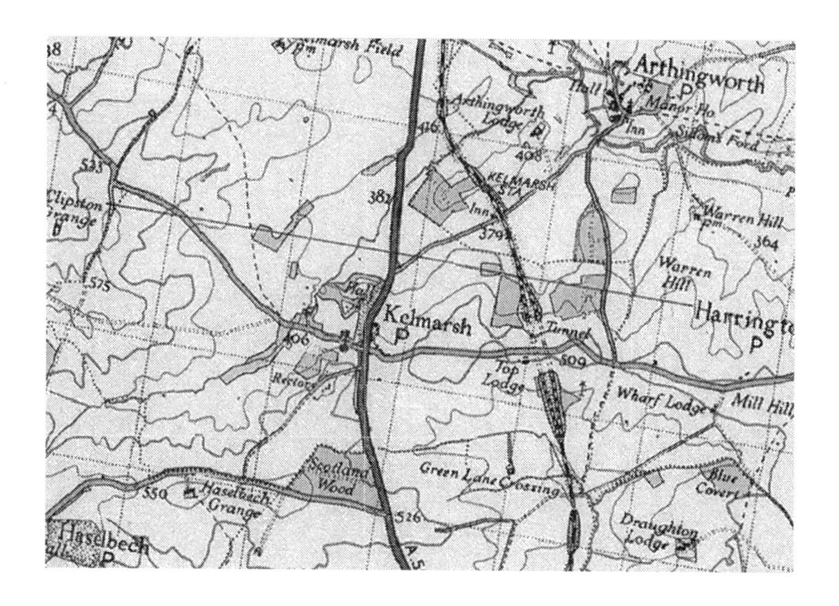

Randel's fight near Scotland Wood

A German armoured car was hit, catching fire. The rest of the enemy reconnaissance group sped away after picking up a crew member from the destroyed vehicle. Randel thought his side should have waited longer before opening fire. They could have easily blown up more of the Germans.

Artillery rounds started dropping on the village and woodlands. Randel was already inside his Sherman and moving south to a location known as Scotland Hill. Enemy armour had also been spotted travelling along the Naseby Road and if it wasn't stopped, it could flank CCA's position in the village. Here, Greyhound armoured cars had retreated from the village of Haselbech, reporting that they'd seen a column of enemy armour moving east. The shells from 105mm guns landed around them as they travelled, but did little damage. Only a direct hit would stop his Sherman.

"Those boys in the M3s will be suffering," said Olaf from his position in the loader's seat.

"Yep, they're open topped and those tree bursts will rain shell splinters down on them," said Freddy Spencer, the gunner.

Randel knew his crew were right. Enemy artillery was working the village over, and there would be American casualties. He put it out of his mind. There was nothing he could do to help. It was up to the US artillery to respond, something that wouldn't happen until the heavy guns arrived.

As they drove along Crowthorne Road toward their new position at Scotland Woods, Randel looked out of his cupola. Strung out behind him were the other four tanks of his platoon. To the east he could see the wooded hill. He would follow this road a little further south before turning in that direction. Looking west he could see across a shallow green valley toward another low ridge, over a mile and a half away. Small black shapes crawled out of the valley toward him.

"All tanks, German armour cross the river to the west," he yelled into his radio.

There were at least twenty panzers coming their way.

"Face the enemy and slowly back toward the woodlands," he ordered.

The Panzer IIIs and IVs advanced quickly. Mixed in with them were at least a similar number of half-tracks. He sent a warning to the headquarters of Combat Command A, then said a short prayer.

"All tanks open fire when ready," he said into his microphone.

Freddy Spencer fired his first shot but missed. The rest of the platoon now faced the enemy and were shooting as well. The Shermans slowly backed up the slight incline toward the forest. Armour-piercing shells skipped off the ground around them. Randel stayed in his cupola. The visibility was better with his head above the hatch and the enemy weren't firing machine guns at them. A clang shook the Sherman and a 50mm round bounced from the tank's armour. The Panzer III's gun couldn't penetrate the front of his tank at this range. Two enemy tanks had been hit so far, one of which was burning. His platoon still had four hundred yards to reverse before they might be safe.

Big Bertha lost a track. As its crew bailed out, a 75mm round from a Panzer IV hit the turret and set the ammunition on fire. Randel wasn't sure if his platoon would make it. He radioed for help but everyone was too far away. Suddenly, a group of tank destroyers contacted him.

"1st platoon B Company, this is Captain Hartman. We are almost at your position. We will be pulling around the southern edge of the woods in a minute," said a voice over the radio.

Randel acknowledged, but he wasn't sure if they had that long. Another Sherman was hit, its crew abandoning the tank as smoke poured from the hatches. Freddy grunted in satisfaction as one of his rounds tore through the frontal armour of a Panzer III. Then the M10s arrived. There were only five of them, and they drove forward to a low hedge and started firing. The 76mm guns immediately destroyed three enemy panzers. Randel now believed his men had a chance. They continued to fall back slowly, losing another vehicle. An M10 also caught fire after being hit in the hull. However, the Germans hesitated. They had lost ten panzers and a half-track. Almost half of their force had been disabled.

Smoke rounds started to explode around the M10s and Shermans. Randel wasn't sure what was happening. He continued to retreat into the woodlands, where his platoon was joined by the surviving tank destroyers. Peering through the artificial white fog his men waited and watched. Eventually the smoke cleared and the enemy were gone. All that remained were the smouldering hulks of destroyed tanks. Randel let out a sigh. Somehow they'd managed to stay alive, yet he knew this battle had just begun.

V

The plane was huge. As it gained speed Major Lang wasn't sure if it could take off. His battalion had been ordered to Crete and was being transported to the island in Ju 252 and Me 323 transport aircraft. Other units were supposed to be travelling to the island by sea. This was all in response to the allied landings, which had taken place overnight and during the morning. His battalion had been hurriedly shoved onto aircraft and sent south. They hadn't even had time to load most of their equipment.

He glanced out the window and saw Bf 109Gs circling protectively above the transports. Getting up from his seat he walked down to the radio operator.

"Is the set alright, Steiner?" he asked.

A tall man glanced up at him. "It will be, sir. I managed to grab a few spares before we were put on the trucks."

"Well done. Keep me informed," said Lang.

Hauptmann Scholler was examining an FG 42 automatic rifle.

"Will it work?" he asked his second in command.

"Yes sir, though we were only supposed be testing the new gun. It should be fine, though its action is far from perfect. The paratroopers who are being flown over also have them. They are loud but will provide extra firepower," said Scholler.

"What about our anti-tank capability?"

“We have two RPzB 43s. We call them Puppchen. It’s all we managed to grab before they put us on the planes. Sir, this is all very rushed.”

“I know. I think we managed to load a few mortars but I don’t know if we grabbed any ammunition for them. Hopefully we will get some from the depots on Crete. I received some vague promises of transport when we arrive. It seems the Allies landed in strength at Heraklion. As you know, the Italians hold that end of the island. American paratroopers have been reported as landing at the airfield.”

“Sir, why didn’t we see this coming?”

“I command a battalion, so how would I know. I heard that during this last two weeks there has been a surge of allied air activity. There have been raids on Malta, Sicily, and Rhodes. Then about seven days ago the enemy started to hit Crete.”

"They sent a regiment from the 2nd Paratrooper Division here, so I guess the High Command must have suspected something was up."

"I spoke to a Luftwaffe pilot the other day. He said it was impossible to get any planes anywhere near the area from Cairo to Port Said. It would take two days for an enemy transport to get here from Suez. If the High Command didn't see this coming, then that wouldn't give much time to respond."

"Still, there have been a lot of our transport planes around in the last three days," said Scholler.

"They flew at least twelve Panzer IVs over to Crete last night."

"So at least we will have some armoured support."

Suddenly the huge plane turned sharply. Lang was thrown to the floor and his men yelled in alarm. The sound of machine-gun and cannon fire could be clearly heard. From the front of the plane the gunner started to fire his machine gun.

Twelve Lightning P38s dived on the transports, quickly shooting a Me 323 down. A second machine was damaged before the Bf 109s caught the American fighters. In a swirling dogfight the enemy lost three P-38s for one Messerschmitt. Unfortunately, the damaged transport crash-landed on the small island of Antikithira, killing half the passengers and crew. Later, the surviving German transport planes landed at Rethimno.

Lang led his men on to the runway, where the rest of his officers were gathering their men and equipment. He could see a group of Panzer IVs and two Wespe self-propelled artillery pieces. Four half-tracks with quad 20mm guns were refuelling nearby. A Luftwaffe Major wearing spectacles drove up in a kubelwagen. He jumped out and saluted, before snapping open a map and handing Lang an envelope.

"I'm Major Fischer. The orders I just gave you will confirm what I'm about to tell you," said the red-faced man.

Scholler and Lang crowded around the map with the Luftwaffe officer. "More men are flying over as we speak, but the enemy is attacking the transports. You and your men are to ride on the back of the Panzer IVs and those half-tracks into the battle. We have also grabbed twenty Fiat trucks and a Sarahiana scout car for your use. It mounts a 20mm gun."

"What about the Wespes? Can they provide artillery support?" Lang asked.

"Sorry, they don't have any ammunition. They flew over with only a few rounds in their racks," said Fischer.

Lang nodded. Maybe he'd get them later. "Alright, what's the situation?"

"The 6th Regiment of the 2nd Parachute Division is in Heraklion, but unfortunately the airfield has fallen. US Paratroopers of the 505th Regiment from the 82nd Airborne Division took the field from the Italians overnight, and the Allies landed at Karteros, Stavromeno, and Gournes. These assaults were made by the Australian 9th Division with support of their Sentinel tanks. The Americans also took Kastelli airfield inland with the 504th Regiment, also from the 82nd. The Americans have landed their 3rd Infantry Division at Malia and Stalida. We believe that armoured columns are racing inland to relieve their paratroopers at Kastelli. The distance is only about fifteen kilometres and Italian resistance has collapsed in this area. Your mission is to advance along the coast road until you reach the positions of the 2nd Paratrooper Division. You will then coordinate an attack to retake the airfield."

"Just like that. We have two regiments against God knows how many enemy units," said Lang.

"You have panzers."

"So will they."

"The Italians will help. They have fought well in this sector. The Siena Division has largely been destroyed but the 185th Parachute Regiment Nembo is in the area for training with the 10th Raggruppamento and its heavy assault guns. Some of these are open-sided vehicles, though they have 90mm guns. There are also some of the new Semovente75/34s. They had about twenty-five of each at the start of the battle. I don't know how many they have now."

"They won't be under German control."

"They've been asked to cooperate."

Lang supressed an eye roll. Why should the Italians do them any favours?

"What about air support?"

The Luftwaffe officer looked away. "We'll do what we can. The Italians are transferring the 51st Stormo to Athens. I don't believe there are many Luftwaffe units to be found, other than those already here. With the renewed fighting in England, the bomber attacks on the north German coast, and the attack on Moscow, to be honest with you, I don't know where we will find any reserves."

Great, no air support and little artillery. At least Major Fischer was being honest with him.

"There are still some units operating," the officer continued. "We had about one hundred serviceable bombers and the same number of fighters a week ago. Another sixty of each were transferred here four days ago, but we have been swamped. We think the enemy are using over two thousand planes, maybe more."

"Against our four hundred, plus what the Italians have here," said Lang.

"Another two hundred, but the Allies still seem very strong. We have shot down two hundred and fifty of their machines, but our losses are only slightly lower. We can't keep up, not unless they send us most of the planes defending Germany and a good proportion of those in England."

Lang wondered if Fischer was making excuses for the Luftwaffe but the situation didn't sound good. If the German Air Force was fully committed elsewhere, then he supposed the Eastern Mediterranean would be the last place to receive resources. The area had been relatively quiet until recently, with most of the action being over in Africa. Even there the Allies had stopped advancing on Tripoli. Maybe that should have been a sign that the enemy were up to something.

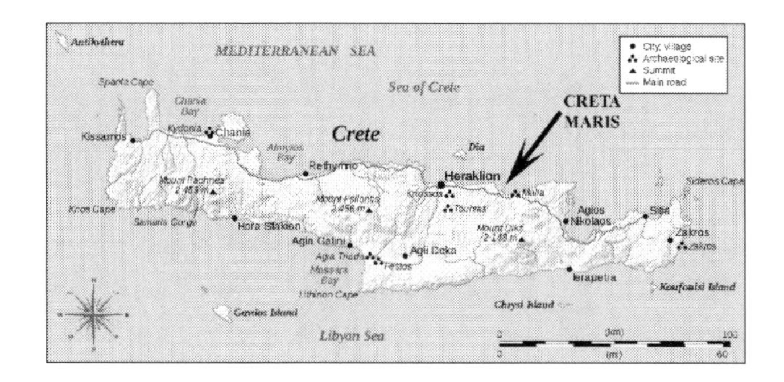

The column of Italian trucks and German armour set out two hours later. It was already late in the day. They had just made it to the little fishing port of Bali when the quad 20mm guns started firing. Lang abandoned his scout vehicle and ran for cover as the two gunners in his car started shooting. A-36 Apache dive bombers from the 86th Fighter Bomber Group fell on the column from out of the setting sun. Sixteen aircraft raked the German vehicles with machine-gun fire. They had dived at a sixty degree angle and landed their bombs among the trucks and infantry. One plane caught fire and crashed into the sea while another headed inland, trailing smoke. Six trucks were destroyed and eight men killed. Lang stood next to one of the half-tracks. The crew of the 20mm gun lay slumped over the weapon, their bodies torn and bloody.

"The vehicle still runs sir, but the gun is useless," said a young Feldwebel.

"Remove the dead and we will use it as a transport vehicle," he ordered.

Scholler trotted up to him. "We have a dozen wounded," he said.

"Put them on a truck and send them back to the air base. There is a large field hospital there. Crowd the men onto the other trucks and the panzers."

"Do you want to stop here for the night?"

"No, the allied planes will attack us during the day. We will drive through the dark. It's only another fifty kilometres by road. We will rest at Gazi. On current information that will be less than ten kilometres from the front. The men will need to sleep and rest. You will drive ahead and try and get us some food."

Scholler grimaced. He knew he'd get little sleep.

Lang slapped his friend on the back. "Cheer up! That means you'll get the first pick. Maybe you will even find us a bottle of wine."

"If I do, I'm not sharing," said Scholler.

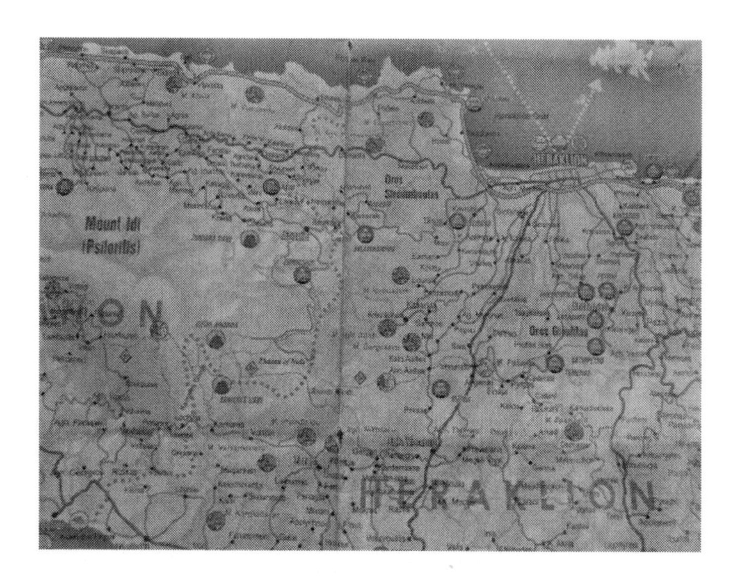

The following day dawned as a bright sun climbed into the sky. Lang's column was already on the move. Overnight Lang heard explosions from artillery and mortars. He didn't know if the ordinance came from his side or the enemy. Offshore there seemed to be some sort of naval battle. He'd discover later that four Italian destroyers had clashed with the same number of Commonwealth destroyers. The arrival of the light cruiser USS Denver, with its advanced radar, tipped the battle in the Allies' favour and only a single Italian destroyer escaped. This battle distracted the enemy, and two German transport vessels with heavy equipment made it unscathed to Souda. However both ships had only been partially unloaded when A-20 Havocs of the 47th Bombardment Group, escorted by Lightnings from the 79th US Fighter Group, attacked them. Italian and German fighters tried to defend the port and six bombers were shot down, two by flak. Two P-38s were also lost and seven Axis fighters were destroyed. More importantly, both ships were sunk and only a third of their cargo had been unloaded.

Overnight, German transport planes had brought more troops and ammunition. A single battery of Wespe motorised artillery tried to drive east at dawn, but two of the vehicles were lost to air attack. At least Lang's unit received a shipment of ammunition. Scholler had also been successful in finding a field bakery from which he took two hundred loaves of bread. He also found a warehouse where the Italians had stored their rations. He found tins of meat, fruit, and fish. Packing his scout car with as much as he could carry, he drove back to the battalion. As a reward Lang let him sleep an extra hour in the morning.

The remains of the Crete Brigade and a brigade from the 7th Mountain Division had already sent regiment-sized units marching east. These were heavily engaged just west of the airfield and in the port of Heraklion itself. South of the city, the 2nd Paratrooper Division, with the help of the remaining Italians, fought the Australian 9th Division, while the 82nd US Airborne regiment attempted to take the centre of Heraklion.

Lang had just contacted General Herman Ramcke when over one hundred B-25s bombed the front line. This was followed by a barrage from the 2/7 and 2/8 Regiments of the Royal Australian Artillery. The twenty-five pounders kept up their attack for twenty minutes. When Ramcke managed to resume contact the general told him to forget his orders. An Australian force had been seen sweeping over the hills to the south of the city. Lang quickly moved his command to intercept the enemy.

The ground here was rough with small valleys running south, getting stepper as they went. Tracks crisscrossed the area but they were narrow and difficult for the panzers to use. The country was dotted with small villas and covered in olive plantations. It took a while to navigate the tracks and by the time they had, the Australians were in front of them.

A Panzer IV was hit by a shell from the twenty-five pound gun of a Sentinel. The Australians used armour-piercing rounds and these struck hard. The low muzzle velocity of the weapon meant that only the front of the turret on the Panzer IV could be penetrated. Still, the weight of the shot caused flakes of steel to break off inside the tank and fly about in all directions. Some of the Sentinel tanks were also armed with six pound anti-tank weapons and these were deadly at short range to the German tanks.

German infantry dismounted and moved forward as the enemy armour duelled with the Panzer IVs. Soon the Puppchen were firing too, the smoke from the rockets clearly visible. Infantry battles occurred at squad and platoon level as the Australians pushed forward relentlessly. Lang had fought men like them before in England. The Australians hadn't been veterans then, but they were now. Months of battles against the Italians in the desert had hardened them. They were led by a successful and famous General, Heathcote Hammer and the 9th Division had never been defeated since it left England in 1940, almost three years ago.

Twelve panzers were knocked out for a similar number of enemy tanks. Lang tried to call for reinforcements but the line was cracking along its entire length. He tried to hold the ridgeline but the Australians called in an artillery strike before charging up the slope. Sentinel tanks blasted away with their twenty-five pounders and Lang realised he had no choice but to retreat. Quickly and efficiently his battalion gathered its survivors and fell back to Gazi. Here they found other German and Italian units, all trying to flee along the coast road. Helicopters were picking up the wounded and flying them west after they had dropped supplies, but it was too late. General Ramcke formed a rear guard with two Panzer IVs and a pair of 88mm guns. He gathered paratroopers and other anti-aircraft weapons and formed a line at the choke point between the White Mountains and the coast. Between the Almiro spring and the sea the paratroopers made their stand. Here a brackish waterway became an anti-tank moat. The bridge across the river wasn't demolished as more German and Italian troops were still using it to escape.

The traffic along the coast road consisted of everything from Italian trucks to civilian cars. Lang even saw carts being pulled by donkeys.

"What a disaster," he said to Scholler.

"We were completely outmatched. Not only that, the enemy has control of the air," said Scholler.

"This may be just the beginning. Unless something changes, Germany is in trouble."

Scholler nodded. “Why do the Allies want the island?” he asked.

“I’ve looked at enough maps of the area when we first invaded Greece. It’s not close to Germany or any industrial centres. The only thing I can think of are the oilfields in Romania. I suppose enemy bombers could reach them from here.”

“We have other sources of oil, don’t we?”

“I don’t know enough about the topic. Maybe we do, maybe we don’t.”

Just then anti-aircraft guns stared firing out to sea. At least forty B-25s were approaching at low level. These were armed with ten forward-firing machine guns as well as the usual cargo of bombs. Scholler and Lang jumped from the vehicle and ran for cover, but the column was flanked by a steep embankment on one side and a drop to the beach on the other. The traffic wasn’t as well spread out as it should have been due to congestion, making the Germans easy targets.

Bullets ripped through the crew of the scout car as it shot at the enemy planes with its 20mm cannon. One of the twin-engine machine was hit and crashed into the slope of the nearby mountain, but the car exploded. Further along the road Lang could see vehicles disintegrating. The weight of led being spat from the cone of machine guns in the nose of the B-25s, destroyed everything. Ahead of him, the road blew apart. A half-track was lifted into the air before landing on its back. He could see men hugging the ground, their hands covering their ears. A shape flashed above his head. There was a huge explosion and then his world went black.

Lang came to. A medic was checking his wound, and nearby a helicopter lifted off carrying wounded men. He could smell smoke and hear the crackle of flames.

"Lay still, sir. You have shrapnel in your arms and legs. I think you might also be suffering from a nasty concussion," said the medic.

Lang leaned on his side and vomited. He wiped his mouth and looked down the road. Ten metres away Scholler lay near the verge.

Two heavy calibre bullets had hit his friend in the chest and a third had taken off a leg below the knee.

"Oh no," he whispered. He pointed weakly. "My friend, my friend."

The medic glanced briefly at the body. "Sorry, he's dead sir. Probably never knew what hit him."

Lang felt himself lifted off the ground. He stared at the sky, tears pouring down his face as he was carried to the helicopter. The whump, whump noise grew as they placed him on the floor of the Drache next to three other badly wounded men. A fourth sat leaning against the wall, his arm in a sling. Blood seeped from a bandage on his neck as he stared. Lang looked out over the ocean as the helicopter lifted off. He had to turn his head sideways. Scholler was dead, most of his battalion had been destroyed, and yet he was alive. The sea below him was impossibly blue. He couldn't take his eyes off it. Eventually he drifted off to sleep. Being concussed, Lang was lucky he woke up. Later, he came to again. Crisp white sheets and a soft pillow cradled him. As he looked around at the other patients, he realised he'd never felt more alone in his life.

V

July hadn't been a good month. Reichsmarschall Kesselring was dreading this conference with the Führer and the General Staff. He walked into the room and saw that only four others were with the Führer. Field Marshal Keitel and General Jodl were there, alongside the leader of Germany. Large maps were spread over the tabletop, and smaller charts hung on parts of the wall. A stenographer sat in the corner recording every word.

"Ah Kesselring, you are here, good," said the Führer. "I want to keep this meeting small. I've scheduled a larger one this afternoon, but I wanted to speak with you alone first."

General Jodl nodded and left the room.

"Crete has been lost," said the Führer.

"I heard," said Kesselring.

"The war is entering a new stage. We are on the defensive now. The offensive on Moscow failed, and we are struggling to hold onto our gains in Russia," said the Führer.

"We will hold the Caucasus region?" asked Kesselring.

"The II SS Panzer Corps was moved to the area. We reinforced it with part of Army Detachment Kempf. The four panzer divisions struggled to hold the Russian advance, we lost Elista in the central north of the region, and the Soviets have opened a corridor to Azerbaijan. The costal road is now safe for them to use. However, we held the oilfields around Grozny. The enemy managed to get to within thirty kilometres of the oilfields, though the 1st SS pushed them back a little," said Keitel.

"And Leningrad?" said Kesselring.

The Führer grimaced and Keitel pointed at the map. "The Soviets have reached the Gulf of Finland at Sosnovy Bor. They have cleared a twenty-five kilometre stretch of the coast. The Soviet 22nd Army has crossed the Neva and reached the outskirts of the city.

We can only supply our troops by sea or through Finland. The 6th SS Division, Panzer-Abteilung 40, the 741st StuG battalion, the 163rd Infantry Division, and the 169th Infantry Division have all been moved from Finland into the city. We were in the process of reequipping Panzer-Abteilung 211 with Panzer IVs, but instead we have been forced to give this unit converted T-34s with Panzer III cupolas. They all have rebored 75mm guns."

"These two attacks and the slow progress of the Moscow assault meant I was forced to cancel the offensive. We have lost most of the ground we took in the attack toward Moscow but that doesn't matter now. I couldn't risk losing those oilfields, especially as they are now pumping fuel to the Black Sea ports we hold," said the Führer.

"And the Soviets attacked and took Poti," added Keitel. Kesselring knew this, as Luftwaffe transports had been involved in the evacuation of the town. Between his planes and the navy, eight thousand Germans and a similar number of Georgians had been rescued. Sixteen thousand German soldiers were captured and the revenge taken out on the Georgians was horrific.

"Those oilfields are more important than ever. I expect the Allies will start attacking the refineries in Romania soon," added the Führer.

Kesselring understood his leader's obsession with fuel. Germany was continually running short and attempts to increase his country's supply was increasingly on his mind as well.

"We need to increase the number of coal to oil plants as a backup," said Kesselring.

"Already those synthetic plants are supplying half of our needs. The Russian fields make up another ten percent, with Romania and Hungary providing the rest, and it still isn't enough," said the Führer. "However, I agree with you, and orders to that effect have been made. To build these new plants will take time, so we must protect the fields in Romania. You need to transfer fighters to the area."

"My Führer, from where? The allied attack in England has taken Cambridge and now the Americans are pushing on Leicester. Luftwaffe units in the area have taken heavy casualties. We also lost many planes trying to hold Crete," said Kesselring.

"England is a side show now. I've told the navy to move their air contingent to the Channel to keep it clear of enemy ships, but for now the land forces will need to cope by themselves. Take fighter units from there," said the Führer.

"Even if I do, these gruppen will be well below strength," said Kesselring.

"Just do it!" snapped the Führer. "Rebuild them in Romania. The US Air Force won't be ready for at least a month."

Kesselring nodded. He didn't like the order and wasn't sure if he agreed with it. Perhaps if he moved more anti-aircraft guns across the Channel, that might partially compensate for withdrawing the fighters. He could easily supply the fighter gruppen with new planes, however finding the pilots to fly them would be a different matter. Maybe if he juggled the units around he could send the less experienced units to central Russia, where the fighting was dying down.

Leaving the meeting, Kesselring rubbed his temples. The Führer was correct. The war had entered a new phase. The Russians were attacking and gaining ground. The Führer was insisting every metre of ground be held. There was another assault which was pushing up along the Volga River to Stalingrad from the southwest. If it reached the Don Bend, the city would be cut off. The Führer had ordered if that happened, the three infantry divisions in the area would turn Stalingrad into a fortress and a counterattack would be mounted to throw the enemy back. Kesselring believed they didn't have the resources to do that. Holding the city would be pointless and the divisions destroyed.

He tried to think of what might turn the tide back in Germany's favour. It was true that the intelligence services were still reporting the Soviet Union was struggling to feed itself. Nearly all of the US aid was in the form of food and clothes, which meant western guns, tanks, planes, and trucks weren't reaching Russia in large amounts. Manpower was being diverted from arms manufacturing into food production, and the growth of the Soviet Army was slowed. Still, the enemy was regaining territory. Kesselring believed it would be impossible to hold on to Stalingrad and Leningrad.

Then there was England. He wondered if it would be better to evacuate the British Isles but knew the Führer would never agree to such a plan. It had been hard enough to convince the German leader to evacuate Crete. In the end, only three thousand soldiers had been flown from the island. A mountain division, most of an infantry division, and parts of the 130th Panzer Division had been lost. A regiment of paratroopers had also been destroyed.

Kesselring still thought there was hope. He was a naturally optimistic man and he believed the enemy could be bled. If the Führer was prepared to negotiate with the enemy, then perhaps an acceptable peace deal could be reached. His own branch, the Luftwaffe, could look forward to better and more advanced aircraft.

The high level interceptor, the Fw 190 C1 was entering service with JG 302, and the early flights of the Do 335 were extremely promising. The engines of the high altitude fighter were still cause for concern, but with the attacks by the US 8th Air Force on northern Germany, there introduction had become a priority.

Fw 190C 1 High Altitude Fighter

The development of the jets continued, but the issues with the engines were still creating difficulty. The Me 262 was an ongoing project and Kesselring didn't believe they would be ready until early 1945. The Germany army was developing a long-range rocket but Kesselring wasn't interested in an unguided bomb. He was putting research emphasis on guided weapons. The Wasserfall rocket was showing some promise as was the Ruhrstahl X-4. The former was a guided rocket fired from the ground, while the latter would be launched from twin-engine aircraft like the Ju 88. These weapons could possibly change the face of warfare if they could be made to work.

The Fw 190 D was now projected to enter service in the early spring of 1944, and the new Ju 188 bomber was reaching both Luftwaffe medium bomber units and Kriegsmarine torpedo bomber squadrons.

The Luftwaffe now had five thousand two hundred serviceable aircraft with one thousand three hundred single-engine fighters, seven hundred twin-engine heavy fighters/attack aircraft, and three hundred fighter bombers. He also had nine hundred and forty twin-engine bombers and nine hundred transport machines. The Kriegsmarine could add one hundred long range Ju 290 reconnaissance machines, forty fighters and one hundred other attack aircraft. He could also count on one thousand five hundred serviceable Italian aircraft, two hundred Hungarian planes, and three hundred Romanian machines. Finland could contribute three hundred more.

Of course, the US were able to put four thousand planes into the air over both Crete and England, and God knows how many they still had in North Africa. This wasn't even counting the extra one thousand Commonwealth aircraft that assisted the USA on both these fronts.

Then there was the growing strength and ability of the Soviet Air Force. The Russians probably had seven thousand serviceable machines. The qualities of enemy pilots in the east was improving and their machines, such as the Yak-9 and La-5NF were a match for any current Luftwaffe fighter. The other issue was the US Army Air Force seemed to grow larger every month. He didn't know how the USA managed this and also fought another campaign against the Japanese in the Far East.

All he could do was fight the war to the best of his ability. Kesselring was determined to get more pilots trained and new weapons systems into battle. This was his best chance of bleeding the enemy and forcing them to the negotiating table.

Chapter Thirteen: August 1943

Major Lang lay prone in bed at the Beelitz-Heilstatten Hospital. He could hear birds singing outside his window. Lang was only fifty kilometres south of Berlin and hoped, when he was feeling a bit stronger, he could go to the capital city. As he lay there watching the nurse's bustle by, Lang noticed a figure striding toward him. General Wagner walked quickly to his bedside, as Lang struggled to sit up.

"No, don't salute. I know you are still recovering from your infection. I believe that new wonder drug helped," said the sharp-faced man.

"Yes sir, I was a guinea pig for the penicillin injections."

The man nodded. "Well, enough of the small talk, you are probably wondering what I'm doing here, alone."

"Yes, sir."

"Let me answer that by asking you a question. How do you think the war is going for Germany?"

Lang was immediately wary. "We could be doing better, sir."

"Ha! Yes we could. Do you think the leadership has a plan to end the war?"

"I don't know, sir."

"Do you think Germany will win the war?"

Lang didn't answer but just stared at the man.

"Are you at all concerned by Germany's policy in occupied land or to certain groups within our society?" continued Wagner.

"Sir?"

"Some officers believe what we are doing to the Jews is abhorrent. I believe it's poor foreign policy, but I think they brought it on themselves. However, I still think destroying an entire people in the middle of a war is a waste of resources. What do you think?"

What was this man up to? Obviously he was not happy with what was happening in Germany, however it may be a trap, thought Lang.

"I would prefer if, where possible, the innocent weren't killed," he said.

"The innocent? If the Russians conquer Germany, do you think they will see our people as innocent?"

"No, they won't. Not after what I saw there."

"I will tell you that there is no plan, just a hope that the enemy will get sick of fighting. The leadership has no idea of what terms they'd settle for. There were meetings between the Russian foreign minister and ours in June, but nothing came of it."

Lang's jaw dropped open. There had been secret peace talks and none knew about them!

"They went nowhere because the Führer insisted the border be along the lines we now occupy, and the Russians wanted the 1940 border restored. There's a lot of land in between those two lines. Our leader wants to hold onto the fuel in the Caucasus and Stalin wants his country back."

"Why are you telling me this, sir?"

"The Führer is a gambler. He believed Russia would collapse. It didn't. He thought the Americans would prove to be a degenerate people, who would have little influence on the war. Wrong again. Now he wants to hold onto nearly all of European Russia. If I was Stalin, I'd say no too. Lang, we can't win. The enemy will grind us into the dust. It might take two years or it might take five, but it will happen."

"Sir, I don't know if I want us to win. I'm ashamed of my country." There he'd said what he really felt. Let this strange general absorb that. The man sat back and stroked his chin.

"If your morals motivate you, then that's fine. I want to save Germany as a country, you want to save her soul. We still have the same goals.'

"Sir, my only goal is to get better."

"Lang, I want you to come and work on my staff at the Replacement Army. Of course our ultimate aim will be to replace the head of the German state with leadership that will work toward getting us out of this war."

"Sir, that's treason. Our oath..."

"The oath to the Führer is a trap. Our loyalty to the nation is more important."

"Why me, sir?"

"I pulled your record and spoke to Rommel. He says you are a good man."

"Is Rommel part of this, sir?"

"Not yet, but he has some understanding of what my aims are. He hasn't reported me. There are other high ranking generals who feel the same way."

Lang's friends were dead. He felt distanced from his family and didn't have a wife or children. His country was in danger and their leader was taking them over a cliff. He had nothing to lose.

"Sir, I'm in," he said.

V

The thunderstorm had swept across the forest only moments ago. The ground steamed but Junior Sergeant Roza Shanina enjoyed the cool sensation on her skin. She still held the letter in her hand from Anna. Her friend was alive and recovering at a hospital in Moscow. Roza sat on the back of one of the new German tanks, a Panther she thought it was called. This one had broken down and been burnt by the Nazis. The view from the turret was of the woodlands, just before the town of Tula.

It was strange to think that after all the savage fighting she'd been involved in, the lines were almost back to where they had started. Roza had participated in the battle before the town. Swept into a group of strangers she'd been placed in a trench with a new partner. Chibek Yahnatov was a young Siberian woman with dark hair and a slim build. Her new companion moved like a cat and had eyes like an eagle. Roza thought Chibek was as good a shot as she was, and both of them now used sniper's rifles. The Siberian woman however, used a captured German Karabiner 98k bolt-action rifle without a scope. Together the two women had killed twenty-eight Nazis during the fighting around Tula. Roza thought that Chibek had probably shot more Germans than she had.

The Fascist advance into the forest drove the Russians back, but many Germans died forcing their way through the minefields and storming Soviet trenches. The first time Roza saw her new partner was when the woman crept up on a Panzer IV and placed a satchel charge on the tracks. After the charge exploded and disabled the enemy vehicle, the crew bailed out. Chibek killed four Germans with her pistol, before stabbing the last man through the throat with a bayonet. The small woman went under a swing of the Nazi's fist and buried the blade into his flesh near the windpipe. She came away covered in blood, her eyes blazing in triumph. Roza was a little frightened of her.

That ad hoc unit had been destroyed, and Roza was allocated to another battalion made up of airborne troops, cooks, clerks, and even artillery men who no longer had guns. Again, Roza was thrown into the line. Her trenches in front of the village of Lipki were hit by an aerial bombardment and then heavy artillery. Then soldiers from the 3rd SS Panzer Division attacked and nearly everyone she fought next to that day had died. No one retreated and the SS men died by the hundreds. In the end, the few Russian survivors were withdrawn.

The Nazis made it as far as the Oka River, then were forced to withdraw. Roza's final battle occurred as the Grossdeutschland Division tried to cross the waterway. Even though this unit managed to grab a small bridgehead, it was at enormous cost and soon the enemy were forced to withdraw. News eventually filtered through that the Soviet Army had attacked in the north and was fighting its way toward Leningrad.

Roza smiled.

"You happy comrade?" asked Chibek. The woman didn't speak Russian well.

"We might be winning. This time the Nazis have been stopped. Our army could take both Stalingrad and Leningrad back from the Fascists."

"Yes, but still lots more to kill," said Chibek.

A Lieutenant whose name she didn't know walked toward the Panther.

"Junior Sergeant, grab your things. You've been transferred," he said.

"Where to, Comrade Lieutenant?"

"Sniper School at Gorki."

"What about Chibek?"

"She's going with you. Truck leaves in ten minutes." The broad-shouldered man passed an envelope to her. "Time to pass your skills on," he added.

"I want to kill more Nazis," said Chibek.

“Oh, I think one day you will. It’s a long way to Berlin,” said

the officer.

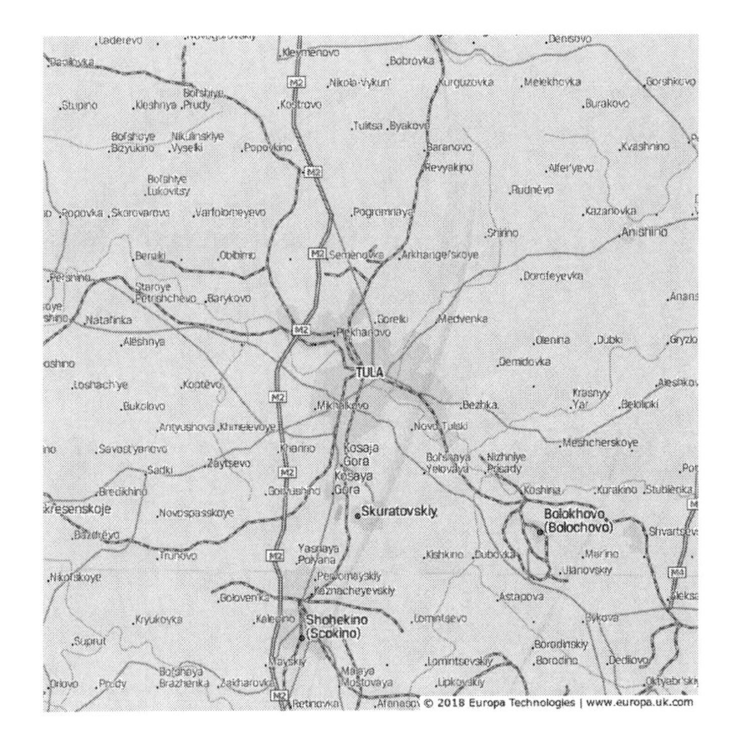

Chapter Fourteen: September 1943

Reichsmarschall Kesselring was happy to have some good news for the Führer.

General of Fighters Werner Molders stood before him. The man couldn't fly anymore after surviving an air crash in 1941. On that day a seat belt had saved his life. The man however, had an exceptional mind, and understood fighters better than anyone else in Germany.

"So, we have confirmed that the Americans lost thirty-six bombers in the last raid?" asked Kesselring.

"It's difficult to confirm all of the kills sir, as some of the enemy planes fell into the sea. However, there are thirty wrecks in the fields around Hamburg. We think, from what the American prisoners have told us, that the raid was made by about two hundred B-17s and B-24s. It was the 376th Bombardment group which took most of the casualties," said Molders.

"That formation was attacked by the Fw 190Cs?"

"Yes, sir. Thirty took off but only twenty made it to the bombers due to engine problems. There were three B-24 boxes of nine planes each. Half of them were shot down. The heavy armament of the new fighters was very effective. Most of the other bombers fell to Ju 88Cs. The Bf 109s armament of a single 20mm gun and a couple of machine guns is too light. Only a few Fw 190 A6s made it to the battle."

"Well, it was a better result than the previous attack made by the Americans."

"Sir, the Wilhelmshaven raid was made in five tenths cloud cover and the direction of the fighters to the enemy bombers was poor. Still, the Americans did little damage to the shipyards."

"We only knocked down eight bombers and the suburbs were badly hit. Don't forget that, Molders."

"Yes, sir."

"Now, the raids on the Romanian oilfields, those had the Führer very worried."

"The latest attack didn't go well for the Americans, sir. I have the latest reports with me."

"Can you give me a summary? I'll read the report in full later."

"Well sir, the smoke pots were quite effective in throwing off the Americans' aim. As you know, the first attacks destroyed twenty-five percent of the refining capacity at Ploesti wells. However, we think most of the damage will be repaired by the end of this month. That attack went through almost untouched, as the Romanians didn't have the necessary air directional capacity. As you know, we have had to centralise our own system and I've now introduced that model to Romania."

"What about their fighter types and pilot skill?"

"The IAR 81 can manage, though they are a little slow. This doesn't matter too much against unescorted bombers and they have a good armament. They also have fifty Bf 109Gs. Their pilot quality is good. They have a number of aces."

"Back to the latest raid, we did better?"

"Yes, sir. Of the estimated two hundred and twenty planes that attacked forty four were destroyed, of these thirty eight fell on land with the other B-17s going down in the Aegean Sea. Moving JG 3 to the area and ZG 76 was successful. ZG 76 has been reequipped with the Ju 88R-2. We don't expect the Americans to try to attack the oilfields again any time soon. It's over one thousand kilometres to the target area and well beyond the range of any fighter escort."

"Hmm, well we can't count on that forever. That's why it is so important that we get the engine on the 190C up to scratch. That machine is fast and with projections of speeds up to seven hundred kilometres per hour at altitude, they will be hard for the enemy to match."

"Hopefully we won't need them, sir."

"Oh, I think we will. Your opinion on the new types is important to me. That's why you are coming with me to view the latest tests of the Do 335 tomorrow."

"I look forward to it, sir."

Do 335

V

Maggie had no time to think of the war. Harvest season was a time for hard work. With the lack of fuel, most of the cutting of wheat and barley had to be done by hand. Maggie wiped her brow and stretched. Her back hurt and she had blisters on her hands. She looked down across the green hill to the bands of forest that followed the river. It was easy to forget the war on a day like this. Grey wagtails darted from branch to branch in a nearby oak tree. Woodlarks chased insects across the fields and a rock pipit watched her from the top of the cross bar of the cart. She smiled and looked over to where here uncle cut barley.

A plane droned overhead, spoiling her mood. Glancing up she tried to work out if it was German or allied. All she could tell was that it had two engines. It was probably a Ju 88, though it could be an American B-26. There was no way of being sure, as it was flying very high.

As they worked, a German came peddling up the driveway on a bicycle. Aunt Mary met the soldier and exchanged a dozen eggs for a small can of fuel. The young man then pedalled away.

Ten Germans from the 207th Security Division were permanently based in Poundsgate now. They had taken over the Miller cottage near the Tavistock Inn. The squad had an old motorbike with a sidecar, and eight bicycles. Their leader was a portly Obergefreiter who enjoyed a pint. At first Maggie had been worried about the presence of these men, but when she saw the Germans her fears fell away. The soldiers were either young with flat feet or poor eyesight, or older and unfit. They all carried Dutch rifles such as the M.95, and the only automatic weapon the Germans seemed to have was an old MP 28 submachine gun.

The squad made a show of searching cottages and farms for the first two weeks after their arrival at Poundsgate. They rode around in a dilapidated truck and generally made a nuisance of themselves, until the Renault AHS broke down. Maggie didn't know what was wrong with it but the vehicle hadn't moved since. Immediately after the truck stopped working, the surprise visits by the German squad slowed and then stopped. There didn't seem to be anything for them to investigate anyway. Since finding the wrecked radio and chasing Maggie across country nothing had happened in the area, and the Germans were distracted by the fighting further north.

Sampson had a radio and often listened to the BBC. He told Maggie of the advance to Cambridge and the liberation of that city by the Allies. There had been more good news recently with the announcement that Shrewsbury had been retaken. In Russia, Stalingrad had fallen, though the Germans still held Leningrad. Crete had been liberated a while ago and now the Allies seemed to be advancing toward Tripoli. Soon Italy wouldn't have a soldier left in Africa.

Maggie was frustrated that she wasn't contributing to the war effort. Without a radio it was impossible to receive orders or send information. Maggie knew her information about the German bomber group transferring through Exeter had been acted on. Local operatives reported a raid by B-25 bombers that had destroyed at least eighteen Ju88s on the ground. That news cheered Maggie, but she wanted to do more. Word had been sent north that she needed a new radio but so far one hadn't been delivered.

So she watched and waited. At least it was easier to sleep at night as the enemy left the area alone. There were a lot more Germans at Exmouth and Plymouth, but the two coastal ports were out of her area.

That night as she sat and ate a meal of cheese and bread there was a knock at the door. Uncle Peter went to open it while Maggie tensed. It was probably just one of the neighbours, and there had been no sound of an engine so it was unlikely to be the Germans. Still, it was hard not to be nervous. Soon her uncle returned with a suitcase sized package.

He put it on the floor and glanced at her. She opened it and stared at a small radio.

"Looks like you're back in business," he said.

V

Lieutenant Randal examined the new enemy tank. It had a long gun and sloped armour. The Panther had the markings of the 2nd SS Division and had been captured after its final drive had broken. This tank hadn't been destroyed by the enemy due to a quick advance by the US 2nd Armoured Division near Naseby. Randel had decided to take a closer look at the panzer, to work out its weak points.

"The armour on the side of the turret is thinner, probably just under two and a half inches," said Freddy Spencer.

"You wouldn't want to take them on from the front," said Private Olaf Magnusson.

"There's a trap shot under the main gun though," said Randel. "That would be an option if the target was close enough."

Randel climbed up onto the turret and dropped into the tank through the cupola. He put the hatch into the open protected position and peered out. The Panther commander would have good visibility but when Randel closed the hatch completely, he realised how slow it would be to open.

Olaf watched as he wound the hatch open again. "Hell Skipper, that took a while. If I was in charge of this beast I'd never close it up."

"The Krauts probably don't. Something to keep in mind," said Randel.

Dropping into the gunner's position, he peered through the sights. He was surprised at the narrow field of vision and noticed there was no other way for the gunner to see what was going on outside the vehicle. This would mean the tank would need the commander to direct the gun onto a target.

He climbed out after checking the driver's position and stretched. The Panther was obviously a good tank but it had its vulnerabilities. Now he'd seen inside one, he felt more confident about dealing with this type of panzer if he met it in battle. So far only about sixty had made it across the English Channel. He walked back to his own tank and wished it had a more powerful gun. The 76mm was supposed to be on the way, though it didn't have the high explosive capabilities of the older 75mm weapon. Randel wasn't sure which gun he'd prefer. Most of the fighting lately had been against German infantry and hidden anti-tank guns. To fight these, a good HE round was needed. Yet, two days ago Combat Command B had faced a group of StuG III assault guns. The unit took heavy losses and found that their guns had difficulty penetrating the enemy armour at distances over five hundred yards. It was definitely going to be trade off where the main gun was concerned.

"Skipper, are we getting any leave?" asked Freddy as they drove back to refuel.

"I don't think so, but we are going into reserve. The Major mentioned we are getting replacement tanks and crews. A new division has arrived as well. The 29th Infantry is taking our spot in the line," said Randel.

"Good, that will give us time to paint those two extra kills on the turret," said Olaf.

"Maybe you'll get to do another interview with that reporter, ehh Skipper?" said Freddy.

Randel laughed as his crew whistled. "I'll be happy for a hot meal and a pint of beer," he said.

The following day the 2nd Armoured Division moved north to Grantham. Here it would rest until being moved to Corby. Later it would take part in General Patton's most successful attack.

Chapter Fifteen: October 1943

The mist drifted through the valley obscuring the river. At this point the Afon Llugwy was about ten yards wide and flowing quickly. The mountains of Snowdonia loomed above the valley as Captain James Stanthorpe led his company of Commandos down to the water's edge. He concentrated on the other bank, hoping the darkness and mist would cover his unit's crossing. The rest of the No. 6 Commando would follow as soon as he fired the right flare combination. He then had to lead his men up the eleven thousand foot slope known as Mynydd Crigau. This wooded hill and the river line was held by the 535th Regiment of the 384th German Infantry Division. The unit was supposedly spread thin and didn't have the usual amount of artillery units. This meant the division used a greater number of mortars, which was fine in the mountainous terrain of Wales.

James still carried his MP 40 and Luger. He'd thought of moving to a Thompson submachine gun or even the new Sten gun, but he liked the action of the German weapon. The British submachine gun he found to be cheap and nasty, and even unsafe. No, James would use the MP 40 until he couldn't find any more ammunition for the weapon.

His company was made up of the most highly trained men of the Commonwealth. No. 6 Commando had New Zealanders, Australians, and a lot of Canadians. It also had men from all over the British Isles. They were all trained to move silently, assault fortified positions, and take the most difficult enemy positions.

The rubber rafts were quickly carried across the forty yards of open ground to the riverbank. Mist swirled around the group, hiding them for the moment. Back in the forest Vickers machine guns were ready to provide covering fire. At this stage they weren't needed. James worried more about mines. None had been reported in the area but you never could be sure. It may have been possible to wade the river, but there were many deeper pools and the current was strong enough in places to knock a heavily burdened man over.

They paddled quickly across the stream, still the current carried them fifty yards past the company's planned landing point to a large pool of still water. The banks weren't high so as soon as the rafts hit the other side, the men were off and running for the woods. There was an explosion. A bright flash lifted a commando off his feet. So there are mines, thought James. Well, they couldn't stop here. He saw men flop to the ground.

"Keep moving," he yelled.

It was only twenty paces to cover. An MG 42 started firing but his company were running. He could see the flash of the enemy machine gun in the dark. The Vickers and Browning machine guns on the allied side of the river started shooting. The big heavy calibre gun chewed through trees and sandbags. The heavier thump of the bigger gun combined with the chatter of the Vickers. The lighter gun was water cooled and so fired slightly longer bursts. Mortar shells fell further up the slope, exploding in the tree branches above the German positions.

James gathered his men by blowing a whistle, then they were in the forest. It was hard to see, but the fleeting flashes of fire from a rifle barrel or an enemy submachine gun gave away the German locations. He held his fire, and instead tossed a grenade into an enemy trench.

"Cover," he roared, before hiding behind the thick trunk of a pine tree. There was a yell of surprise, followed by the flat crump of the grenade. The commandos swept on up the slope, overrunning German foxholes and trenches. James had to halt his men as the mortar shells from their own side continued to fall in front of them. James fired a green, then a white flare. This signalled that the covering fire needed to stop and the rest of the battalion could cross.

"Right, Sergeant Conway, lets push on," James said to the tall Canadian next to him. They followed the slope upward until they hit a forestry track that ran sideways across the slope. Crossing the path, the two men were suddenly thrown backward as an explosion tore apart the tree next to them.

"Trip wires," yelled the big sergeant.

German machine-gun fire came from further up the slope, forcing the men around James to hug the earth. The forest was thick here with leaf litter and low shrubs covered the ground. James could see the brief flashes from the machine gun and even heard a grenade explode.

"Move along the slope to the left, men," he yelled. "Keep low."

All twenty men started to crawl. James hoped that they could find their way around the mined area and work past the flank of the German machine gun. He guessed they had moved about two hundred yards from the river. The rest of the battalion would be crossing by now.

"Private Jackson, get down to the river and warn the major of the trip wires. Tell him we are moving to the left," said James.

The man repeated the message and crawled away down the hill. James wished he could use the radio but most of his headquarters' group had become separated from him in the dark. He could hear other fire fights as commandos and German infantry fought small scale battles in the dark.

Gathering more men, James led the commandos to the left. They crossed the track and moved back into the forest without setting off any more explosives. Pushing through the forest his men ran into a small clearing. Ahead, Germans ran to bunkers while a man in a peaked cap yelled orders.

"Charge," screamed James.

His forty men burst on the enemy headquarters. Thompson submachine guns exchanged fire at short range with Germans carrying MP40s and rifles. A big New Zealander started firing his Bren gun from the hip. An enemy officer fired a pistol, but was chopped down by a stream of bullets. It was chaos as men threw grenades into bunkers or wrestled with the enemy. James grinned like a wolf as he picked his targets. Germans put their hands into the air, but he kept shooting. Other commandos did the same and soon every member of the enemy headquarters was dead.

James gathered magazines for his submachine gun from dead Germans, while other men searched the enemy for documents or useful weapons.

"Sir, there's a track running up the hill behind the clearing," said Sergeant Conway.

"Gather everyone you can. We will follow that track," said James.

He blew the whistle and waited ten minutes as commandos started to appear from the foliage. The sky lightened and it was clear that dawn was approaching. James could hear the crump of mortar shells and he guessed the enemy were dropping them on the crossing area, near the broken bridge. That's what he would do. This would slow and disrupt the rest of the battalion.

"Right, on we go. We can't waste any more time," he ordered.

Scouts were put out in front but they didn't find the enemy. Eventually, a private returned and spoke with Sergeant Conway.

"Sir, there's a gravel pit next to another track just around the corner. It's about seventy yards across. The Germans have some carts hidden in the woods around the edge of the pit. The area is fairly flat with a few old mounds of stone. There are about five ponies tied to the trees and a squad of Jerries there watching over them," said the tall Canadian.

"It's their company's baggage train. They'll all be armed with rifles. Right, we will take them on the run," said James.

Again they surprised the enemy, but this time the Germans gave up swiftly. James considered shooting the prisoners. He remembered the blue eyes of a nurse disappearing under the ocean and thought of the German torpedo that had killed her. Suppressing his rage he took a deep breath. Men would have to be left to guard the enemy and he needed every soldier to take the peak. This would give the Allies a one mile bridgehead across the river and domination of the next valley. The ability to cut the A470 and advance to the River Afon Leldr would be an added bonus. He shook his head. Best not to get ahead of one's self.

He decided his men wouldn't approve of killing prisoners, but he wanted some questions answered. Walking up to a Feldwebel he pointed the gun at his head.

"Is there a track to the top of the peak?" he asked in halting German.

The man ignored him. James lowered the barrel of his MP 40 and squeezed the trigger. A single round hit the man in the leg. He howled in pain and rolled on his side.

"Sir!" yelled Sergeant Conway.

James turned and glared at the man. "This may save some of our lives," he growled.

He looked down at the enemy soldier. "Let's try again. Is there a track to the top and who is up there?" he asked.

"There is a track. A squad holds the summit. I've never been there but they spot for artillery," said the man through gritted teeth.

"Right, bind his wounds and let's get going," said James.

The Sergeant signalled for one man to treat the injured German and another to guard the other ten prisoners. The tall Canadian eyed his officer warily, but James ignored him. He led the commandos through the final stretch of forest and out onto the bare slope. A path led between a lower point and the highest peak. The enemy would have them in their sights any moment now. The thirty commandos climbed to a crest and followed the trail down into a bowl of almost flat ground between the two peaks. Suddenly an MG 42 fired down on them and two men fell. Bullets sent pieces of rock and stone flying, as his men desperately sought cover. The Bren began shooting back but the Germans were well hidden with plenty of cover.

James was at the rear of the column. He signalled the few men nearby to follow him.

"Sergeant, keep their attention," he ordered.

Climbing back along the slope on the other side of the ridge James kept a careful eye on the lay of the land. He had to take a path to the top to give him and his men the most cover. A ridge allowed him to hug a rock shelf until he reached some open ground. Peering around the corner, he spotted the German observation position. A long aerial stuck into the air. The Germans were protected by rocks and a few sandbags. A camouflage net was draped over the top of their position.

James signalled one of his men with a rifle onto the top of the rock, and told two others to provide covering fire.

"The rest of us will charge. Then, we will double back and take out the machine gun," he said. The men nodded but James could see the fear in their eyes. He would lead the way.

Springing around the corner he started to sprint up the slope toward the enemy position. He could hear the sounds of running feet behind him, and then the two riflemen and the submachine gunner started firing at the enemy sandbags. James was firing his MP 40 but it was difficult to shoot accurately while running. An enemy rifleman fired back. Behind him there was a grunt, then another German stood up and shot with a pistol. Dirt flew from the ground to his left revealing where the bullet had struck. Stopping, James crouched and fired his submachine gun. One of the enemy fell backward.

"Down," screamed a man. A German grenade landed nearby and another soldier screamed. Two grenades flew in the other direction, exploding next to the enemy position. James had reloaded his gun and was up again. He ran forward firing short bursts. Sand spurted from holes in the hessian sacks that surrounded the German trench. He kept shooting until he was only ten yards from the enemy position. An enemy soldier stood up and pointed a rifle at him, as he struggled to ready another magazine. A single rifle cracked and the German fell. James tossed a grenade into the trench. An explosion tore the camouflage away and threw the ripped sandbags down the slope.

He walked to the observation point and saw the wrecked radio and three dead Germans. The code books lay nearby, torn and partially burnt. It looked as though the enemy had tried to destroy them, but James picked up what was left and stuffed them in a large pocket.

"Taylor and Anderson are dead, sir," said one of his men. Turning around he saw the two commandos lying on the slope.

"Grab their discs and cover them. I'll send some men back later," he said. "We still need to deal with that machine gun."

By the time James and his remaining men had circled behind the enemy position, the Germans were gone. He could see three men in the distance making their way toward the forest on the southern face of the mountain. They were about two hundred yards away but clearly visible to his squad. He nodded at the two men with the rifles and they took aim. Rock and dirt flew from the ground near the three Germans. One fell and James could see he'd been shot in the middle of the back. The other two abandoned their equipment and sprang down the slope like mountain goats. This made them difficult targets but Corporal Thatcher hit one of them in the shoulder just as they reached the trees.

James walked down to his men, grinning. "A job well done," he said.

Enemy artillery started to fall on the peak. James spun around as shells exploded near the old observation post. The Germans would have the range of that position to the inch. He was glad he had moved away from it.

"Right men, back to the reverse slope," he ordered.

The commandos fell back and waited out the brief enemy bombardment, then they moved forward and occupied Mynydd Cribau. Another part of the British Isles had been liberated from the enemy and more importantly, more Germans were dead. James smiled grimly. The enemy would pay for what they'd done to his country.

Notes

Roza Shanina was a Russian sniper in World War Two.

Unfortunately, she didn't survive and died from her wounds in East Prussia in January 1945.

Roza Shanina

The absence of a hatch for the loader in early model Shermans is a fact. They were actually called 'doors', though I use both terms in this book. General Patton wasn't against modifications being made to American armour, and many late-war Shermans can been seen with extra plates of steel welded to them. Then of course, there was the addition of the Rhino tusks, added so American tanks could push through the bocage in Normandy. This prevented the Shermans from exposing their bellies to enemy weapons as they pushed over the thick embankments.

The Fw 190 C was a possible high-altitude interceptor that the Germans could have developed. Why they didn't is open to debate. It seems as if there were problems with the engine, but these were overcome when the same power plant was used in the Me 410.

Figures for German aircraft strength are based on the Luftwaffe Data Book by Dr Alfred Price and then inflated by five to ten percent. In this timeline the Luftwaffe is better organised and had narrowed down the types it uses. This allowed them to concentrate on building more, rather than dispersing their efforts. Also, in this alternate history, there is no British night bomber offensive. This means the Luftwaffe could send more twin-engine planes to support the army.

The Americans are trying to make most of the Allied planes to support both the war in the Pacific and the campaign in the west and south against Germany. This slows the pace of the build-up, though American divisions are quicker to reach action because of the ongoing campaign in England.

During the summer of 1942 and into the early part of 1943 there was a food shortage in the Soviet Union. When the Stalingrad offensive swept the Germans back, food-producing areas were recaptured. This allowed the Russians to sow crops in the reclaimed land and the problem eased. In this timeline they don't recapture these areas, at least not in the same time frame. This means the Americans had to feed them.

To write alternate history books I do a lot of research. There are many different opinions on everything from the best tank to the effectiveness, or otherwise, of the allied bombing campaign. Sometimes these debates become quite heated. I don't participate in them as I'm not qualified enough in the area, but I do find them informative.

These books are written to entertain. I try and stay within the bounds of plausibility, but in the end a story has to engage the reader. In the end my hope is that my audience enjoys the experience and goes away thinking, what if?

America Victorious Part B should be out some time in 2021. Hopeful it will be a better year than the one we have just had.

Printed in Great Britain
by Amazon